Finding their Place

Missing Link 2

Lynn Burke

Contents

1. Haley — 1
2. Garrett — 17
3. Wyatt — 27
4. Haley — 38
5. Garrett — 48
6. Wyatt — 58
7. Haley — 71
8. Garrett — 89
9. Wyatt — 101
10. Haley — 113
11. Wyatt — 133
12. Garrett — 148
13. Haley — 158
14. Wyatt — 170
15. Garrett — 181
16. Haley — 190
17. Wyatt — 202
18. Garrett — 217
19. Haley — 232
20. Garrett — 243
21. Wyatt — 256
22. Haley — 269
23. Garrett — 283
24. Haley — 296
25. Wyatt — 306
26. Garrett — 318
27. Haley — 331

28. Wyatt — 342

29. Garrett — 359

30. Haley — 370

31. Wyatt — 382

32. Garrett — 397

33. Haley — 405

34. Wyatt — 413

35. Garrett — 423

36. Haley — 438

37. Wyatt — 451

38. Haley — 468

39. Garrett — 483

40. Wyatt — 494

41. Haley — 505

42. Garrett — 515

43. One Year Later — 520

About the Author — 533

Also By Lynn Burke — 535

Chapter 1

Haley

"Go suck a dick!" I hollered at my roommate from where I slumped on our couch. Didn't he realize I was on the phone?

My cousin snorted a laugh in my ear, her giggle like a happy bell. "What's all that about?"

"Garrett," I muttered at the same time he did from his bedroom—something about where he'd put his bag of Blow Pops. The man had a serious oral fixation and hadn't wrapped his lips around a cock in…I didn't know how long. "When are you coming home?" I whined at Lily who'd flown out to the East Coast a week earlier. "I need a girls' night with *all* the wine."

"Soon," she promised. "Then again, knowing these two, who the hell can say."

The two she spoke of were the lovers she'd been seeking since moving out to California from Philly to share my apartment. Well, the lucky little bitch had gotten what she'd been dreaming about, then left me alone without a roommate again.

Enter Garrett...a gorgeous sweetie who somehow weaseled his way into my head and had gotten me to open up within a matter of weeks of moving into the room Lily had vacated. Add in that the guy knew how to cuddle like a koala, and I'd landed in heaven.

But of course, Garrett preferred dick.

If only I could find my place in the ever-changing flow of humanity around me like my cousin had.

Something banged from back in the hallway, interrupting our conversation again.

"Hal!" Garrett hollered at me again, and I muttered at my cousin that I had to go.

"Girls' night. Wine," Lily promised and hung up.

"What?" I yelled at my roommate, staring unseeing at the TV I had muted to call my cousin.

"I can't find them!"

"You put the new bag in the cabinet beside the stove like always!" I added a bit of grumble into my voice as his footsteps shuffled into the open kitchen area behind me.

Nothing about Garrett pissed me off. I just pretended to be prickly because he said he liked me that way. No man ever had—including my dad who'd abandoned me after Mom got put into a psych ward.

He'd claimed I was exactly like her—overly emotional.

Too *much*.

Garrett flopped onto the couch with his head on my thigh, wet hair from his shower soaking the hem of my long sleep shirt. I was half-naked as usual, but so was he. Nothing but lounge pants slung low on his hips.

That V of muscles drew my focus quick as hell as he sprawled out, erasing all thoughts but those of him from my mind. Abs that would even make a straight man swoon pulled my focus up over prominent pec muscles. My mouth watered to sniff the scent of his woodsy bodywash, to lick along the smooth, clean skin he showed off nightly.

He peered up at me with dark eyes that reminded me of luscious chocolate, and his lazy grin around his lollipop stick made my panties damp.

Every. Damn. Time.

I had a serious thing for kissing, and Garrett's plump lips were made to be tasted. Savored. Every guy that looked at him without a doubt thought about having them wrapped around his cock—fuck knew I would if I packed what he did between his thighs.

I scowled down at Garrett, overwhelmed by the love/hate emotions I had for my roommate.

He sucked the pop free from the mouth I longed to lick, twirling the stick in his fingers. "Pet me," he demanded like the needy brat he was.

There wasn't much I didn't know about Garrett Moore. He was a TMI dumpster, and his openness had rubbed off on me shortly after our first meeting. I'd ended up sharing the entirety of my bullshit, making him the only other person to hear it all outside Lily.

"Hal," he whined when I didn't move fast enough.

"You're a pain in my ass," I muttered as he put the candy back into his mouth. I ran my fingers through his dark hair. My fingernails scratched at his scalp exactly as he liked.

"Mmm." He all but purred, black eyelashes fluttering down to brush at the tops of his cheeks, one of which bulged from his lollipop.

At least the jerk gave me a reprieve from those orbs that seemed to peer right through me.

"Tell me about your day," he said while shifting his ass to get comfortable along the couch to my left, flexing his damn abs in the process.

I took a gulp of my wine to swallow down the drool he set into motion.

Why did he have to be gay?

Why?

Garrett Moore was as far from a narcissistic prick as possible, and that was all I'd been able to find on hookup and dating apps for almost over a year. He never rolled on about himself, his shit, and his accomplishments, and instead, he asked me about my day. My feelings.

My wants and desires.

Shit, if he knew the truth of those final two, I doubted we would have such a comfortable friendship that was perfectly platonic. If only my insides agreed with what he and the rest of the world saw.

Straight woman, gay man—best of friends.

I sighed and focused on the words scrolling across the bottom of the news station I had muted. The top story had prompted my call to Lily.

Abraham Quell had gotten what he deserved according to the law. Life in prison. The fucker should have been tied up with his dick sliced off and tongue ripped out for the shit he'd done at the cult's compound in the sticks of New Hampshire where Blaine, one of Lily's lovers, had grown up.

Child abuse. Rape. Murder.

And the list went on.

Blaine hadn't needed to testify in witness against Quell, but he'd gone back east to support his sister who'd kept her chin up and eyes flashing while sharing her story on the stand broadcasted over the world. Lily and Greyson had sandwiched Blaine in their courtroom seats, a gorgeous, supportive triad that filled me with jealousy.

Couldn't I just find *one* decent guy?

"Day, Hal." Garrett shoved his right hand beneath my thigh, giving me a little squeeze closer to the back of my knee while sliding his pop to his other cheek. The candy clacked on his teeth during the move. "Tell me."

Clutching the stem of my wine glass, I rested it lightly on his abs, which contracted.

Of course.

More drool erupted, another swallow bobbed my throat, and I tore my gaze off his torso.

I needed dick.

Badly.

"The clothing order that was supposed to be delivered yesterday didn't come in today either. Gretchen gave me shit about all my extra hours last week—even though *she* demanded I stay to cover for her—and the new employee I finally talked her into hiring was a no-show. She didn't answer her phone either. So, guess who ended up working two hours past her quitting time again today because daddy's spoiled princess had a dentist appointment?"

Garrett made an apologetic noise of sorry in his throat, his thumb rubbing the back of my thigh. I ignored the goosebumps skittering down to my ankle.

Gretchen came from money. Lots of it—old Hollywood cash her father handed over like…well, candy. She'd opened her upscale boutique which barely made it out of the red every month thanks to her bad business sense.

She spent more than she could afford on the store, that was for damned sure. The woman didn't deserve what she had. Didn't work for it…just demanded her employees slave away without proper compensation or showing us appreciation.

But I kept my mouth shut because I was lucky to have such a job. GED, no college to speak of, a resume hardly worth looking at…yeah, I plastered on a plastic smile and dealt with the bitch who had everything.

"Then, while I'm driving home," I continued since I knew he'd want every last detail as always, "I pass that new boutique down on Vine Street that just might put us out of business, and who do I see, but Gretchen and her two besties walking out with bags on their arms!"

"Lying bitch."

I grunted an agreement. "Toxic Twat." I tacked on the nickname I'd given her years earlier.

Trigger after trigger hit me daily with that goddamn woman. If I didn't need my job at *Pieces* to provide for my ass, I would have left years earlier. But without a good education, I couldn't do much beyond working for minimum wage.

Landing the manager role had been huge for me, but I put up with a lot of bullshit in order to keep it— including Gretchen's selfishness serving as a daily reminder of how my parents had been.

Since birth, they had left me alone to wade through the waters of my existence. Without a footing, without a floatie, I'd floundered. Still did. I had no damn clue where my life headed or how to get there.

I needed a true north holding onto my hand—as did Garrett.

My roommate and I were identical twins when it came to feeling as though we aimlessly wandered the earth without direction. We both had jobs but hated them in equal measures.

Garrett pulled the pop from his mouth with a smacking noise and licked his lips free of the cherry flavor I could smell on his breath. "Tell Gretchen to either hire another part-time manager to help carry your load or give you a pay raise. You work too damn hard and get taken advantage so easily."

"It's my own fault," I muttered.

Garrett's eyelids shot open, and he frowned up at me. "So then do something about it, Hal." He used his candy like a pointer at my face. "Your complaints are going to continue to be the same every day unless you stand up for yourself."

Something I'd never been able to do. Mom's mental illness had fucked me up to the point I didn't know how to defend myself. She'd battered me emotionally until I had shut down and became that quiet child who walked on eggshells to keep the peace between her and Dad—who also couldn't get his head out of his ass to recognize another soul suffered at her hands along with him.

Mom's downfall had started with depression, which led to narcissism, manipulation, and lies. She'd finally tumbled off the deep end and landed in a psych ward where she couldn't continue to tear me to shreds.

My problem? The damage had been done, and I couldn't afford therapy. Add in the fact bleakness had started to hover over me as well, and I clung to whatever other emotions I could to keep it from taking me on the same path she'd gone.

Pissiness became my favorite teddy bear, and I clung to it internally.

Stubbornly so.

"I'll tell her tomorrow," I stated firmly even though I knew I wouldn't.

Garrett popped the stick back between his teeth and grinned at me. "That's my girl."

I swallowed some more wine at his word usage. My girl.

If only.

"Any luck today?" I asked, needing to change the subject from my aggravation.

Garrett's lips parted as he let out a heavy exhale, and I got caught up in imagining them running over my neck, my breasts, his red-stained tongue leaving behind a damp, sticky trail along my skin.

Stop, Haley.

I swigged my wine again, tearing my focus off the face I wanted to lick as much as the rest of his body.

"None," he finally answered. "Both open calls I went to were a bust, and that agent looking for new clients didn't do more than hear my name before turning me away. I swear, it's like I'm beating my head against the wall."

Garrett had moved from Pennsylvania to California with dreams of being on the big screen like thousands of other wannabe actors did every year. He'd landed a couple commercials, then had fallen into bed with an up-and-coming producer who'd promised all sorts of shit.

The *shit* had never panned out, but a different pile of poo hit the fan, one he refused to share with me no matter how much I asked. Garrett ended up getting his ass tossed out of their home and living in his car for a week.

Enter my post about needing a roommate of the female sort, and in desperation, he'd begged, assuring me of his gayness.

Melancholic over Lily leaving me, Garrett's pitiful eyes, and the fact he wouldn't ever attempt to manipulate his way into my pants made the choice an easy one.

Eight months after moving in, he'd become as necessary in my aimless life as coffee.

No…wine.

Yeah.

Okay, so maybe both—definitely a codependency which I greedily wished was more.

I swallowed down the rest of my chardonnay and leaned forward to put my empty glass on the coffee table. My unbound breast pressed against his cheek.

"Shit. Sorry." I sat back quickly, cursing the hardening point beneath my T-shirt.

"No worries." Garrett didn't open his eyes, but his damn lips curled with that sexy, slow smirk around his lollipop stick again.

I was going to need a change of panties.

"So, was that Lily on the phone?" he asked, rolling to his side and facing the TV, his warm face against my bare skin just south of my shirt's hem.

"Yeah." My voice sounded rough, and my hand found his damp hair again.

"When are those gorgeous men of hers bringing her back home?" The candy clacked against his teeth as he shifted it around in his mouth.

"Not soon enough," I muttered.

We sat in comfortable silence for a time, my fingers eventually falling away from his head. His hot exhales coasted over my knee, and I leaned my head back, closing my eyes.

Discontentment weaved its way through my mind like always, making me wish for things I couldn't have. Unease followed on its heels as usual. I had no sane reason to feel as miserable as I did. Sure, my boss was a bitch, but at least I had a decent paying job. I had a roof over my head. A roommate I got along with, who cleaned up after himself better than I did. I had healthy organs, clear skin, a good figure...a lot of women would kill for my life.

So why couldn't I just count my blessings and be happy? Why did I wake up every morning feeling as though something was missing?

Greediness for more had always been an issue for me, and I blamed Mom and Dad because I'd never gotten enough of anything good from them while growing up.

I'd longed for physical touch and kind words, a firm, guiding hand to help me traverse through life. All Mom had given me were lies and bullshit. Dad hadn't been anything but a shadow, and even that had disappeared when he abandoned me.

Lily had been my comfort during her stay with me, but Garrett had slid into the place she'd vacated without difficulty.

It had been easy to open up with him because with him loving dick, I didn't have to worry about ulterior motives of getting me out of my clothes.

I just wanted to find the person who would make me feel complete, damnit. Or persons. I needed to figure out where I fit with the other puzzle pieces around me. Surely, that would bring happiness and keep a downward spiral away, right?

It had for Lily.

But attempting to connect with a man or two would mean taking down my walls, leaving myself vulnerable to lies and manipulation that came with conditional love, the only kind I'd known.

Depression snuck its way back into my head with that truth, and I swallowed hard, sure I would never find peace of mind—same as my mom.

Chapter 2

Garrett

Nothing smelled better than Haley fresh out of the shower, her warm, silken skin slathered in lavender lotion. Eyes closed, I soaked in the warmth of her bare thigh beneath my cheek and breathed her in, thankful I'd jerked off earlier. Even emptied, my balls still stirred life to my dick when she had accidentally pressed her breast against my face.

It wasn't the first time it had happened, seeing as how I often used her legs for pillows, and I sure as hell hoped it wouldn't be the last.

At least I could roll to my side, effectively hiding my boner while thinking about suckling and nibbling on her nipples. My mouth watered, and I sucked my Blow

Pop instead, swallowing the taste of cherries instead of the woman I wanted.

Her fingernails scratched at my scalp, and I closed my eyes against the news station, forcing myself to pretend I really *was* gay, that I had no feelings for my roommate whatsoever, and that I wasn't the type of liar she would despise if she ever learned the truth.

While I wasn't usually one to bullshit my way through life, I'd been desperate for a place to stay within a week of Alec kicking me out of what I'd thought had been our dream home.

He'd gifted dozens of things to me over our year together, but I hadn't deserved to take anything more than the single suitcase I'd carried out to California from the sticks of northern Pennsylvania.

Alec had trusted me to look out for his sister, and I'd failed.

Big time.

My stomach hardened like it always did whenever I thought about that night, and I hated that I couldn't go back and fix the trauma I'd caused. I was lucky to have escaped him and his family without anything more than a broken heart and buckled pride.

When I'd left my conservative grandparents back east, it had been Hollywood or bust, and I carried no backup plan in my pocket like I did Blow Pops. All my hopes, my dreams, had me on the big screen, falling in love with my costar and having a happily ever after with either Cinderella or Prince Charming.

I thought I'd found the latter in Alec, but Haley, my prickly cuddle bug...well, I wished things were different.

Much different.

I longed for complete honesty between us, to spill my guts, but I wasn't willing to lose her. Having been kicked out of Alec's life, Haley had become my everything. Best friend. Confidant for all but that one bit of truth about my greatest mistake, and the unrequited love that ached my entire body. She was the lifeline who kept me from drowning—even though she claimed to need a buoy of her own to cling to.

Insecurities weaseled into my brain like they always did when I thought too hard on how I'd lied to her about my sexuality, and I crunched my lollipop down to the gum.

Yes, I liked men and had told her as such, but I'd left out the part about finding women sexy as hell too.

Especially Haley Foster with her dark eyes and constantly changing hair color. The current purplish-red in a messy bun atop her head was one of my favorites. It pulled out the same hints of color from her irises. Add in her petite body, the flash in her eyes whenever her little claws came out, and stick a goddamn fork in me, I was done.

A heavy sigh sent me deeper into the couch.

"Are you okay?" Haley dragged her fingernails over my temple and down the scruff lining my jaw.

I fought off the blood wanting to rush straight to my dick again. "No."

"Give it to me."

Fuck, when she said those words...

I bit back a groan and focused on what she really asked for—an unloading of my thoughts.

"I'm thankful I have a job," I started, "even if it is washing dishes at the busiest diner I've ever set foot into, but it's not fulfilling in the least bit. Yes, it pays the bills—barely—but this isn't what I want for my life. I had high hopes. Big dreams."

Haley didn't offer me bullshit encouragement about it not being my time yet, that I would make it one day.

I wasn't good enough, bottom line.

For Hollywood or for her.

One stupid mistake had ruined my life, and I wasn't about to tell her the truth and screw up what I had found as her roommate.

"Life is good," I stated quietly, knowing I ought to really think so. "But I want more. A real-life happily ever after with someone I'm hopelessly in love with."

"You will." Haley pinched my cheek gently. "You're too damn cute to stay single for long."

The problem was, I couldn't have the one I wanted.

We were stuck in friendship land.

"When's the last time you went on a date?" I asked, expecting we had to be in the same boat since I'd never seen her go out.

"Nine months ago."

"Shit. Seriously?"

"Yeah."

I angled my head back to catch her gaze. "Hookups?"

"Eight months."

"Shit." I grinned, chewing obnoxiously on my gum to annoy her. "Those battery-operated boyfriends in your bedside table must be getting a workout. Not that I haven't heard the truth of that for myself."

She punched my arm, scowling down at me.

"Ow." I feigned being hurt, rubbing my shoulder. "Okay, so maybe I haven't."

I totally had.

"I need dick," Haley muttered.

Fuuuck.

I damn near choked over the offer of my own wanting to spew from my lips.

"How long can a woman go without it before losing her damn mind?" she asked, staring at the TV.

"Eight months?" I suggested, barely able to keep from chuckling.

"Brat." She hit me again, and I let out my amusement.

"If you need to get laid that bad, then *do something about it*," I stated even though it killed me to suggest she go fuck some random asshole who might end up taking my best friend away from me.

"Lily found the loves of her life on Missing Link. Maybe I ought to give that a try."

"Isn't that app for poly relationships?"

"Yeah. So?"

I chewed on my gum for a few seconds, hating how quickly the sugary content dissipated and the pleasure of it on my tongue turned into a workout for my jaw. "It's tough enough finding one person. Imagine looking for two?"

"My usual sites haven't suggested anything worth a shit, and Missing Link panned out for Lily."

"And she's one lucky bitch." I spoke the truth, recalling her two gorgeous lovers.

"There are singles on there. I saw hundreds when I was helping Lily search through matches. Who knows?" Haley shrugged and scooted from beneath my head to get off the couch. She stood right in front of me, the hem of her long sleep shirt inches from my face that now lay on the cushion rather than on her warmth. "Maybe I'll get lucky and find two of my own."

My mouth watered over the creamy skin of her inner thighs and the shadow beneath her T-shirt. I'd snooped in her drawers a time or ten and knew her panties preference.

Silk.

In a rainbow of colors.

I rolled onto my belly to hide my once more thickening dick.

"Want anything?" she asked, still standing right in front of my face.

Fuck, did I ever. *You*, I wanted to say. *For us to get our shit together and figure out where we belonged in life.* I swallowed hard. "Another lollipop?"

"You're going to rot your teeth out," Haley muttered and finally left, allowing me to breathe.

Talking my hard-on down, I grabbed the remote off the coffee table and flicked through the channels a bit.

"Nothing." I clicked.

"Nothing." I pressed the up button again.

Robert Downey Junior stood in all his shirtless glory, perking me right the fuck up. "Ooo! Iron Man!"

"Move it." Haley tapped my foot, and I pushed to sit up.

As with every movie night, I sprawled into the corner of the couch and welcomed her with open arms.

New lollipop on my tongue, I snuggled Haley against my side. "He's so fucking fine." I was the first to state what we'd both agreed on countless times before.

"Mmm." She sipped her wine, the low moan radiating like electricity over my skin.

I grabbed the throw pillow to cover my groin.

Haley snorted with laughter. "As if I haven't seen you get hard before."

Heat rushed to my cheeks. Anytime I sported an erection in front of her that didn't go unnoticed, I blamed the nearest man—in person or on screen.

"It's okay." Haley pressed in closer. "I totally understand the draw. That dark hair begging to be mussed up, that mouth of his." She shivered, and for a second, I imagined it was the heat of my skin along her side that roused her. "I'd do him for free."

I moved my lollipop around in my mouth a few times, sucking down the sweetness, hard as fucking nails. "So would I," I agreed.

But only if you were there with us.

A man could dream.

Chapter 3

Wyatt

Rhett Stirling and his partner Ashton had a gorgeous house on a cliff overlooking the Pacific Ocean. Since they were my longest customers, I still took care for their grounds bimonthly on my own.

It had been Rhett's recommendations countless times that had helped me build up the business my dad had handed over to me five years earlier. Named after Dad, Lionel's Landscaping had grown substantially since I had taken the reins. We'd gone from mowing lawns to caring for other landscaping needs, including laying patio and outdoor living areas for the rich and famous.

I'd even landed a contract with Sunrise Condos and had my best worker making everyone smile at the retirement community. If I could have cloned my employee Blaine, I'd have done so a dozen times over. The man knew how to work, keep his mouth shut, and take guidance from his boss.

While he didn't seem the submissive sort, he certainly liked not having to be the decision maker.

My kind of guy—it was too bad he was spoken for. Twice over.

I wasn't a Dom but I definitely enjoyed being in charge and taking care of people who looked to me for guidance.

I had offered Blaine the position at Sunrise, which pushed him outside his comfort zone, but I didn't have anyone else I could trust like I did him to get shit done.

I finished up the irrigation repair in Rhett's backyard and headed around front, ready to call it a day.

Sweat soaked my green T-shirt that stuck to my back. It had hit 82 degrees, hot for March, and I wasn't anywhere near prepared mentally for the months ahead. While I loved the sun, sand, and surf, the heat got to me.

"Wyatt!"

I pulled up short.

Rhett stepped through the slider, a couple of beer bottles in hand. "Want a cold one?"

"Fuck yeah." I left my tools laying beside the walkway leading out front and joined him beneath the second floor's balcony. The shade welcomed me with a cooling caress, and I sank into one of the cushioned chairs beside him.

He handed me a beer, the glass chilled and sweating. "Cheers."

We clicked our bottles together, and I sucked down half the beer in one go, the chill sliding straight to my stomach. "Goddamn, did I ever need that." I swiped sweat from my brow with my forearm.

"If you want to borrow some trunks, you're welcome to hop in."

The water in the kidney-shaped pool in front of us lay still as glass, blue as the sky. While the offer tempted me, I'd had enough of the sun. "This is good, thanks." I lifted my beer and swigged. "Fuck, this is hitting the spot."

"How's business?"

"Busy, and finding a good worker is damn near impossible. I have a handful of guys I can trust on a job without constant supervision, but more and more people these days don't want to be bothered with landscaping." I stretched my neck and enjoyed another long pull from my beer. "I'm starting to think it's time to hire someone to take care of all the office shit too. I hate paperwork and my current billing system, having to make calls after hours...I'd rather be out sweating. Working with my hands."

I glanced over to find Rhett's face pinched and laughed. "When's the last time you labored out under the sun?" I asked him.

"High school—and never again." He grinned and clinked his bottle against mine a second time. "Ash and I used to rake and bag leaves in our neighborhood back in Massachusetts."

"Where is Ash?"

He and his partner were usually connected at the hip. I rarely saw them apart, and every single time I caught how they looked at each other with undisguised love, jealousy stirred inside me.

They'd been together since middle school and still couldn't keep their hands to themselves.

My goal was to find that kind of a relationship.

"He's on the phone with his mother," Rhett answered.

I nodded as though it made sense even though I didn't know the man well. The two of them had grown up back east, so I expected they didn't get to see their families all that often.

My mom lived less than twenty minutes from me, and I still had to carve out a solid half hour every week for a chat over the phone, and that was atop the weekly Tuesday night dinners with her and Dad.

"She's on her grandkid kick again, and Ash is just as determined to have a kid of his own."

"Shit." I chuckled and drank down the rest of my beer. "I haven't heard that one from my mom yet, but I can't tell you how many times I've been told it's time to settle down with a nice girl or guy."

"She doesn't have a preference?" Rhett asked, sitting back in his chair, long legs stretched out.

"She and Dad don't give a shit about my sexuality, and seeing as how I can't decide which I prefer…"

My mind flitted to Blaine again, that damn jealousy creeping in. He had a man *and* a woman in his bed every night, the lucky fuck.

"Why not both?"

I glanced over at Rhett but couldn't make out his eyes behind his sunglasses. Not that he could see mine either for the same reason.

"That's what Ash and I created the Missing Link app for."

I'd never considered a triad before, choosing to hook up with whatever sex I was in the mood for at the time.

"So, you and Ash…?"

"We're both bi and have been together a long time, and although I don't feel a need for more than him, he wants those children…and not from a surrogate."

"And you would give him whatever he wants." I didn't need to ask that question. It was as clear as day with how Rhett looked at Ashton.

Ash was his person, his peace, his home.

"He wants an angel to pamper like I do with him, and you're right. It's the finding part that's proving difficult."

"High standards?" I asked. "Because I gotta imagine you've got women tripping over themselves to land between the two of you."

Rhett snickered. "It'll take a very special woman to make a permanent place in our bed. All I have ever needed is Ash. We've shared women in the past to spice things up a bit from time to time, but I'll take his ass and mouth over a wet pussy any day."

I chuckled at his blunt honesty. Rich as fuck, posh and suave, Rhett Stirling surprised me quite often.

"I shouldn't admit this, but the app hasn't worked for us—yet. But maybe you ought to give it a try considering the thousands who've ended up happily in polyamorous relationships," he suggested and drank down a few swallows of his beer.

"Maybe," I agreed without really giving it any thought while glancing over the placid surface of their crystalline pool.

"There are all kinds of people profiled. Couples seeking specifics, but the bulk of our customers are singles like you and wanting to explore. There are separate groupings according to needs and desires, filtered down until the best possible matches can be found."

"So, I'm not the only greedy asshole who can't make up his mind?"

Rhett smirked and lifted his beer in the air as though toasting. "Why choose?"

Why indeed?

Rhett's question rang in my ears long after I left his and Ash's home in the hills.

Blaine had spilled his love life to me the summer before, and he too had thought the need to decide between Greyson and Lily would rise up before him.

Good thing his best friend and their girl had already fallen for each other by the time the three of them got together. Once the walls came tumbling down, he'd found out he wouldn't *have* to choose.

Rhett was right. Why force myself to decide between male or female? Why not try for both? That was the reason Missing Link had come to fruition—two men wanting a woman to fill that missing portion in their lives.

Or rather, Rhett wanted to please his lover and find the perfect woman to bear those children Ashton wanted.

Talk about dedication and love.

I desired that. Someone to love and need me to clasp their hand through life. Two someones would be even better. A woman who drew out my tender side and a man I wouldn't have to hold back with.

But finding even one had proven a tough chore. Guys loved my dick, but that was it. No one was looking for longer than a one-night stand, and women...well, the ones I'd dated had been clingy as fuck and not in the needy way I hoped for. I had a lot of love and affection to give, but having both *demanded* of me left a sour taste in my mouth.

Perhaps I'd been looking in the wrong place. Hookup apps and bars almost always offered me the opportunity to get off, but emptiness followed on their heels—and more than just my balls.

Rhett's suggestion stayed with me on my way home, and later that night, after showering the sweat from my body and downing a half-pound of ziti broccoli, I sat in front of my MacBook. The process of creating a profile on Missing Link proved easier than I'd expected.

The questionnaire started out in broad terms—sexual identity, what I hoped to find, sexual preferences, general location, and how far I was willing to travel. A second screen of multiple choice dove deeper but wasn't nearly as thorough, as I'd expected it to include limits and all that shit. But maybe that sort of information wasn't necessary since I hadn't clicked off the BDSM as an interest on the first page.

Finally, I ended with a brief write-up, a little introduction of myself. The image I chose was one from the summer before my mom had taken of me while out to dinner with her and Dad.

I'd worn a button-down dress shirt, blue like my eyes, and she'd caught me in a candid laugh. While I knew I was a good-looking guy, it was by far the best picture I had of myself.

An image of me shirtless and flexing probably would have gotten me more action, but I decided if I was going to download yet another dating app, it would be for the real deal. I'd grown bored with hookups and living alone and sick of the silence in my house. I wanted to wake up with a warm body beside me, someone I could hold—two someones that Rhett had made me realize I ought to try for.

Because why the fuck not?

Thousands had used Missing Link, and the feedback I'd seen while scrolling through the reviews promised what Rhett had stated—poly relationships were doable.

I just had to find my perfect matches who were as dedicated to finding their place as I was and willing to put in the time and effort to make a triad work.

A trace of adrenaline trickled through my bloodstream as I clicked on the finish button.

Let the hunt for happiness begin.

Chapter 4

Haley

I hugged Lily long enough that the other patrons in Shadow's Lounge started to stare at us through the dim lighting, but I didn't give a shit. I'd missed my bestie while she'd been back east. She was the only person besides Garrett who loved me unconditionally, and the second she had walked in, my eyes and nose had burned with the need to cry.

"Sit your ass down and tell me everything," I demanded, finally stepping out of her arms.

As always, she smelled like vanilla and chocolate mints, her eyes twinkling with light and happiness.

"Chardonnay?" she asked about the drink I'd ordered for her while settling into the chair across from the one I'd been sitting in.

"Mmm hmm. So should I ask why you were late?"

"My boys were feeling horny, and I was hungry."

"You're a cum slut."

"Only for them," she stated rather than offering an apology for keeping me waiting ten minutes longer than our agreed upon meet up time.

I rolled my eyes, the ugly green giant of jealousy and depression rousing in the back of my mind. If I had the kind of love and affection that she did at home, I would have been late too.

Lily sipped, eyeing me over the rim. "So, which do you want first? The courtroom shit or the dinner shenanigans?"

"Fuck the Quell/cult fuckery. I saw enough of that on the news, and I'm ready to put it all behind me as I'm sure your men are—but how are Blaine and his sister doing after everything?"

"Better than I'd expected. I thought for sure that seeing Quell again would stir up shit in Blaine's head, but he hasn't had a single nightmare about his childhood. He's just relieved to finally be able to move on entirely from the whole situation. His sister Sarah is still at Franklin's grandparents with him and his siblings."

Lily enjoyed another swallow of wine.

"They're getting married at the end of the summer on the farm in Maine," she continued. "Nothing major, no big celebration, but she wants Blaine to walk her down the aisle they're going to mow in a grassy field."

The thought of such an intimate ceremony tickled all my happily-ever-after dreams and poked at the enviousness I tried to keep caged up. "Aw! That's so sweet."

"Right?" Lily let out a sigh. "I'm so…full to overflowing it's almost sickening."

I wouldn't know the feeling she spoke of, and that truth brewed the shit in my mind some more. "Okay, now give me the goods about that dinner Grey set up with your ex and his husband because I've been *dying*."

And I needed a change of topic from weddings and happiness.

Lily laughed, her voice like a tinkling bell. "So, the second Levi opened their front door, I went flying up their walkway and jumped into his arms, leaving Grey and Blaine behind."

I smirked and enjoyed a healthy swallow of my wine while Lily recounted forgetting all about her two lovers for the sake of hugging Levi again—but how she noted that any sexual attraction she'd once had for her ex-fiancé had completely disappeared. She'd just missed the friendship they'd carried beyond their engagement ending.

All four men had greeted each other without any sense of jealousy or hostility, keeping the situation from being awkward.

"Just sitting there while they shot the shit at the dining room table, thinking about how each and every one of them had at one time put their hands on my body made me fantasize about having my own harem."

I snorted, almost choking on my drink.

"Just kidding." Lily laughed. "I don't want Levi or his husband's hands on me ever again. Grey and Blaine are all I need."

"Greedy dickmonger."

"You're just jealous." She fake-simpered and winked.

"Damn right, I am." I didn't mind admitting that truth to the one person who knew me better than anyone—Garrett included.

"So, how's your dating life going the past couple of weeks?"

I flagged down our waiter, ready for another drink. "Nonexistent."

"Are you at least trying?"

"Why bother?" I glanced over those drinking at the bar to the left of our high table but found nothing of interest worth a second look. "I'm doomed to just pick up another narcissistic asshole who will only try to manipulate his way under my skirt."

Lily's gaze bored into me with concern furrowing her eyebrows.

"What?"

"How are you doing, Haley?" She was well aware how depression often attempted to grab me by the pubes and hold on for dear life.

Maybe it was time I started to wax on the regular. "I'm okay, but everything kind of sucks right now."

Just not me…

I clung to the buzzed thought since it wasn't gloomy, then tacked it on out loud to my last sentence to get Lily to laugh.

She did. "And how about Garrett?" she asked rather than helping bemoan my lack of action.

"He's still got a sucking fixation—*just not on me.*"

We both busted into laughter.

Fuck, had I needed a night out with her. I felt lighter already.

"Seriously, though," Lily said once we settled down, a smirk still on her face. "Are you still crushing on that sexy roommate of yours?"

"Bad. Like, *really* bad, but maybe it's just because my love life is in a serious drought, and I'm dying for kisses that will curl my toes." I sagged into my chair, leaning onto our table with my elbow, chin propped in my hand. "It doesn't help that he walks around in nothing but sweats, showing off those abs and that V I would pay to lick."

"He *is* fine."

"Fuck fine," I snorted my disagreement. "He's divine perfection."

"DP."

We laughed our assess off again, and I knew I'd be changing Garrett's name in my cell to DP.

"It's a lovely thing, isn't it?" I asked, knowing it was my tale of a threesome I'd had a couple years earlier that had enticed Lily into moving to California and seeking out two lovers instead of one.

"Sometimes it hurts like a motherfucker," Lily said quietly, leaning toward me, that light back in her eyes, "but watching my men fall apart together inside me while they're sucking on each other's tongues...yeah." She shuddered and sat back, fanning her face.

"Bitch."

Lily flipped me the bird while grinning.

The waiter arrived with new drinks, and we clinked our glasses together. "To Haley getting her man."

"Two men would be better," I said, "but at this point, I won't be greedy. Finding one is hard enough."

"They'll both have to be hard to—"

"God, Lily!" I barked out, dissolving into laughter yet *again*.

One thing about my cousin, I could count on her to take the heaviness away even if we acted like immature dorks.

Same as cuddling with my sweet koala...

I sagged again, letting out a sigh. "Do you think Garrett knows how hot I am for him but just ignores it since he's gay?"

She shrugged and sipped. "It's possible, but I've seen the way he looks at you too. He adores you...you're definitely his safe place, and he wouldn't ever do anything to fuck that up."

"Why can't he be straight?" I whined, something I rarely did.

"There's such a thing as gay for you. Maybe you could talk him into being straight for you?"

"I wouldn't ever attempt it. He's like...my platonic person, and I can't jeopardize our friendship."

"Fuck."

"Yeah, I wish. Over the back of the couch, against the door..." I let out a heavy sigh. "He's the perfect a guy... almost everything I want. He doesn't have a manipulative bone in his body, and while he lacks in direction like I do, that bulge of his I catch tenting his sweats when we're watching hot guys on TV...fuck to the yes, please, fill me up and wreck my mouth with your tongue."

Lily lifted her wine again and held it toward me. "Then let's make a vow—we're going to find you your man—or two—both hotter than Garrett who will love you unconditionally and hold your hand through life. Oh." She giggled. "And may they have a bigger, thicker dick than your roommate's too."

I wasn't sure I would want anything more than what Garrett packed between his muscular thighs, but desperation had begun to creep its way into my core.

"And how do you propose we do that?" I asked, clinking my glass against hers.

"Missing Link."

A half hour later, I had an active profile on the latest poly dating app.

The wait began, fingers and toes crossed for luck, something I'd been shortchanged on since birth.

It was about time fate gave me a break and offered a path different than the one my mom had gone down.

Chapter 5

Garrett

"I'm sorry, Mr. Moore, you're not what we're looking for."

"Nothing about you fits the criteria."

"You don't have the energy we want."

"Perhaps you ought to return to Pennsylvania."

That last not-so-gentle letdown was the icing on the cake for my day of going to open calls.

All four had been for a built, dark-haired guy my age, two with cocky swagger I had no issue portraying when needed and cliche gay male which I'd proven over the previous eight months living with Haley I could rock in my sleep.

And yet I wasn't what the producers were looking for.

I thought of Alec and his family's influence in Hollywood. Was it possible he'd somehow gotten me blacklisted in retaliation for my shameful mistake? Was there some secret network of whispering behind the scenes that kept people from being hired?

It had been that final interview where they'd asked me if I was the Garrett Moore who'd been involved with Alexander Henley. Like a moron, I'd answered with the truth—then seconds later had been told I should head back to the sticks where I'd come from.

I'd deleted Alec's number from my cell, but I knew it by heart.

Hoping like hell I'd assumed wrong, I shot off a text the second I climbed into my car, my chest tight as my heart pounded beneath bone and tissue.

Was my being blacklisted your doing?

My phone chimed a notification before I turned the key.

Payback's a bitch.

"Fuck." I slammed my head back on the headrest, jaw set tight. I'd known Alec was a ruthless bastard when it came to business, but I'd never considered being on the receiving end of his anger.

He'd been enamored with me once upon a time—or so I'd thought.

That showed how fickle the heart could be.

My mind heavy and shoulders slumped, I pulled out of the parking lot, admitting defeat.

There would be no *Garrett Moore* in Hollywood's lights, no billboards featuring my face as the hottest leading man on screen.

My eyes burned with the need to release my emotions, but I choked them back, thinking it made me strong.

I'd been putting on shows since I could remember, dancing and singing, however off tune, for any I could talk into watching me perform.

And now I wash dishes for a living.

Could I be any more pitiful?

But I'd made my own bed—because of one stupid choice that had ended up ruining my life and leaving me on a path to nowhere.

I'd been on a fast track to attaining my dreams, Alec being my boyfriend only a plus, then I'd left his bitch of a sister alone at a party at her insistence. It helped that the guys she'd plastered herself to had kicked the shit out of me when I'd attempted to drag her ass home, but that hadn't mattered in the end.

She'd been sexually assaulted after I'd abandoned her.

And I'd been blamed.

Never mind that Alec's sister was the most stubborn girl I'd ever met, a selfish bitch of the worst sort who'd been spoiled since the day she'd been born. Silver spoon and the whole nine yards, Sindy got what she wanted when she wanted it.

But so did Alec, which was why I found myself unable to land a job in the entertainment industry and I struggled to find my way in life.

It had been poor judgement on my end to not call him about his sister's tantrum and insist he help me since I hadn't been able to get her to listen. I'd left her to her own demise after countless battles between her and I in the past.

And I'd paid the consequences along with her.

Anger roused inside me, pissiness at Alec for refusing to see there might be another side to the whole story. Even though I was to blame for what happened to his sister, I felt like a victim too.

Or was I being a selfish bitch?

Dragging my ass toward Haley's and my apartment, I decided that regardless of my thoughts toward the entire situation, I was done chasing a dream that wouldn't ever come to fruition. Maybe I did need to move back east to where no one knew my name and I could find my way onto boring stages in local drama clubs and such.

My grandparents wouldn't ever accept my sexuality though, so I wouldn't have any freedom to be completely me. The thought of having to suppress part of who I was tingled fatigue through my limbs. I'd done that the first eighteen years of my life and had no wish to backpedal.

A tear finally trickled down my cheek as I shoved the key into our apartment door.

Haley stood in the kitchen when I walked in, her sleep T-shirt hanging mid-thigh—same as always when she got off work in the middle of the afternoon.

She frowned at the look on my face but didn't say a word, simply hurrying toward me.

I dropped my bag and caught her up in my arms, burying my nose in her neck and squeezing her tight.

The scent of lavender lotion filled my nose, and I shuddered from anger, heartbreak, and arousal in equal doses.

There would be no joining Pennsylvania drama troupes since it would mean leaving her behind.

"What happened?" she murmured, rubbing my back while I sniffled and cried against her soft skin, hating everything about my life outside her.

"I'll never work in Hollywood ever again," I said, setting her back on her feet, thankful as fuck my misery had kept my dick from going stiff as an oak.

She grasped at my scruffy jaw with her small hands. "Why do you say that?"

"Alec."

A frown furrowed between her eyebrows as she swiped tears from my cheeks with her thumbs. "Are you shitting me?"

"No. I texted him asking if he'd gotten me blacklisted somehow. He replied that payback is a bitch."

Haley let go of my face and set her hands on her hips. She didn't wear a bra, but I couldn't be bothered to think about her breasts in my headspace that Alec had shit over. "What really happened with him, Garrett?"

I hadn't told her the entire truth or revealed my worst mistake. She would find out what a selfish asshole I really was at my core. "It's a long story and not worth repeating," I went with while kicking off my shoes, hoping she would allow me my secret.

"I have a couple bottles of wine and all night," Haley said, stalking on my heels as I made for my bedroom to change into sweats.

I yanked off my button-down shirt while stepping over the threshold, my stomach tight. "I don't want to talk about it."

"Well maybe getting it off your chest will help."

I glanced over my shoulder at Haley who stood in my bedroom doorway, arms crossed beneath her breasts.

A messy bun held most of her hair atop her head, and a few purple-red strands escaped around her face. She'd put on makeup for work earlier that morning, creating a beauty I had a hard time not staring at.

Given the chance, I would worship every inch of her delectable body with my mouth and hands. But even without her face made up, Haley would have held my eyes captive. I had to tear them off her to pay attention to what I did—unzipping my skinny jeans and glowering at the chub growing between my thighs.

Haley cleared her throat.

"You're the one who followed me in here," I reminded her, hands in my waistband ready to drop my jeans to the floor.

"You could have closed the door," she said with a shrug.

As if that would have stopped her from treading on my heels when she'd sunken her teeth into a conversation I wanted to escape. The woman was a pitbull when she set her mind on something.

Just out of spite, I shoved off my underwear along with my jeans, giving her a view of my ass.

I swore I heard her breath catch—and it made me feel just a slight bit better while I tugged on the sweats I'd discarded earlier in the day.

I turned back around in my usual home garb.

Haley's cheeks were a bright shade of pink, her nipples poking against her shirt.

Jesus Christ.

I scrubbed a hand down over my face, scruff scraping my palm as I took note of the hunger in her eyes.

Can't. Go. There.

"Wine," I croaked out, and she nodded and scampered away, leaving me cursing in my head and fighting the chub that refused to deflate.

I stretched my neck side to side, so damn amped up on emotions I wanted to get drunk. Or fuck.

Preferably both.

"Damnit, I'm a mess." Still muttering to myself and dick once more as discouraged as my mind, I went out to the living room, collapsed on the couch, and listened to Haley pop the cork and pour two glasses.

"Feel free to bring the bottle," I told her.

"Already done." She rounded the couch and handed me a glass—then a Blow Pop she'd tucked the stick in alongside the glass's stem.

My girl.

I swallowed hard then guzzled my wine down, wishing for something stronger.

"Come here, baby." Haley patted her thigh, and I sank into my usual spot when I was the one needing comfort, the lollipop firmly enclosed in my mouth.

Her hand twined into my hair, and I closed my eyes, breathing a sigh of relief.

"I love you, Haley." The words escaped from my heart without thought, but I'd never been so damn honest with her.

"Love you too, Garrett."

Her echo tightened my throat again rather than making my heart soar because I knew we would never share the kind of love I wanted more than anything.

Chapter 6

Wyatt

Maybe I was just too damn picky, but I'd spent hours throughout the week searching all Missing Link had to offer and couldn't find jack shit. Or maybe some inner fear I refused to face made me hesitant to poke any of the hot guys or women I'd seen pictures of—because experience had told me that rarely did a person appear as good as the image they'd uploaded to snag a fish on their hook.

Looks weren't everything.

I wanted someone or two someones I would click with emotionally and mentally.

A married couple hoping for a boy to smother with love had caught my attention in the couples bin of possible match ups, but I desired to be the one of the triad being the main giver.

Thanks to parents who'd offered affection and unconditional love without hindrance all through my life, I had a lot stored up, ready to be lavished on whoever owned my heart. As an only child, I had one hundred percent of their attention and hadn't lacked like my employee Blaine had while growing up in that damn cult.

He'd found the two who filled his empty emotional vat, and I wanted someone who needed me in the same way.

That married couple who'd snagged my attention briefly got tossed back into the bin without a poke.

Friday night, I sat alone on my couch and scrolled the app while sipping a beer rather than hanging out with some friends at the bar. I'd attempted hookups their way and had enough.

I'd finished up my paperwork for the week, aggravation over the tedious work making me want to rip my hair out.

Not that searching an app for my forever girl or guy proved any easier.

A new match popped up ten minutes into my disheartening hunt.

SWF wanting to find her place.

That bio line caught my eye—resonated big time because it's exactly what I'd written for mine with the F swapped out for the opposite sex.

I clicked to check out her profile and to bring the tiny avatar pic of her into better focus.

Her devilish smirk caught my attention first, no bright lipstick or gloss, just natural lips curled upward with a dimple in one cheek. Dark eyes with a mere hint of makeup, long lashes, and hair a funky maroon color drew out the freckles over the bridge of her nose.

Cute as fuck.

Gorgeous tits that would fit in my hands without spilling over stretched her white crop top, but it was the boyish figure from her chest down and in jean shorts that really did it for me. No wide hips or a waist to speak of...more straight and sexy as all hell to my eye.

"Fuck." I sat up and quickly scanned through her bio.

Haley was tired of hookups, wanting to find her person —or persons, preferably two men. Interaction between the males was more than welcome. Pink-collar working woman who enjoyed the beach and waves but could do without the sun. Honest as fuck too, in stating she could be a bit needy affection-wise if someone managed to get her walls down. A big chore, she'd written, but she promised would be worth the price for someone truly interested in a real connection.

I hit the poke button without a second thought, excitement bubbling inside me. Knowing I would have to wait for a response rather than immediate gratification—or letdown—like hitting on women in bars, I set aside my cell and grabbed another beer from the fridge.

Haley had poked me back by the time I sat again.

My pulse jacked up, but I made myself twist off my beer cap and take a long pull before opening the messaging system that unlocked between the two of us because of the returned poke.

"Okay." I put down my drink, rubbed my hands together, and went for it. A damn grin stretched my mouth wide.

Me: **Hey, Haley. Thanks for returning the poke.**

Haley: **My pleasure—I hope, anyway.**

I chuckled, wondering if she flirted or was being dead honest about connecting instead. I decided to let the sexual shit sit on the back burner since I hadn't gone on the app for hooking up.

Me: **As you must have seen, I'm hoping to find my person or persons, same as you.**

Haley: **Your write up didn't state if you wanted MMF or MFF?**

Me: **I'm bi and don't prefer one over the other, but if we hit it off, I'd gladly be open to bringing another guy in if that's your preference.**

Haley: **Yes, please, but I've never done this before, so I'm clueless where to go from here.**

"Same, woman, same." Sure, I'd had lots of dating apps take up my time over the years but nothing for serious adventures.

Me: **How about we leave the stress of meeting up together for a couple weeks and just chat a bit to see how things go?**

Haley: **That sounds so damn refreshing, you have no idea.**

I settled back in the couch, swigged my beer, but another message came through before I could respond.

Haley: **All the guys I've gone out with lately have had one thing in mind...getting between my thighs asap. Don't get me wrong—I like sex. Too much, but wine and dine me first, for fuck's sake.**

I almost typed back that there was no such thing as too much sex but didn't want to give off the impression I was like the last couple of jerks she'd gone out with who'd only been after pussy.

Me: **You go first. Tell me all about you—your wants, your hates, your needs.**

Haley: **Are you going to cut me off halfway through to talk about yourself?**

Her reply came back in a snap as if she used speech to text—and I could hear the wariness in her typed words.

Me: **I'm guessing you've been out with a lot of selfish assholes lately.**

Haley: **Understatement of the year.**

I was no narcissist, but I could be honest. **I might drop in my two cents here and there if something you say hits me in the right way, but it won't be an attempt to turn the conversation to me if that's what you're concerned about.**

Haley: **I'm untrusting because of past experiences, that's for damn sure, so sorry in advance if I'm a bit prickly. My cousin and roommate use that adjective for me all the time.**

Her blunt honesty turned me on.

Me: **Some of nature's delights grow thorns to protect themselves from predators.**

Haley: **Wyatt just earned a checkmark in the plus category.**

I laughed and let her know her frankness earned one on my tally card too.

Haley: **I could ramble on, but it's weird texting out my life. How about we play fifty questions instead and see where our score sheets end up at the end? If we're still interested, we can do the whole spilling of our stories over the phone one night.**

Me: **I'm game if you have time.**

Haley: **Coffee or tea?**

She started out in the same place I would have. **Coffee.**

Haley: **Same.**

Morning person or night owl? I asked next.

Haley: **Afternoon delight. You?**

I choked on a laugh, shaking my head. **Morning person**, I replied, hoping that didn't get a negative checkmark like it usually did with anyone I dated. Nothing better than the sunrise over the ocean though. **Politics or religion?**

Haley: **No thanks, but I'm all about equal rights and keeping the second out of the first.**

"My kind of girl," I stated quietly, grinning again like an idiot.

Haley: **Old white men have no place telling me how and what I can or can't do with my body, thank you very much.**

Me: **I'm not big on either of those topics, but I'll hold your hand while you're up on that box for however long you need, Haley.**

Haley: **You have no idea how happy I am to hear that. Summer or winter?**

Shit, that was a hard one. **Summer**, I went with, **but only because it's the busiest time of year for me.**

Haley: **What do you do for work?**

Me: **Landscaping, and it gets too damn hot in the summer. How about you?**

Haley: **I'm a winter girl, and I manage Pieces, an upscale boutique downtown.**

Me: **Do you enjoy it?**

Haley: **It pays the bills, but my boss is a bitch, and finding good help is hard as fuck.**

A woman with a potty mouth as my mom would say. Definitely a plus in my opinion.

Me: **Tell me about it. Just my two cents here…I've hired and had to let go over a dozen guys in the past five years since I took the reins of my dad's company.**

Haley: **Maybe you ought to start hiring women.**

She included a smirk and wink emojis—and she had a point.

Me: **Looking for a new job?**

I asked her as a half-joke but bookmarked her statement for later thought.

Haley: **My roommate might be. He's a struggling actor who's washing dishes at a diner rather than shining behind a camera.**

A male roommate.

That had to be an interesting situation. Rarely did the opposite sex living together remain platonic or not have weird vibes going on. I left that one alone for the time being too and went back to the fifty questions thing, learning she didn't care for sport of any sort—

possible checkmark on the negative, but I didn't really need that in a woman to enjoy her company.

We both liked the outdoors, a good glass of wine—mine with dinner mostly while I preferred a cold brew for chilling. Movies and relaxing were high on the list of our favorite to-dos, as was eating out because we didn't like to slave away in the kitchen.

She mentioned her roommate cooked, and my mind went back to their relationship. I decided I had to ask before she drew me in even deeper than she already had and he ended up being the kind of negative checkmark that could break what we'd begun building.

Male roommate, huh? I went fishing to see what she'd give me in response.

Haley: **He's gay, unfortunately.**

I mused over how she'd worded her answer for a few seconds, wondering about possible unrequited love.

Me: **Since you said it's unfortunate, I'm guessing he's either hot as fuck or he's everything else you want in a man.**

Haley: **He's both. You should see him in a pair of gray sweats.**

Yeah, I was all about men in sweats—but I had a definite preference when it came to build and how said pants hugged their ass and groin. **Body type?** I asked, still fishing and expecting bluntness like she'd been giving me throughout our messaged conversation.

Haley: **Ripped as hell but not bulky, luscious abs, the sexy as fuck V…he's a total thirst trap.**

I found myself laughing again.

Me: **I think I need to meet this roommate of yours.**

Haley: **Nope. Nuh uh. Not until I decide if you and I have a shot at something first because that delicious asshole will entangle all your feels, and you'll both leave me on the side of the road.**

Outright laughter burst through my living room.

Me: **I like you, Haley.**

Haley: **You've got more pluses than checks, so I might like you too, Wyatt.**

"Fuck." I still grinned and shot off another message before I overthought what went through my head.

Me: **I know we said we'd chat and get to know each other before meeting up, but I'm intrigued as**

fuck. Love your honesty, and you've got a shit ton more checkmarks on my fuck yeah list than not. What do you say? Up for dinner and drinks one night sooner rather than later?

I waited, and the more time that ticked past made me question my suggestion. Perhaps I'd jumped the gun. Maybe she thought I wasn't a man of my word after asking her out when I said we'd go slow for a couple weeks.

Haley: **It's a date, Wyatt.**

Haley: **Just don't get your hopes up or have plans to weasel your way inside my panties by night's end.**

Chuckling and dick swelling, I messaged back my assurance that I could be a patient man—if the prize would be worth it in the end.

She promised it would.

Chapter 7

Haley

I sat curled up on my bed rather than in my usual corner of the couch while messaging with Wyatt.

Garrett lounged in the living room watching a movie, and even though he knew I'd started up a conversation with a potential guy on Missing Link, I wanted to keep Wyatt and all things about him to myself for a while.

Whatever had happened between Garrett and Alec had definitely fucked with his head. I had shown my roommate Wyatt's photo before poking him back. Garrett drooled over my cell, same as I had—then went on to state he was done with dick for the foreseeable future.

He'd refused to open up beyond that statement, but I knew it had to do with his ex.

I'd gone back to studying Wyatt's pic, allowing Garrett his secret. Dark hair and light eyes always did shit to my insides, and Wyatt had worn a blue shirt in his pic that made those orbs of his pop. Add in black, thick lashes, and I knew I would sit and stare at him in person given the chance.

And those lips...don't even get me started. Bowed on top, slightly plumper than the bottom—I wanted them on mine, licking and nibbling, blowing my goddamn mind.

We definitely clicked through messaging, and I allowed myself a bit of hope that he wasn't like the other assholes I'd found on dating sites before Lily had moved out.

I was ready to end my dry spell, and after an hour of back and forth banter, I was interested in giving him a chance.

Even if Wyatt wasn't as hot in person as his pic suggested or he turned out to not be the world's greatest kisser like I hoped for, we seemed to get along great and had a lot in common too.

But I still wanted that phone conversation first.

At the end of our messaging, I gave him my cell number, and we agreed to chat the next night—and meet up for a date Sunday if things continued to run smoothly. We'd gone from an agreement of a few weeks of taking things super slow to a date in less than forty-eight hours, but I had a good feeling about Wyatt.

"So how'd it go with Mr. Hot Stuff?" Garrett asked as soon as I sank onto the couch beside him.

I had a nickname habit—and I'd given Wyatt one the second I'd seen his profile pic.

"Mr. Hot Stuff seems like a sweetheart, but time will tell."

"Did you let him past those ten foot high walls you've got around your heart, or did you keep things on a superficial level?"

I curled up against Garrett, and the stench of the diner he worked at hit my nose. "Ugh. You stink."

Same damn thing I'd said when he'd first gotten home.

"I still haven't showered yet—I wanted to be available the second you finished up your conversation in case you needed an ear."

God, did I love him.

Rather than snuggling in closer, I leaned away and elbowed his arm. "Shower. Then talk. I need my koala, and I'm not getting any closer until you wash that stench off your skin."

"Thought you liked my skin." He smirked, running a hand over his bare, ripped as hell abs.

"Asshole." I poked said muscles, swallowing a mouthful of drool. "Shower. Now."

"Yes, Mommy."

"I'll be your mommy, boy...but you might not enjoy my heavy hand." I gave him shit right back.

He snorted out a laugh while standing and striding through the hallway toward the bathroom we shared. "Strap on a rubber cock, and I just might let you be my sugar momma since I'm no longer interested in men with real dicks."

Arousal, hot and combustible, shot through my core at his joking, and I couldn't find a comeback before he shut himself away.

Closing my eyes, I slumped back on the couch and groaned. "Oh my *fucking god,* that man will be the death of me," I muttered.

Garrett had never gone so far in his teasing, but maybe he lashed out because of the recent knowledge of what his ex had done. I hated to see him so down about his life, but what could I do to make things better?

Wyatt said he was in the market for another laborer, but Garrett didn't seem the dirt and landscaping type.

But what if I could help him in other ways?

I nibbled my lower lip as ideas starting pinging around in my head all thanks to that comment about a goddamn strap on.

One bit of heartache wouldn't truly turn a gay man off from sex for the rest of his life...I felt sure Garrett would get over his disinterest in dick and be back at the hookup apps in a matter of weeks.

Would he be interested in a poly relationship where the only sexual contact would be between him and another guy? He found Wyatt attractive—he'd grabbed a pillow and clutched it to his groin when I'd all but sat on his lap and had shown him Wyatt's write-up and picture.

But would I be willing to share Wyatt with Garrett—sex with one and a platonic relationship with the other if the fake dick thing *was* just a joke? Any time I considered a triad, I saw me with two men bracketing my body. Always.

But...

I loved Garrett and wanted him happy. He might have teased about allowing me to peg the hell out of his ass, but maybe he and Wyatt would connect on a different level than I did with both of them. Perhaps Garrett needed a nice guy to get him get over Alec.

"You're putting the cart before the horse, you moron," I grumbled at myself and tore down my sloppy bun to re-twist my hair into a new updo.

Still messy but less strands falling into my face.

I needed to see how things went with Wyatt first.

Then, I would maybe consider opening another door that included one of my best friends in the equation.

* * *

I'd never had such a first good conversation with a potential date. Had I been focused on sex rather than connecting, I'd have been playing with myself while Wyatt spoke, getting off on just his smooth, deep voice alone.

Saturday night, and I once more sat on my bed in a long T-shirt sipping on chardonnay. A few candles lit around the room created an intimate vibe for what I'd hoped would be a telling chat. I didn't want to waste either of our time if we didn't click.

I'd messaged my cell number to him the night before, and he called right at seven o'clock p.m. on the dot.

He had that deep gravel that hardened nipples and dampened panties with a simple hello.

Or perhaps I just needed to get laid.

After a bit of small talk, Wyatt insisted I go first in telling my shitty life's tale—my adjective, not his—and I agreed. I expected him to cut me off once he grew bored like anyone else did whenever I allowed myself to be vulnerable. Or, he would find the first excuse to hang up on a woman who was just too damn much for her own good.

Garrett had insisted I just open up and share, put all my issues out on the table with the blunt honesty he and Wyatt claimed to appreciate. Since I wasn't about drama and had decided games were a thing of my past, I went with it, even though my stomach twisted as anxiety ate at my insides.

I fucking hated spilling my guts.

About being an only child to a psychotic cunt who lied and manipulated to get her own way and a chickenshit dad who'd done nothing about it. How I had been nothing more than a wall piece in the theatrics of my parent's marriage. How their lack of parenting skills and selfishness had left me needy as fuck and clueless on how to build a life of my own.

Wyatt listened without interruption, not even offering his two cents or tossing out empathy tales from having any similar situations in his past.

"My mom is doing her second stint in a psych ward near Philly, and I haven't spoken to my dad since the day he took off on both of us," I told him without any embarrassment or regrets. My past existed, and nothing I said or did would change it. Sure, anger filled my voice, but that was how I'd survived the pain of my childhood trauma.

Wyatt went quiet when I finished.

"Well? What do you think of me now that I've just spewed the shit of my life's foundation?" I asked, my tone still pissy as I readied to hear how Wyatt was going to take off from the psycho bitch from hell who had more issues than he could count.

"You like honesty?" he asked, his tone steady. Sure.

"Always," I didn't hesitate to answer, a bit of hope weaseling its way into my heart.

"You sound really angry and bitter. I'm not saying you shouldn't be," he hastened to add. "I would be if I were in your shoes."

"Anger is my armor." I went with the truth too. "It's what I cling to when I start to spiral down in the dumps. It keeps me from depression. Probably not healthy." I shrugged even though he couldn't see me. "But it helps me stay afloat, so it can't be a bad thing."

"So, who is your family now since your parents are no longer in your life?" Wyatt asked, sounding truly interested.

"You're ready to move onto the next conversation even though I just revealed how much of a handful I can be?" I asked, wondering if the man on the other end of the line was real.

"If you want to talk about your past and the emotional trauma some more, Haley, I'll listen all day long. Whatever you need."

Fuck, this man.

My heart raced. It would be so damn easy to fall for him. But rather than wallowing in my past, I wanted to move forward in the flutters he'd woken back up inside my belly. "I have a couple of friends—acquaintances, really—but my cousin Lily and most recently Garrett are the two who know me best and love me regardless of my prickliness."

"You don't sound prickly to me," Wyatt argued. "Just wary, as anyone who'd been exposed to such a childhood would be. Dating these days is tough, and finding someone of substance who's interested in the same things as you, let alone honest, is damn near impossible.”

“Preach,” I snipped even though his words filled me with warmth. “But enough about me. Tell me about you.”

“There’s not a whole lot to share.”

“Don’t feign humility,” I said, crossing my stretched out legs in front of me, a smile pulling on my lips over what sounded like a true character trait.

“I’m serious. I work and have a good group of friends I go out with on occasion, but that’s about it. I’m boring, really.”

“You’re one of the sexiest men I’ve seen, Mr. Hot Stuff, so I’m calling bullshit.”

He laughed, the deep chuckle making my belly flip in the best way. “Thanks.”

“My pleasure.” I barely held back my purr that would have taken us down the phone sex route like it always did with guys. “Back to your tale.”

“I’m an only child, but I got lucky in the parents aspect of my life. Neither are judgmental about my sexual preferences, and they've been nothing but supportive. If they'd been able to have more children, we'd have been the picture-perfect family."

"You're one lucky bastard." My jealousy didn't come through in my voice, but I felt it in my chest.

"I am—but I'm hoping to share them with someone or someones sooner than later."

My throat went all tight at the longing in his voice, and I picked at a loose thread on the hem of my old sleep shirt. Wyatt sounded like a giver—not a taker. Definitely a plus in my book.

"They had me in their early forties, so Dad handed over the landscaping business to me a few years ago when he was ready to retire. It's been an uphill battle but one I can honestly say I'm winning."

"Winning—explain," I demanded.

"I don't like to brag." His honesty reflected in his quiet tone, one void of manipulation.

"Tell me your accomplishments you have every damn right to be proud of, Wyatt."

"Fine." He exhaled loudly in my ear. "I have ten employees, five work trucks—all paid off—and I bought myself a house last year."

Wyatt had his shit together—a *massive* checkmark on that pro list.

I didn't know more butterflies existed to join in the ones already fluttering around in my insides. "Do you enjoy your work?"

"I do. Sweating and being physically tired at the end of the day makes me feel like I've accomplished something."

"Exercise." I made a disgusted noise in my throat as I reached for my glass of half-empty wine on my bed stand beside me. "No thanks."

He laughed again as I sipped. "So, what do you do to keep your body in shape?"

"Sex," I tossed out the truthful answer.

Wyatt choked on another laugh.

"Seriously, though," I hurried to add, my face heating, "I haven't hooked up in over eight months, so maybe I ought to consider hitting a gym or something."

He didn't respond right away, and I wondered where his mind went. If I'd fucked up something I'd thought might be a good thing...

"Too crass?" I asked, my hand tightening around my glass's stem as those fluttering wings in my stomach crashed and burned.

"Not at all. I told you I like your bluntness."

"But?" I held my breath.

"You...kind of sent my mind down the path we agreed to put on hold even though we've both been in serious dry spells."

"Mmm," I hummed as warmth spread through my body and settled between my thighs. "Do tell."

Wyatt's deep inhale came through loud and clear, and I bit the inside of my lip. "Two conversations into whatever this is," he said, his tone lowering, "and my dick is more than willing to give you a good workout."

Fuck.

I bit down harder to keep from moaning the word dragging out in my head. While dirty talk usually just made me snicker, Wyatt's husky voice did my arousal factory in. Damp heat hit my core with intense need.

I'd definitely lived too long without the real thing.

I set aside my wine and slouched on my bed. "Now you've got my mind going and my body all warm and tingly," I grumped out the words, wishing we'd travelled my usual route of fucking first, chatting later.

"Do tell," he repeated my suggestion, and I swore I could hear his smirk.

"Shut up," I snipped.

"You started it."

"Don't be an ass."

"I've been told I have a *great* ass."

"I want to see."

Wyatt didn't shoot back another rapid-fire response.

"Well?" I pushed, those wings taking to flight in my belly again, a grin on my face.

"Tomorrow," he stated firmly, "*if* our wine and dine goes well."

"Fine," I simpered, hoping he heard my eye roll. "What other *great* attributes do you have other than those gorgeous blue eyes?"

"What's that you said about your roommate? Abs and a luscious V?"

My armpits prickled with excitement. "Shut. Up."

"I've been told I look damn good in sweats too."

I laughed, squeezing my thighs together. "Now you *are* bragging, you arrogant ass."

"No brag, just fact. It's what happens when you have the job I do."

"Fuck, Wyatt. I thought we weren't going down this road," I said, my tone back to serious.

"It's what we both wanted if things went well, and I'll be honest..." the sounds in my ear went muffled as though he shifted to get comfortable, "we're hitting it off better than anyone I've met on any dating app before."

My smile returned, and I snuggled down beneath my blankets, more at peace than I'd expected after a first conversation. "I feel the same way."

"Since we're in agreement there—then just in case, I should let you know I always use condoms and test regularly."

"Same," I agreed. "I refuse to let a man's dick near me without protection until the day I'm *sure* he's the one I want for the rest of my life."

"Good girl."

I gulped, my skin set ablaze by his rumbled words.

"While I'd love to discuss the rest of your preferences when it comes to sex and all the things that turn you on—"

"Kissing," I blurted and bit my lip to keep from spewing I also had a praise kink.

He chuckled. "I've been told I'm pretty great at that too."

Fuck. Me.

I didn't bother holding back my groan that time. "Change the subject before I beg you to come over here and end my dick drought."

"Tell me three must-haves for your forever man or men."

I let out a sigh over the lighthearted feelings welling up inside me—then I proceeded to repeat to Mr. Hot Stuff all the character traits he'd spelled out about himself.

A man who listened to *hear* rather than respond.

One who wanted to hold my hand through life and take care of me physically and emotionally.

Someone who had their shit together since I didn't.

Garrett had that first in spades but lacked the most basic of all requirements for more than a platonic relationship.

But for the first time in a long fucking time, hope sprang to existence in my heart.

Within twenty-four hours, I would know if Wyatt had put on a façade or was a mythical fantasy come true.

Chapter 8

Garrett

I sat in the living room and pouted, the TV on mute so I could perv on Haley chatting and laughing with Wyatt. While I couldn't make out distinct words, I knew her tones, the different noises she made while enjoying herself, and she seemed to be having a blast.

No moans or groans hit my ears, thank fuck, and I wondered if she and Wyatt had actually stuck to their agreement to keep things on the lighter side of dating for a few weeks rather than having phone sex.

She seemed pretty gone on him just after their messaging the night before and had told me everything she'd learned about Wyatt. He was confident and seemed to have his shit together—

sounded like the type of man who could take care of her.

Compared to Wyatt, I fell short of everything she wanted and needed by about ten miles. I would never be good enough for Haley even if our relationship went beyond friendship. Yes, I knew I met a lot of her emotional needs, but he filled in the gaps where I sorely lacked.

Wyatt seemed like a decent guy from all she'd said, but I wondered how much of a front he'd put on to weasel his way between her thighs.

Because let's face it—guys did whatever they had to in order to land pussy or ass when they set their mind on getting some.

Alec had been a smooth talker too. Made promises and manipulated me into giving him what he wanted all the damn time—me under him because he lusted after my spectacular backside.

Not once did he let me top, but I'd contented myself with our relationship because of who he was and how much I'd adored him.

Haley barked out a laugh through the wall separating us, deepening my scowl. Whatever I'd thought about my ex in the beginning didn't compare to my feelings for her. What she and I shared went deeper than sexual experience, a closeness I hadn't found with anyone before, blood relations included.

My grandparents had raised me and would never accept my sexuality. Strict Baptists, they didn't approve of my "choice" to like guys but at least they hadn't disowned me. Family gatherings were awkward as fuck, and I really had no desire to go back to the land of suppression.

And leaving Haley wasn't an option.

But with how she hated manipulators and liars, I was doomed for constant regret when it came to her.

Fuck my life.

I pushed off the couch and took a shower, having heard enough of another guy making my Haley happy. Jealousy turned me into a grump, and I shut myself into my bedroom once I used up all the hot water, pillow over my head to wallow in the shit hole I'd created for myself.

I lived in a mess of my own making, and I didn't know how to clean up or fix the disaster.

Sleep eventually came, but I dreamed of Haley dancing on the beach, flowers in her hair, her lips smiling for me. Hands beckoning me to play in the lapping waves with her, to just *be* in the moment of love and contentment from finding where we belonged.

With each other.

I woke hard and just as brokenhearted as I'd been the night before.

And shit only got worse.

Haley never crawled out of bed before me on mornings she didn't have to open *Pieces*, but she met me in the kitchen with a steaming cup of coffee and bright eyes. "Morning!"

I couldn't bring myself to smile at her odd display of early jolliness, but I at least thanked her for the hot mug.

"Did you get off with him over the phone last night or something?" I muttered and slumped onto the couch, keeping my back to her so she wouldn't see how her happiness over Wyatt knifed at my chest.

"We definitely could have but chose not to. I'm telling you—" Haley melted onto the couch beside me with a ridiculous sigh, cradling her coffee in her hands "—he's definitely got my mind and panties all twisted up."

"He's one hell of a catch, huh?" I asked, my tone bland, thank fuck.

"A girl can hope, right?"

I didn't need to glance her way to know she had hearts in her eyes and a dreamy smile on her lips that I had fantasized of kissing since the day we'd met.

"We're going out to dinner tonight," she tacked on and took a sip of her coffee while curling her bare legs beneath her body.

Fuck.

"What happened to getting to know each other over the phone for a few weeks?" I definitely sounded like a moody prick.

"We've connected. Really hit it off. I went with honesty like you suggested and unloaded all the shit of my life into his ear. He didn't run away. Asked me questions— told me he was there for me if I ever needed to talk. I'm feeling really good about taking the next step." She didn't sound as though she'd picked up on my mood or the dented skin between my eyes.

Haley tended to fall fast and hard for guys and regretted her choices more often than not when considering more than a hookup.

Uneasiness slithered atop my heartache, and I hated myself for having told her to be vulnerable. It's what had made me lose my heart to her too. "Just be careful, okay? Don't go back to his place—and text me his license plate number."

Haley leaned over and kissed my bare shoulder.

I refused to focus on the softness of the caress on my skin that blazed fire through my veins. "Better yet, bring him back here like you said you and Lily always used to do with hookups."

"Ew. I do *not* want you to hear us and have you fantasizing about being the one impaled by Wyatt's dick."

Jealousy stirred like a hornet's nest, wiping all other emotions from my head, and I forced myself to enjoy a swallow of coffee before I spoke and ousted exactly how I felt.

"I really wish you weren't gay, Garrett Moore," Haley said before I could think of a reply.

I choked on my mouthful of coffee and coughed a few times while she beat her fist on my back. "Why's that?" I asked, my voice rasped from the hot liquid going down the wrong tube.

"Because if you weren't, I could almost believe in happily ever afters," she said with a sigh, once more sinking into the couch.

My mouth opened to spill my guts—and I snapped my jaw shut just as fast. I'd already dug my grave with Haley. Admitting to lying to her for the previous eight months would put me on her shit list, ruining the near-perfect man she believed me to be.

No more best friend, no more snuggle bug, and definitely no more roof over my head.

Stomach churning and chest tight, I swallowed hard, hating what I was about to do. "I'm hooking up with a guy tonight—met him on Grindr," I tossed out, forcing myself to sound nonchalant in continuing on with my bullshit life.

She backhanded where she'd smooched. "Why didn't you tell me you were going after dick again?"

Because I'm not.

I shrugged, having enough of my own lies for the day. "I won't be home, so don't hold back on bringing Wyatt here if things go well. My ears won't be around to listen in to tempt me to jerk off."

Haley relaxed and leaned into me, filling my nose with the scent of lavender and sweetness. "I'm so glad you aren't letting the Alec situation hold you back from finding love."

I'd already found it—but my place wouldn't ever be beside her because I was nothing but a jaded liar.

I can give her one truth…

"Alec's sister was sexually assaulted because of me." I blurted out my life's worst mistake, needing some sense of honesty for all the shit I'd been spewing at Haley lately.

"Fuck." Haley set her coffee aside—something she never did until the mug emptied—and wound an arm around my chest to squeeze me tight. "Give it to me."

So I did, puking out words and emotions in the hopes I would feel better about myself.

The party Sindy had been told by her parents to not attend. A phone call from Alec asking me to go pick her up, his words something along the lines of trusting me to keep her safe. How my ignored plea for her to leave with me had ended with my body battered by the three guys she'd been there with.

She had laughed the entire time boots battled with my guts.

I had held back the curses I'd wanted to scream at her and left the second they'd allowed me to stumble away.

Those men later took advantage of her, and I'd been blamed because I didn't have big enough balls to make her go with me.

"She lied about what happened. Alec's little sister told him that she would have listened to me—*if* I'd shown up." Anger burned inside me as I spilled the rest of the shit from the following days.

The text demanding I move out and how the whole affair had landed me on the damn blacklist in Hollywood.

"What a fucking asshole," Haley muttered. "He wouldn't even listen to your side of the story?"

"She's his little sister, the supposed angel the entire family adores. They never met the nasty side of her like I did."

"Why did she let you see beneath her mask?"

"Sindy is a needy little bitch and hated that I took her big brother's attention away from her. She put on a sweet front for the family, but any time she happened to catch me alone, those true colors raged. I secretly always wondered if she had...unhealthy feelings for him."

"Spoiled princess, fake ass cunt," Haley muttered, her support warming my chest.

"That sums her up perfectly." I set aside my empty mug and tipped my head back, closing my eyes. My fingers entwined with Haley's atop my heart, and I soaked in the moment of closeness without the usual arousal. The sweet contentment was almost as good as sex.

"I'm sorry," she whispered, her breath hot on my shoulder where her cheek rested.

"Yeah, me too."

"So, what are you going to do with your dream about becoming a movie star?"

"That dream died. I'm a master of washing dishes, haven't you heard? I've had offers from dozens of five-star restaurants and everything."

"What other skills do you have?"

"Sucking dick." I muttered the poor truth of my life.

Haley snorted a laugh and snuggled closer, bringing on the beginnings of that attraction I couldn't control. "That's one thing we have in common."

I barely bit back my groan over the image in my head of her sinking to her knees between my thighs and closing her lips around my girth. It wasn't the first time I'd fantasized—and certainly wouldn't be the last.

Time to move.

"Gotta shit."

"Ew!" She leaned away and backhanded me again. "TMI. Seriously."

Maybe, but it got her off me so I could hop up and escape before I sported a boner I couldn't reason away since the TV's screen sat black and silent and there were no men around to blame.

Shit, showered, shaved, and balls emptied, I closed myself in my bedroom on a mission—find a reason to escape our apartment that night.

Fuck knew I couldn't deal with jealousy over Wyatt touching the body I longed to love on more than I wanted another dick.

Chapter 9

Wyatt

I'd woken up Sunday morning with butterflies like I was in middle school again and crushing on a girl for the first time.

Was it possible to be smitten with someone after only two conversations? Sure she had some issues in her life, unresolved shit, but who didn't? It was like a part of her reached out through cyberspace and through the phone line, snagging hold of my heart. I wanted to clasp her hand tightly in mind. Give her the support she needed while facing down her demons.

Haley had managed to make my head spin internally, and I couldn't keep from getting my hopes up that we had serious potential. While leaning against my kitchen counter drinking my first cup of coffee, I opened the app to stare at her picture again.

A little red heart in the app's notifications let me know Missing Link had found me another match. Since there was nothing wrong with having a backup plan, I decided to just click on the profile and take a peek.

I choked on my coffee as the woman's picture showed on screen.

"The fuck?" I set my mug aside and zoomed in closer at the smiling dark-haired woman with blue eyes. "What the actual fuck?" I burst out again, my tone high like someone had squeezed my balls.

She was me—but with longer hair.

The same cowlick I had swept hers to the side. An identical dimple on one cheek. Her slightly off-center nose and the arched upper lip, fuller than the lower...

I rubbed my eyes, sure they played tricks on me.

A mirror image of me still smiled when I opened them again. Zooming in revealed the same golden ring around our pupils—and the tiny mole at the corner of an eye.

Scrubbing a hand over my mouth and scruffy jaw, I considered the implications. While I'd heard the myth every person had a twin on the earth, our similarities were...uncanny. Like we'd been cut from the same cloth...

I poked to open the lines of communication between us, because what other choice did I have? The green circle above her name let me know she was scrolling the app—and she poked back within seconds, a message popping up immediately afterward.

@RiverAngel: **Rowan?!?**

Wyatt, I replied, my forehead dented. **Who's Rowan, and why the fuck do I feel like I looked into a mirror when I checked out your profile pic?**

@RiverAngel: **Shit. I can't believe this. Okay...so... were you adopted by any chance?**

A fucking elephant sat on my chest as my mind raced. Mom and Dad were both fair-haired, one with dark eyes, one with hazel—but I'd never questioned the fact that I was their opposite looks-wise. I'd never been anything but their son, no question from friends or other family members, since half of Dad's relatives tended toward dark hair like mine.

My hands shook as I struggled to reply. **Not that I'm aware of, but I'll be honest—I look nothing like my parents.**

"Fuck." I rubbed at my scruff again, curses spilling from me. Mom and Dad hadn't called me anything but son, hadn't suggested a single time that we didn't share blood.

But as my heart thumped, I realized they might have lied to me. I freakishly towered over everyone in my small-statured family. Not a single aunt, uncle, or cousin had blue eyes either.

I hit the video option for the woman who'd opened up my mind to what I'd never given too much thought before.

"Answer...please fucking answer." I whispered, hoping and dreading she did.

The call went through, and I sank to the floor, my cell clutched in my hands. There was no denying the woman on my screen could be my identical twin was as her eyes filled with tears.

"My brother and I were in the system and separated when we were two," she stated in greeting, the words barely escaped her trembling lips.

I let out another curse.

It was highly possible my real name was Rowan.

$$* * *$$

Talk about toeing the line of a fucking identity crisis.

If River was right, I had no goddamn clue who I was, who my *real* parents had been—neither did River, but at least her adoptive parents kept her birth name and knew her mother's surname.

River hadn't ever gone looking for the woman who'd given her up, but her adoptive parents had told her at an early age that she had a twin brother who had already been adopted. They were honest with her, had her trust, and she'd never felt the need to find the woman who'd abandoned her.

She'd spent years searching for her brother, but there was no Rowan Angel to be found.

Because he didn't exist.

Or did he?

Numbness had settled over my mind, and I struggled to wrap my head around the fact I might be her missing twin even though she stared back at me through my cell in vibrant colors.

River and I were on the phone for hours, and I couldn't believe how our thoughts aligned, how we finished each other's sentences...talk about a mind fuck. As the minutes slipped past, I found myself believing I'd been adopted, that she was a piece of my soul I'd been missing and didn't even realize until fate slammed us together.

And until we exchanged numbers and agreed to meet in person in the near future, I was convinced River was my sister.

Emotions slammed into me like a goddamn sledgehammer in the sudden silence after hanging up. Elation. Hurt...a sense of betrayal for having been lied to—and being abandoned by the woman who'd given birth to us.

I couldn't decide if I was happy River and I had found one another, angry that my entire life was a lie, or just plain disappointed in the two people I had trusted without question.

Well, I had a shit ton of wonderings going on in my head.

Who had given birth to me and River?

Why hadn't my adoptive parents told me?

What was their purpose in keeping my real identity from me?

Did they have my birth certificate?

Had they known about my twin sister?

Was it their decision to separate us, to take away the one blood relative I had?

Suspicion wrapped around my stomach and squeezed like a vise, keeping me on the verge of nausea while I hopped in my truck and drove the twenty minutes to my parents'.

Mom and Dad.

Tina and Lionel.

I never had to knock, so I let myself into my childhood home without thought. While glancing around, I realized everything about the front door, the entryway, the family photos hanging on the wall along the stairs to my right were no longer my life's foundation or my truth.

A gaping hole widened inside me, slowing eating away at what I thought I'd known, all I had based my entire fucking life on.

Dad—Lionel—sat in his recliner to my left watching baseball. Pots clanging in the kitchen toward the small house's back told me Mom—Tina—cleaned up the lunch dishes.

My home—my cornerstone.

All crumbled to dust—

"Hey, son," Lionel greeted me, a big grin on his face.

I stood and stared, studying the only face of a father I could remember. River had convinced me, but I found myself hoping...

Lionel's smile flatlined, worry pulling his eyes into a frown at my lack of greeting. "Is everything okay?"

"No," I bit the word out, my chest aching, blunt fingernails digging into my palms at my sides.

Tina came into the living room, drying her hands on a dish towel. The light in her eyes at seeing me faded just as quickly without doubt from the unease that had to radiate off me like blinding sun rays. "Wyatt? What are you doing here?"

"Did you lie to me? This whole time? My entire *fucking* life?" My voice cracked, and I swallowed hard.

I rarely cursed in front of them—color leeched from Tina's face.

"What's going on?" She glanced at Lionel before turning back toward me and closing the distance between us. "Wyatt?"

I held up my shaking hand to stop her from entering my personal space, nausea rising up the back of my throat. "That's not the name I was given at birth, is it?" I barely managed to rasp out.

Tina swayed, the towel dropping from her hands, and Lionel got up from his chair to grasp her elbow before she fell over.

"Sit," he murmured, leading her to the couch. He settled beside her, clutching her hand. Both had paled, their eyes gone wide.

Their immediate lack of denial twisted my insides into a tight knot, and I clenched my jaw to keep from cursing again. The sense of betrayal rose to choke me. Anger, bright and life-giving lit inside me, and I grabbed hold of it so I wouldn't break down.

Armor of anger.

I had a deeper understanding of Haley in that moment and couldn't fault her for clinging to an emotion that would keep her head afloat.

Lionel swallowed audibly and found his voice first. "Your mom couldn't have children—"

"Tina's not my mom!" I snapped out, uncaring of being insensitive.

"How can you say that?" Tina cried, but Lionel shushed her, pulling her against his side.

"We tried for over ten years and couldn't conceive. Adoption was our only final option."

I'd been a last choice for them.

"Why didn't you tell me?" Wetness gathered in my eyes, hazing the vision of them, and I clenched my fists tighter to keep from breaking down.

"You were—*are*—our son regardless of our not sharing blood. We didn't want you to deal with the trauma that I did as a child."

I reeled back like I'd been slapped. How many secrets had they kept from me? "You were adopted too?"

Lionel nodded.

"The fuck?" I tipped my head back to escape their stares, blinking away tears and taking note of the popcorn ceiling Lionel and I had repainted over the winter. We'd laughed. Drank beers. Dripped one too many splotches of white on Tina's hardwood floors we'd installed three years earlier. Even though weight lay heavy on my shoulders, it felt like I free-fell through uncertainty. "I—I can't process this... *Fuck*."

I lowered my focus onto the two people I had trusted the most and inhaled until it hurt. "Were you aware I had a twin sister?" I asked, my voice no more than a ragged whisper.

They shared a look, and the agony on their faces said it all. That ache in my chest turned to a twisting knife, and I swallowed hard.

"You fucking lied to me." My inhale stuttered on a near sob. "I—I don't even know who the hell I am anymore."

"You're our son," Tina cried, tears rolling down her cheeks.

On paper. I wanted to lash out but couldn't find my voice through the thickness closing off my throat.

"Wyatt—please." Lionel motioned toward the recliner he'd vacated to comfort his wife.

He'd chosen her, caring for her emotions over mine.

My thoughts, my feelings, scattered on a brisk breeze. I had to leave before I lost my shit.

Legs weak and eyesight hazed by tears, I spun on my heel, ignoring the pleas of the people who'd raised me, to escape what the sight of them did to my head and heart.

No matter the miles, the distance I put between us physically didn't ease my confliction over my existence and where I belonged.

The crumbling of my entire foundation left me devastated and stumbling through the rubble of what I'd thought had been a good life.

Chapter 10

Haley

Excitement over seeing Wyatt kept me grinning all day long, and it had nothing to do with how hot his body might be or how good-looking he was. I genuinely couldn't wait to sit and chat in person like we had so effortlessly over the phone.

Like Garrett, Wyatt kept the shadows in my head at bay, like a shield of happiness shining with blinding light.

I'd thought I would be content with just talking and hanging out with Wyatt, but as each hour passed by, whittling down the time until we met face to face, I couldn't stop the arousal train his voice had dragged me onto.

Once he'd set desire in motion, there'd been no stopping it.

I wanted to taste his lips, prayed to all the fucking gods of the universe he knew how to make a woman's knees weak with his mouth. A nice-sized dick would definitely be a check mark in the positive category, but I didn't really believe in mythical creatures.

That didn't stop me from hoping.

Garrett left for his hookup mid-afternoon, and I'd wished him luck since he'd been a pissy bitch all morning long.

And I'd thought *I* needed dick.

I envied the fucker he took off to meet, wondering if he'd be allowed to feast on Garrett's lips and that V like I'd often dreamed about while he used my thigh as his pillow and I played with his hair.

Pushing aside my jealousy came easily because of the night ahead of me and all its possibilities.

I considered getting myself off in the shower so my thoughts wouldn't be overshadowed by wet panties during my date with Wyatt but decided against it. If we went further than expected after that wine and dine we'd agreed on, I wanted to be edged to the point that any climax would rob me of strength and cognitive abilities.

That meant no getting off until later.

Hopefully with Mr. Hot Stuff wrecking me with his mouth and dick.

My skin tingled and pulse thrummed while getting ready, which caused my hands to shake. I messed up my eyeliner three times before getting it right. At least I didn't poke out my eye with my mascara wand.

Lily texted me a good luck, and I shot back two thumbs up and a promise to call her—but told her to not wait up.

Just in case.

In my excitement, I sat ready to roll an hour before Wyatt and I had agreed to meet, and I couldn't find distraction to save my life.

My cell rang, and the sight of Wyatt's number and blue-shirted image I'd saved skyrocketed my heart rate and stretched my lips in a wide grin.

"Hey," I answered, breathless like I'd sprinted a mile even though I'd been lounging on my ass channel surfing on the TV.

"Hi. So, I got some fucked up news." His voice sounded scratchy, like he'd been crying for hours on end.

I sat up on the couch's edge while muting the TV, all trace of my smile gone. "Are you okay?"

"Not really, no. Fuck, I don't know what to do," he muttered as though to himself.

"Talk to me, Wyatt. What's going on?"

He cursed again, his voice breaking. "I'm sorry, but I— I'm not really in the right frame of mind to meet you for dinner."

My heart fell, but my concern for his well-being overrode disappointment. "What can I do to help? I mean, if it's too private, tell me to fuck off and I will."

"No. It's fine." He blew out a huge exhale, and even that sounded shaky. "I found out earlier today that I was adopted."

The words he'd used to describe his parents flashed back through my mind—how awesome they were, how supportive of his coming out as bi. He'd been lucky in the parent department.

And his identity had been ripped from beneath his feet.

I could hear the agony in his words, the underlying anger, the inability to find emotional footing.

"We're going to dinner," I told him, my tone not allowing argument. "We're going to enjoy a nice meal, a bottle of wine, and you're going to unload all the emotions you're feeling right now onto the table so I can shoulder them with you."

"Goddamnit, Haley. You barely know me..." Wyatt choked on a laugh that still held evidence of tears. "Are you for real?"

I wondered the same about him and suddenly wished Garrett could go along with us because he was better equipped to comfort Wyatt than I was. But my roommate's story wasn't mine to tell.

"Meet me at Shadow's Lounge like we agreed on, and you'll find that out for yourself."

Another heavy sigh filled my ear. "I'm not going to be the best of company tonight."

"How about you let me decide on that, okay?"

"And if I'm nothing but a disappointment?"

Empathy swelled in my heart, creating a sad smile on my face. "Then I'll cling to your hand and act as your leaning post."

"You're like five-foot nothing to my six-plus."

"Then you'll get onto your knees so I can hold the rest of you up."

He snorted a laugh that sounded a hell of a lot lighter than when he'd first called.

I pushed aside the thought he might be lingering on that knees comment and what it might look like in his head.

"We've got reservations at six, but I'm ready now if you want to meet earlier," I offered, thinking he might need that ear sooner than later.

"The stress of this day has made me sweat, the anxiety coming out of my pores. You'll want me to take the time to shower. Trust me on that."

"Go pretty yourself up for me then, and I'll meet you there."

"Thanks, Haley. Seriously. Less than five minutes of conversation with you and I'm more settled than I have been all day long."

"Imagine how you'll feel after sitting across from me for a few hours," I teased.

"What if I'd rather be beside you, sharing body heat?" His tone suggested he didn't mean snuggled on a table's booth, thighs and shoulders pressed tight while we perused the menu.

"You had to go there, didn't you?"

I could almost hear his shrug and the smirk I'd studied on his profile picture. "Sex *is* a great way to take your mind off shit."

He had a point, but Wyatt carried a lot of heaviness in his heart that needed to be eased first.

"Wine and dine," I told him. "Six—and don't be late."

"Oh my fucking God," I groaned, wide-eyed and staring at the sexy as fuck man who walked into Shadow's Lounge at the exact minute I'd told him to.

Wyatt knew how to wear a pair of jeans, and the button-down black shirt with its sleeves rolled to show off thick, tattooed forearms had me sitting straighter in the chair I'd been waiting on like a sugar-high toddler.

His dark hair was longer on the top, fading down to the length of the neatly trimmed scruff along his jaw. Those lips...

I licked mine—and his blue-eyed gaze landed on me.

The slight furrow between his eyebrows eased as a slow smirk curled one side of his mouth.

Ruined panties stuck to my pussy, same as Garrett's similar grin always affected me—and Wyatt and I still had a good thirty feet separating us.

He headed toward the high table where I sat shivering, his steps sure. Confident.

But with those wide shoulders and prominent pec muscles as well as the massive thighs flexing beneath his jeans, what man wouldn't be sure of himself?

He had the type of eyebrows a woman would kill for, thick and perfectly arched above eyes that would cause any human to swoon. Pale blue. Lashes so thick and black they appeared wet.

Was there such a thing as *more* than divine perfection?

Absolutely criminal.

"Haley." His rumbled tone raised goosebumps over my arms as he neared, and I slid off my stool onto weak legs to greet him.

Five feet of crackling energy between us. Three....

"Hey," I squeaked out.

Wyatt came right into my personal space without asking, but I wouldn't have denied him. He wrapped those arms around me like they belonged there, lifting me off the ground.

Good. Fucking. God.

Wyatt smelled of soap and male virility, his hard body there and gone before I got a chance to catch my breath and cop a proper feel.

"Thank you for pushing me to get out of my house and stop wallowing, Haley. I needed this."

Warmth flooded my face as he set me onto my feet again. "My pleasure." I tipped my head back to hold his gaze as his hands settled onto my waist.

"Sorry for grabbing you up like that—I just really needed a hug," he murmured with his rumbly voice licking heat over my skin.

"And it was entirely too short to satisfy if you ask me," I shot back, one of my eyebrows arching in suggestion that he try once more.

Wyatt's smile grew, flashing pearly white teeth, and he snagged me up off the ground a second time, his nose in my hair, those strong arms of his banded around my back.

Had we been anywhere but Shadow's, I'd have wrapped my legs around his waist and set to rutting against his hard body until I erupted.

"You smell good," he murmured, his voice a rumbled groan emanating from the chest beneath my ear. "Like flowers and springtime."

I filled my lungs with all things spice and man, melting inside over how delicious he felt against me.

Same as Garrett.

An inner sigh went through me at the thought Garrett might already have some guy on his knees, but I pushed against the sting in my chest, determined to focus on my date.

Rock hard arms smothered me against an equally granite-like torso that had every single one of my arousal buttons flicked the fuck on.

Wyatt was damn delicious—and I hadn't seen or touched his skin.

Once he set me back on my feet and we separated to sit down, I decided my body's reaction to touching his had nothing to do with my dry spell.

Clear skin, a beauty mark at the corner of one of his eyes, full lips, corded muscles even in his neck...the hint of tanned, bare chest I could make out between the opened buttons.

Muscular shoulders stretching the material of his shirt.

Inked forearms.

My mouth watered.

"Eyes up here, beautiful."

Cheeks heating again, I gave his face my attention. "You're pretty damn fine yourself."

We both laughed lightly, my insides squirming like a three-year-old who'd been told to sit still. Both of our smiles slowly faded, and I leaned onto the table, crossing my arms. Wyatt glanced down at my boobs, and I totally took advantage of my posture to plump up my cleavage, but I ignored my desire to tease further.

"How are you doing, Wyatt?"

A heavy sigh sank him back into his chair, and he lifted his focus off my chest. "Floundering."

"I can imagine. Will you tell me what happened? Sometimes it's easier opening up to a near stranger to unload what's weighing on your mind." Again, I thought of my roommate and how he would better understand than me.

"You don't feel like a stranger," Wyatt stated quietly, those intense orbs of his studying my face, "and believe it or not, I wanted to talk to you. I had already decided I would word vomit the shit of my life today over the phone if we ended up putting our dinner date off for a later time."

My throat tightened, my eyes stinging at the glaze creeping over his. He felt as invested, as connected as I did. How the fuck was that possible after two conversations?

Then again, I rarely conversed. Just went for the dick.

Pleasant flutters rose in my belly over the prospect we might actually have found something worth the effort of exploring outside of sex.

"What can I get you to drink?" The waitress interrupted, and Wyatt glanced at the glass of chardonnay I'd been nursing since I showed up ten minutes early in my anticipation of our date starting.

"Just water for now," he told her, offering her a smile that didn't reach his eyes.

She ambled off.

"Let's figure out what we want to eat, then settle in," I suggested.

Wyatt rubbed his palms down his thighs and nodded, eyeing the menu. "Sounds good."

Less than five minutes later, we had our order put through to the kitchen, and we once more caught each other's gazes across the table.

Quiet music filtered through hidden speakers, light jazz and dimmed lighting creating a sexy mood, but heaviness seemed to hang over Wyatt's head. I tended toward selfishness when going out with hookups, but something inside me cared about his emotions. Having shit for parents amped up my empathy, and I found myself leaning forward as though closing the distance between us might help him deal with what he'd learned.

"Give it to me," I said.

One of his eyebrows arched, and I rolled my eyes.

"Tell me what happened," I amended my words with a smile.

"This morning," he began and blew out a steady exhale before starting again. "I was excited about our date, flying high, and got on my cell to check social media while drinking my first cup of coffee. A red heart notification let me know someone had poked me on Missing Link, so I brought up their profile just in case…"

He motioned between us, and I nodded, refusing to allow jealousy to grumble in my mind. Honestly, I probably would have done the same if a guy had poked me.

"The second I laid eyes on her profile picture, I went to the floor. Literally. It was like looking in a mirror, but she has longer hair."

"Oh shit," I whispered, my eyes popping wide as I realized where he was going with his story. What were the chances?

Wyatt went on to tell me how he put through a video call to the woman who'd poked him and ended up learning his real name.

Rowan Angel, twin to sister River.

His eyes went all misty again while talking about her, sharing every bit of information he could recall from their hours-long conversation, including not knowing where their birth mother or father were.

That sadness dissolved when he moved on to the confrontation with his adoptive parents where he told me he clung to his anger, that sense of betrayal, exactly as I did whenever the hurt over my parents became too much.

Our gazes stayed locked, the words and emotional connection between us becoming a living, tangible entity.

The waitress brought our food, cutting Wyatt off mid-sentence about how his dad—Lionel—had coddled his wife Tina rather than going to Wyatt. While steaming plates were delivered in front of us, I tried to imagine how insignificant he must have felt in that moment.

For any child, no matter their age, being second choice hurt like fuck.

I knew that all too damn well, my own heart aching whenever I thought too hard on my chickenshit dad who'd chosen self-preservation rather than me whenever dealing with my psycho mom.

When our waitress moved off, I reached over the table for Wyatt's hand.

He wound his calloused fingers through mine, and I squeezed, my smile uncertain, eyes watery.

"Are we going to pray for our dinner?" he asked with a lopsided smirk.

"Fuck no." I snickered and squeezed his hand again. "Just offering what support and affection I can right now. I can't imagine the emotions you must have been dealing with all day today."

"Anger, disappointment, elation at finding out I had a sibling I've always wanted…betrayed and bitter…it's overwhelming to say the least. I know you understand quite a bit of all those feelings too."

I held his steady gaze as that tether between us leaked from my hand into his and vice versa, tying us together. While I wanted to poke and prod, dig into his brain about his plans for seeking out his birth parents and getting together with his sister, I chose to let the matter rest.

Wyatt needed a break from all the negativity in his mind, same as I often did when depression came knocking. I desired to give him a distraction to ease the tension in his shoulders.

But what if he still needed to talk about it?

"I'm all ears as promised," I said, "but if you're wanting something else, a change of topic so you can enjoy your dinner, I can do that too."

Wyatt lifted my hand to his mouth, lightly pressing his soft lips against my knuckles and sending shivers clear through my body. "Thank you, Haley."

My hand tingled, the warmth of his kiss lingering after he released his hold. "My pleasure." At least, I certainly hoped it would be.

He grinned as though reading my thoughts—or maybe my arousal leaked out in those two words. "Let's eat, then maybe we can get out of here, and we'll snuggle the hell out of each other until my mind grows quiet."

Snuggle. Naked. Warm skin and wandering hands...

"I can think of a few ways to distract your mind faster than a cuddle fest," I said, biting back a suggestive smirk, my pulse thrumming with heated blood.

Wyatt narrowed his gaze. "You're a little tease."

"It's not teasing if I plan on delivering," I promised, having decided to fuck going slow. I liked Wyatt, we *definitely* had one hell of a connection, and I wanted a a lot more than just his hard body and dick.

One of his eyebrows arched, those thickly-lashed eyes going a shade darker.

Arousal once more coursed through my body, and I shifted on my chair.

"I thought we were taking our time with this," Wyatt murmured, the deep timbre of his voice pebbling my nipples to tight, aching points.

Thank fuck for padded bras.

"I'm using the excuse that it's empathy making me want to soothe you," I tossed out with a bit of sass. "Trust me—I understand your need for distraction."

He chuckled while shaking his head and turned his focus on his steak. "Eat, Haley. Then we can decide where and how far we're going."

"My place because Garrett is out for the night, and going *all* the way is a good option," I added, a lot more breathless than I could help, hoping like hell I could get Wyatt to agree.

"God, Haley." He shook his head, hand clenched around a fork and serrated knife. "What am I going to do with you?"

I didn't think he meant to really question me, so I bit back the words that tickled my tongue.

A good, hard fucking would be nice.

Chapter 11

Wyatt

I'd never met the whole package before, the type of woman who could listen without interruption, ask questions because she truly cared, and who looked as delicious as a luscious slice of coconut cream pie.

The beguiling curl of her lips begged my tongue to take a taste. A gentle slope of tanned skin along her neck peeking at me through maroon-colored tresses made my teeth itch to scrape the flesh. Slender shoulders and a perfect amount of cleavage from her low-cut white shirt caused dampness to coat my palms time and again.

I'd been on a goddamn roller coaster of emotions since early that morning, but just chatting about our favorite TV shows—reality for both of us—settled my insides better than any pink chalk-like liquid medicine.

We got into the latest dating show that had taken the US by storm, but Haley lost the sparkle in her eyes.

"Jessica Braddock is a bitch, a complete narcissist."

The latest bachelorette to join in the house where the cast of singles had been shut in together for two weeks. Forced proximity hadn't worked out well for finding any happily ever afters, and I had to agree with Haley's thoughts on the newest addition.

And Haley would know the TV star's character. She'd told me all about her mom the night before.

"She's making every goddamn thing about her, and don't get me started on the tears." Haley rolled her eyes. "Manipulative little whore. She got caught lying to save her own ass—twice—and the men are still falling at her feet because of honeyed words. How can they not see the red flags she's waving like those guys do at the end of car races?"

I didn't correct her about them being checkered but let her go on with her tirade. Haley's mom had done some serious damage to her heart. Broke down her ability to trust easily. The narcissistic woman had made it hard for Haley to lower her walls and be vulnerable.

But she'd shared with me more than I expected—and I saw firsthand how her emotions played out on her face.

Her eyes couldn't lie, and her going off about some random woman on TV gave me information into her inside workings I craved to understand.

"You seem super empathetic," I said when she paused to take a bite of her dinner. "Have you ever put yourself in that woman's shoes? Tried to figure out why she behaves that way? Not that I'm condoning cheating or anything."

"And why the fuck would I? She's just like my mom." Haley's anger coated every word—wrapped around her like that armor she spoke of to protect herself from the hurt.

"I'm just saying that our pasts oftentimes dictate how we react. The words that leave our mouths. Sometimes it's involuntary, and if a person isn't aware of their problems…"

I shrugged, deciding psychoanalyzing probably wasn't the best thing to be doing on our first date.

"There are no excuse for lies and manipulation. Period."

I'd finished my dinner and sat back, watching Haley's expressive face as she continued to go off about a girl she hadn't ever met.

Dark eyes flashing, furrowed brow, lips pouting and spouting curses...I shouldn't have been turned on by Haley's understandable tantrum, but she wore the pissed off look well.

"That Joshua Richards isn't much better," she spewed, waving her fork. "They're a fucking match made in heaven if you ask me. Selfish prick, narcissistic bitch. They ought to just put a ring on it and be miserable together."

I shouldn't have been enjoying myself as she unintentionally bared herself to me, but I couldn't bite back my grin.

Haley caught the humor on my face anyway. "What?" she snipped, fork still upright in her hand, those eyes of Jameson like liquid fire.

"You're fucking gorgeous when you're riled up."

Haley narrowed her gaze, and I lost my ability to keep from laughing.

"Christ, Haley, I like your spirit. Your fire. You're one hell of a woman."

The pissiness leached away from her face, and she went all soft in less than two heartbeats. Yet another telling reaction I soaked the fuck up.

Haley craved edification and attention—and I had a shit ton to give if she'd let me. "You aren't so bad yourself," she murmured, pink on her cheeks.

"Not so bad, huh?" I raised an eyebrow, deciding I'd had enough of the serious conversations and getting to know your likes and all that shit continuation from what we'd shared on Friday and Saturday night.

She'd promised distraction, and even though she'd already delivered more than I'd expected over our dinner, she left me aching.

Wanting more.

Haley seemed to be on the same page because her focus dropped to my mouth.

I rubbed my thumb over the corner of where she stared as though to wipe away a bit of steak sauce, gently pulling my lip from my teeth.

A shudder rippled through her, dilating her pupils.

I dropped my hand and bit on my lower lip, slowly allowing the flesh to slip free.

"Oh. My. God." Her groan sent a rush of blood to my dick.

"Hmm?"

"If you're trying to ruin my panties, you already did that," she said, turning her flirting eyes back on mine. "The second you walked in and I caught sight of you, my body was ready for round one."

Blood rushed to my groin. "How many rounds do you think you have in you, sweet Haley?"

A shiver raised goosebumps over her bare arms. "Six, at least."

"Six?" I barked a laugh even though she sounded serious as fuck. "I'm not seventeen anymore."

"Then you can have two—*if* you can," she said, those dark eyes of hers once more twinkling and teasing.

"Just for the record, twice for me is *easily* done."

"Fine then. I'll take care of the other four by myself while you watch."

"The fuck you will," I argued, my voice going low as I leaned forward. "I'd thought you wanted my dick six times in the next twelve or so hours, but since we're talking climaxes, I promise you a half-dozen is only an appetizer."

She stared slack-jawed, eyes once more going wide.

"Don't think I can get you off like that?" I asked, pulling my wallet from my back pocket and tossing some bills on the table since the waitress hadn't been back to check on us.

"You're pretty fucking confident in everything else, so I wouldn't be surprised." Fuck, did her husky tone send lust jolting through my entire body.

I stood and held out my hand. "I'm ready for a little more of that distraction if you are, gorgeous—*more* than ready."

And not just my body either. I craved Haley like I'd never experienced with another person before. Forget only burrowing into her body—I wanted inside her head, her heart, my own soul wrapped around hers like an octopus and holding her through life.

She slid her slender fingers through mine, sending another bolt of pure need and excitement through my blood. Tucking her in close to my side as we turned toward the exit seemed as natural as breathing. Haley's much smaller body fit against me perfectly, and I couldn't wait to see if I felt the same once I had her stripped down and beneath me.

Or maybe I would lay back and allow her to take what she claimed to need so badly. Would she be a bouncer or a grinder? Would she play with her own nipples and clit or demand me to map out her body while she rode me? Would she bend over my torso and let me kiss her while she chased her orgasm?

I wanted her cum smeared all over my groin, lusted to hear the wet sounds of fucking into her pussy and her whimpers. Her cute little ass cheeks would fit perfectly in my hands, and I would knead the hell out of them while slamming up into her to find my own release.

Holding her stare, watching her come undone time and again so I could memorize her beautiful releases was a must.

Dick entirely too thick for my jeans, I stepped out into the night's warm air, filling my lungs to steady my nerves.

I'd gone too long without loving on someone, and the desire to strip Haley down bare, kiss her mouth, and worship her with my hands kept me on the edge of trembling.

Haley had taken an Uber to the restaurant, so I opened the passenger door of my Corvette, the one splurge outside my house I'd allowed myself for all my hard work, and helped her climb aboard. I grinned before shutting her in.

"What?" she gave me a narrowed-eyed glance—suspicious as hell.

My girl had an edge to her, one I knew how to soften when I wanted. "You look good in my car."

She bit back a smirk. "I'll look even better on *you*."

I groaned as my semi went to granite again as all that imagining I'd done at the table slammed back into my brain. Shutting the door cut off my ability to maul Haley right there in the parking lot. A few deep inhales while rounding the car's front didn't cool my blood, and I had to rearrange my junk before my dick strangled itself in my jeans.

"Problem?" Haley asked sweetly as I climbed in beside her with a grimace.

"I'm hard as hell with a damp spot on my boxers—call it what you will," I muttered and roared the engine to life.

She let out a soft, devil-like chuckle while I pulled out of the lot. "I'd call that delicious," she purred.

"Christ." I shot her a quick glance.

She leaned toward me, one elbow on the console separating us. "I want a taste."

"Fucking hell." I clutched the steering wheel with one hand and pressed the palm of my other down against my aching groin.

"Let me help." Haley caressed her hand over mine, and I shifted, deciding I didn't have it in me to wait either. I wanted her hands, her mouth on me with the kind of need that made a person go all tunnel vision, the shit of their day long gone from the mind.

With both sets of my fingers wrapped around the steering wheel, I clenched my jaw and focused on the road while Haley made herself familiar with the bulge in my jeans.

"Mmm," she hummed appreciation before even popping my button.

"Take me out," I rasped the demand after three seconds too damn long of her teasing fingers.

"Needy little boy," she murmured with humor in her voice.

I was hardly little and far from a boy, but something about the nickname sent tingles down my spine and a rush of desperate arousal through my blood. *She* made me that way—and I fucking loved it.

My hips lifted as she took care of the button and zipper, my abs tightening as she moved her warm, smooth fingers down over my happy trail.

A hiss slid from my lips as she wrapped her hand around my girth and worked my length free from its prison to stick straight up toward my belly button.

"Oh God," she damn near croaked, her fingers a feather touch up and over my dick. "This gorgeous thing is just as perfect as the rest of you." Haley's voice had gone breathless as fuck, and I groaned, shifting my hips upward into her touch.

She un-clicked her seatbelt, and I was too damn horny to give a shit. A shift of her body laid her over the console, and wet heat surrounded my length in one downward motion of her head.

"Christ!" My balls seized, and I clutched at the steering wheel, fighting to keep my foot from pressing harder on the gas pedal. "Jesus—fuck, Haley."

Cheeks hollowed, she lifted, her tongue swirling on its way up to the aching head.

"Haley...fuck. Your mouth feels so fucking good."

My eyes wanted to roll back, but when she lowered, shoving my throbbing shaft into her throat, they bugged instead.

Curses flooded from my lips as she swallowed, and I shook my head, my entire body on the verge of combustion.

"*Too* good, Haley...I'm gonna come. Shit."

"Mmm," she hummed around me, her soft hand shoving into my jeans to rub my balls.

"Fuck!" Like a damn virgin teen getting his first blow job, I shot off like a geyser, flooding her mouth—struggling like hell to keep my eyelids open, semi-focused on where I drove.

She swallowed without complaint, without gagging, without a single drop of my spunk dribbling onto my groin.

"Fuck. Me." I groaned, head back, arms stretched out straight to where my knuckles remained white against the steering wheel. At least I'd kept to the speed limit.

"Mmm," Haley made that goddamn noise again, still rubbing my balls but lifting up to blow her hot breath over my ear. "Distracted?"

Not one thought fluttered through my head.

She snickered and kissed down my jaw. "I'll take your stunned silence as a yes."

Longing to turn my head and taste myself on her tongue roared through me, but I held steady. When I claimed her mouth for the first time, she would be my sole focus, and I would devour until sated.

If that was even possible.

She put my jeans back to rights and settled into her seat before I could trust myself to look at her.

Even though she hadn't sucked my dick for a long period of time, red flushed her lips, and those gorgeous eyes of hers had been overrun black by swollen pupils. Lust still ruled her body, but more resided in her dark orbs, a wanting, the same type of craving I felt for her in the deepest parts of me. It was as if my bone marrow thirsted for what only she could give—but I longed to give her what she needed even more.

"I think I more than like you," I nearly groaned the words.

She huffed a laugh. "That's the post coming-like-a-tidal-wave feels talking."

"I'm serious, Haley." I reached over to wind my fingers through hers, pulling our clasped hands atop my thigh. "Gotta hang onto you right now to make sure you're real."

"I know what you mean," she murmured, and I wondered over the emotions inside her and whether they mirrored mine.

A little bit anxious, a whole lot of excited about the possibilities.

But I also had a strangling bit of fear. My real parents had abandoned me—and that shit fucked with my head and doubtless would for a long assed time. Would I ever be able to trust a relationship?

I'd fallen hard and fast for Haley.

I prayed like fuck she felt the same.

Chapter 12

Garrett

Had Haley and Wyatt finished dinner?

I glanced at my ancient watch, barely making out the hands in the club's dim corner I'd hidden myself in. Twisting my arm toward the dance floor allowed strobe lights to help me see the tiny numbers on the watch's face.

Nine o'clock.

Surely they'd headed home already. Maybe Wyatt had already fucked my Haley. Jealousy over the thought of another man's hands on her twisted my insides, and I downed the rest of my martini.

Would he hold her afterward, prove himself to be a Prince Charming by snuggling her how she loved, the way I always made her melt against me?

"Fuck." I muttered a few more curses to myself while stretching my neck side to side in an attempt to ease the tension riding me.

I'd had no intention of scrolling an app for dick, but once I'd left the apartment early to get away from all things Happy Haley, I'd had nothing better to do.

Sitting on a bench near the beach had only made my scowl deepen.

Watching lovers and kids play in the sand while the sun sank on the horizon had sent a pang through my chest I didn't know how to deal with.

So much for that dream about Haley dancing in the sand with flowers in her hair.

Loneliness had nagged at me like my grandmother used to about taking out the trash, and a shit ton of self-pity had sent me scrolling and clicking on the first guy in the area who was on the prowl for some action.

But he never showed, and I ended up in a corner all by myself while men made out on the dance floor, their groping hands and swiveling hips doing nothing but creating an even bigger pity party inside my head.

Could I catch a damn break already?

I pulled out my cell to check if Haley had texted to let me know her date was over, that I could come home without having to fear listening in to a fuck-fest I would want to break up.

Or join in.

The air fled from my lungs with a grunt.

Wyatt's pic suggested the dude was hot as hell, a rugged pretty boy—yes, there was such a thing. He looked like a glass of ice water I would thirst for after a day on a sunny beach. While I had told myself I didn't want dick again, a bi man had to be dead to not find the image of Haley's date appealing.

Lips pursed, I pushed aside thoughts of how hot he and Haley would be together. I refused to linger on the images flashing in my head of Haley getting herself off riding him.

I kind of wanted to not just be in Wyatt's shoes, I realized in that moment, but Haley's as well.

I enjoyed the male body too damn much, the roughened hands and the lack of restraint I could allow myself when in bed with another man to say no to dick for the rest of my life.

Maybe I needed to get onto that damn app Haley and Wyatt had met on.

Missing Link—all things poly for those who loved a bit of kink.

Perfection for a bi guy like myself. Dick and pussy. Me in the middle having both or my length shoving into a guy's ass while he filled the woman beneath him.

Both fantasies made me hard—but it was Wyatt and Haley there with me in my mind.

I groaned, tipping my head onto the table I occupied by myself. Shit, I was a goddamn mess.

If only I'd been honest with Haley from the start—

No. She'd have denied me the second bedroom in her apartment, and I never would have found my best friend in the whole fucking world.

I would take what I could when it came to her, any scraps she offered me… How much of a perv would I be if I did listen in on her fucking another guy?

My dick twitched at the idea, and I sat back, my feet itching to walk out the door and head home—

Alec.

My pulse jackknifed.

"Shit." I stared at the dance floor, watching my ex grind all over the backside of a cute twink half his size.

The fuck was he doing at Jackson's Hole? Alec never went out of his upper-class neighborhood, never fraternized with those below his pay grade. Except he had with me because I'd been his kryptonite—his exact words on our third date, the night he'd begged me to move in with him.

It had been my mouth, my ability to swallow down a dick without gagging that had snagged his heart, I didn't doubt. My personality and nurturing spirit had jack shit to do with why he'd wanted me in his bed.

Perhaps it was the cute as hell twink shoving Alec's hand all over his dick while they danced together that had drawn him south of the Hills where he'd refused to hang out before. Maybe the kid could take dick like a champ too.

My guts churned as I glowered at the two of them practically fucking on the dance floor.

Alec had been there for a while, I realized. Sweat plastered the longer hair atop his head to his forehead, making the blond strands appear almost brown. His wide shoulders dwarfed the guy in front of him, but he managed to latch his mouth onto the twink's neck.

The boy would be marked, for sure, bruises on his hips and thighs if they ended up fucking.

Of course, Alec would glance my way while I sat vulnerable, frowning from…I had no fucking clue what. There was no allowance of time for me to school my features. Glancing away with a feigned sniff of indifference would be seen as the lie it was.

My anger couldn't be contained in that brief moment—and I realized it wasn't jealousy over Alec on some other guy's ass. Nothing about him turned me on any longer, nor did I want him.

I just yearned to smash his face in like those three assholes had done to me while Sindy had watched with laughter on her lips and lust in her eyes.

Psychotic cunt and her douchebag asshole of a brother.

Losers. Both of them.

A smirk curled Alec's lips, and he turned the twink, arms wrapping around his slender body. The ass grind turned into a frotting fest, and he watched me with a calculated gaze, that goddamn smile on his lips like he read my mind.

He thinks I'm jealous.

I held back my barked laugh and reminded myself that while I'd never made it in Hollywood, I *was* an actor.

A damn good one.

The lines on my face smoothed, and I stared back with the indifference I knew would piss Alec off since it would take the upper hand away from him. Even better would be finding myself someone to fuck with—to see how Alec handled the sight.

I slipped from my chair and ambled toward the dance floor, the scent of liquor, cologne, and sweat filling my nose. Music throbbed in my ears, the flashing lights making for a slow-motion effect over the swaying dancers.

I spotted what I was looking for within seconds. On the smaller side, effeminate, a definite bottom if how he moved like he wanted a thick dick up his ass was any indication.

One rub of my groin against his backside, a deep command against his ear for him to dance with me, and he melted against my chest like I'd hoped for.

Unlike Alec, I kept my lips to myself, my hands above the boy's belt—but I moved with him like he writhed beneath me, begging me to fuck him deeper. Harder. My ex hadn't ever allowed me control, hadn't once given me the option to be more than his willing hole.

I showed Alec who I truly was beneath dizzying strobe lights and thumping bass. Versatile, more than capable of topping. Not at all submissive like I'd been with him. I portrayed my inner confidence he'd never seen before, moving the boy beneath my hands exactly how I wanted him.

And I felt fucking glorious, getting off over how Alec stared, his smirk long gone. But I didn't allow any satisfaction to grow on my face, didn't feel the desire to let him know I cared what he thought.

Because I didn't give a rat's ass if Alec was jealous.

The fuck am I doing?

I pulled away from the twink who'd been putty in my hold. Caressed of his ass with a gentle squeeze and once more spoke in his ear—thanking him for the dance.

Turning away, I headed toward the exit, done.

With hookups.

With Alec.

With the emotions he used to rouse inside me.

My heart went light as I stepped outside into the night, and I breathed easier than I had in months.

But that feeling faded as I pulled out my cell to call an Uber.

Another hour had passed, but surely Haley and Wyatt were still in her bedroom—if they'd even made it there to begin with.

Fuck knew if I'd gotten either of them in my bed, I wouldn't let them out until morning.

Scrubbing a hand down over my face, I warred with my mind. Find another bar to hide away in or be a selfish dick and head home where I might get a chance to hear Haley come from something more than her dildos and vibrators?

My dick thickened.

"And there's my fucking answer," I muttered to myself. "Shit."

Chapter 13

Haley

I felt a little guilty over nudging Wyatt toward the sexual realm of our getting to know one another. We'd agreed to not go there so quickly, but goddamnit, the man was too fine for his own good.

And mine.

He'd proven to be damn near perfect, and even if I'd learned over dinner that he'd put a face on in order to manipulate me into bed, I would have gone there willingly because he was just too delicious to say no to.

Never had I felt drawn to a guy in such a way, with strong emotions to the point I wondered if I'd gotten knocked upside the head.

He was downright beautiful. Tender and kind. No walls blocked me from seeing through his eyes—even if I wondered over possible fears of abandonment after learning what he had that day. Any grown ass man would call into question their identity after finding out his adoptive parents had lied to him.

If anyone understood the effects of being lied to, it was me.

And my heart ached for Wyatt even as my body did for his.

I hadn't been able to control myself and had gotten him off while he drove his sexy Corvette across town. The noises he'd made, the force of his ejaculate hitting the back of my throat, had only intensified my lust for release.

Should have gotten myself off in the shower.

We climbed the stairs to my apartment, my backside burning from his gaze. Panties soaked and already breathless from raging desire, I couldn't unlock the door fast enough. Couldn't get across the threshold to hide us in privacy as quickly as I would have liked.

Garrett's car had been outside, but he'd taken an Uber earlier in the day. The lights were still off when I let myself into our apartment, so I didn't bother calling out to see if he'd gotten home.

It wasn't yet nine—

A warm hand wrapped around my waist and pulled me back against a hard chest as the door snicked shut behind Wyatt.

"I'm dying to kiss you," he whispered against my ear before I could hit the lights, and I gulped over how his low tone sent tingles straight to my clit.

Could a woman come from a sexy voice rumbling things like that in her ears?

"If you kiss me now, you'll taste your cum in my mouth."

"I'm bi, sweet Haley." Wyatt nuzzled his nose along my neck. "I like the taste of spunk, even better if it's mine on your tongue."

A curse rang in my head and escaped like a hiss off my lips.

I turned on weak knees and sagged against him, peering up at him in what little city lights filtered through the closed blinds. "Then kiss me."

"Your lips or all over every inch of your rocking body?"

A shudder ripped through me, leaving a field of goosebumps in its wake. "Yes."

Rather than claiming my mouth, Wyatt lifted me into his arms, and I finally got the chance to wrap my legs around his trim waist. His bulge settled against my core, and I shivered.

"You're hard again," I murmured, grinding against him.

"It's all you," he said, his lips against my forehead. "Where's your bedroom? I'm going to strip you down and lay you out like a feast before devouring you."

Fucking hell, Wyatt knew how to push my buttons.

"First door on the left—if you can find your way there in the dark."

He strode forward like he had night vision, nudging my bedroom door open with his foot. "Lights?"

Guess he wanted to see that feast before he ate it.

"Shift right," I told him, and when he did so, I reached out to flick the switch.

Blinding white light flooded my bedroom, and we both blinked the glare away.

Pink had risen to his cheeks when I'd blown him, and the color still remained, giving him a flushed, sexy-as-fuck appearance that had me wanting so damn much my head swam.

He stood me on my feet beside my queen-sized bed, his focus on my face. "We haven't discussed kinks or limits..."

"I thought I had a shit ton, but with you?" I shrugged, unable to help my smirk from the butterflies in my belly. "At this point, I'm not sure there's anything you could do that would turn me off."

"You're just saying that because you haven't had dick in eight months."

Neither has Garrett...but he probably is right now.

I shook the thought from my mind.

"Nah." I fumbled with the buttons on his shirt, needing to get my hands on Wyatt's body and forget about the other man I wanted. "You're just damn...perfect."

Wyatt grabbed my hand, stilling my intentions of stripping him naked. "No man is perfect, Haley. Please don't put me up on some pedestal that I'm going to tumble from and leave us both miserable."

"You think I've fallen that hard already?" I asked with a snicker, pretending to hold onto those walls he'd crumbled down so easily, same as Garrett had done.

"I have." Those blue eyes of Wyatt's peered into mine, full of vulnerability and longing.

"Goddamnit, Wyatt." I grabbed hold of his neck and yanked him down, needing distraction of my own.

Our lips met in a hard kiss, both of us moaning.

Absolutely criminal, just like I'd thought.

His tongue swept into my mouth as his arms banded around my waist, and my back bowed to arch the rest of me closer to him. Hands clutching at his hair, I swooned, going limp except for my lips and my core pulsing with every probe of his tongue along mine.

He tasted of sweetness and man, a heady mix—and fuck, did the man know how to kiss. Luscious slides of his lips over mine, a tasting, was further proof of how we connected.

A leg shoved between my thighs, and I whimpered, rubbing my pussy against him. He'd worked me to the breaking point before we'd reached my apartment...I was about to get that first taste of an appetizer.

I was going to come—

"Fuuuck," I groaned into his mouth as my climax shuddered through me, and he cursed along with me, grabbing hold of my hair to angle my head.

"One down...dozens to go," he murmured and claimed my lips again before I fully settled down from my high.

No more Mr. Nice Guy.

Wyatt ate at my mouth with the perfect blend of licking and nibbling, the lack of drool smearing over our flesh solidifying his perfection status.

A-plus kisser, Wyatt wasn't just a rare specimen, but he was also the knight in shining armor atop that horned steed.

With a deep groan, he tore his mouth off me and stepped back, leaving me weak-kneed and shaking. "Take off your clothes," he demanded in a husky, low rumble.

I cocked an eyebrow, ready to remind him he'd wanted to undress me—but he fisted his hands, a slight tremor breaking his stance. Did he not trust himself, or was he just so turned on again that he needed a moment to gain control?

Slowly, I shed my shirt. Kicked off my sandals. Peeled my capris off my legs.

I stood before him in a matching nude-colored panties and bra set, my skin pebbled, my heart racing.

"Fuck," he groaned the word, his hands unclenching to flex where they hung at his thighs. "More."

I unsnapped my bra and dropped it to the floor, and Wyatt licked over his lower lip before sucking the flesh in between his teeth again.

Sexy. As. Fuck.

"Panties," he rasped, and I obeyed, my hands shaking as I slid my thumbs into the waist band and pushed them until they fluttered around my ankles.

"Christ, Haley, you're even more perfect than I'd fantasized. Every sweet, achingly beautiful curve of you." He swallowed audibly, the tension between us quivering his body, his words leaving me breathless. "Get on the bed."

I tended to be the bossy one in the bedroom to ensure I got what I wanted, but I lusted to kneel down and bend to Wyatt's every whim. Anything to keep that heat and raging passion in his eyes, those words of praise he rumbled that did silly things to my insides.

Turning, I gave him a view of my backside and climbed onto the bed.

He released a few curses, and I made sure to sway my ass while crawling to the center of the mattress.

A soft roll landed me on my back, and I spread my legs, unable to keep from touching where I ached.

Wyatt zoned in on my fingers as I traced my wet slit, up and down, up and down. "Fuck."

"Get your ass over here and stick your dick inside me," I finally let loose since he stood there staring rather than moving.

His gaze flicked to my face, one eyebrow raised and a smirk on his face. "On the edge again already?"

"Yeah, and if you don't hurry, number two is going to have me creaming all over my hand instead of your cock."

"Can't have that."

He tore the shirt from his body, and I moaned like a whore while pressing two fingers into my sopping pussy. He was a little taller than Garrett, but their builds were similar—cut muscles...dips and valleys I wanted to lick. Bite. "Show me the rest," I whispered, my hips rising as I finger fucked myself.

He shoved off his jeans and kicked them aside, and the second he wrapped his big hand around his dick, my pussy pulsed—and I came.

"Oh fuck," I groaned, my back arching, losing sight of his gorgeous body as my core squeezed around my fingers. "Wyatt...please. Forget that feast—" I gasped through my climax. "It's been t-too long. Fuck." A hard swallow accompanied my last body tremor. "Just fill me up. Wreck me."

A crinkle of the condom wrapper sounded, and panting, I came down from my high in time to watch him crawl over the bed toward me, shoulder muscles flexing. Smoldering blue eyes catching my skin on fire.

I grabbed hold of his length to put him where I needed him, and he took my mouth, sliding deep into my slick core in one slow push.

Goddamn...

I moaned long and loud, and he cursed something about how tight I was. Hearing beyond the ringing in my ears wasn't possible. He filled me to my breaking point, and the second he rocked his hips, thrusting a little deeper...

"Oh...fuck, *yes*," I hissed. All the feels shuddered over me—butterflies, euphoria, contentment and yet longing for more.

Wyatt was a book boyfriend come to life, too good to be true. And holy hell, was I into him as deep as his length in my core.

His drag along my inner walls while backing out sent shivers over my skin, and I clutched at him with my heels and hands.

"No," I whimpered, desperate to keep him inside me.

He propped onto his elbows, taking some of his weight off me. "Not going anywhere, sweet Haley." Wyatt glided into my pussy, his eyes on mine, both of us gasping for breath. "Are you going to let me love on you all night long?"

"Yes…oh God, Wyatt…" His name came strangled from my throat as he began to thrust in steady rhythm, every snap of his hips at the end of his thrusts brushing the tip of his dick against my cervix. Just shy of painful and a total fucking turn-on.

No man had been inside me so deeply, and no man had moved like he did, every grind of his hips rubbing his pelvis over my clit.

Wyatt wrapped his hands around my head, his thumbs brushing over my lips before taking my mouth in a kiss that curled my toes.

I was good and truly fucked—in more ways than one.

Chapter 14

Wyatt

I needed a diversion from the distraction Haley had promised and delivered. She felt too fucking good clasped around my aching dick. The flowery scent of her skin and sweet musk of her cum was an aphrodisiac that tightened my balls up, ready to release again like I was some teenager rather than a thirty-year-old man who'd been around the block a time or ten.

And her mouth...goddamn, I loved the feel of that bit of flesh on mine almost as much as I liked the sass and honesty she let loose from her lips.

Thrusting into Haley's tight sheath while fucking my tongue with hers was like drowning and coming home at the same time.

I'd been floating aimlessly all day long in a sea of emotions, and Haley offered grounding. Focus, when I'd floundered in my new reality.

I wrapped her up in my arms, but I wanted her inside my soul, offering me comfort when I needed it most.

"You feel so fucking good, Haley." I groaned and thrust harder, needing to be deeper—so fucking imbedded inside her she couldn't get rid of me. Wouldn't be able to abandon me. "So wet. So tight. So fucking *right*."

"Wyatt," she breathed against my lips, the sound of my name on her lips seizing my balls even higher. "Touch my clit. Wanna come again."

Unable to keep from clutching her against me, I shifted my hips and ground over her pelvis, giving her what she needed.

"Oh fuck...yes. Just like that." She whimpered, trying to arch in my hold.

"I've got you, sweet girl." I repeated the motion, over and over until she trembled. "Want you to come." My voice had gone haggard, on the verge of breaking along with the rest of my body. "Need your cum all over my dick—"

"God!" Haley's pussy clamped down on my length.

"That's it…such a good girl," I growled into her neck, letting my body take over. I pounded into her, drawing out every wave of her climax until only flutters pulsed around my cock.

"Let go," Haley whispered against my ear while clutching at my back, and my balls gladly gave into her command.

Cum shot into the condom with spine-tingling spurts like I hadn't just come into her mouth less than an hour earlier.

Each shudder through me pulled a groan from my lungs, and I clasped at her tiny body, completely… fucking…lost.

But feeling more settled in my head than I'd been all day. Peace swept over my mind and heart as I finished with a deep groan. I clutched her close and rolled to my back, still embedded, her small body plastered to my front.

"Such a gentleman," she murmured, a smile in her voice.

Guess she figured out I feared crushing her but needed to go boneless and just *rest* for a few seconds.

We both breathed heavy in the comfortable silence between us as she lay like a blanket over my body.

What a fucking release—my balls, my mind...

I made a rumbling of appreciation deep in my throat while running my fingertips down her back to her pert ass cheeks.

"Somebody's content."

I chuckled while kneading the soft flesh of her backside, every muscle in my body lax. "More than."

"Mmm. Me too." Haley tried to snuggle closer, but she was already plastered to me, face to toes.

I gave a little squeeze, loving how well she fit against me, how easy it was to just *be* with her. "I didn't hurt you, did I?"

"No."

A heavy exhale deflated my chest beneath her cheek. "You're so tiny I was afraid I was going to split you in half."

"I'm tougher than I look."

I believed her firm statement. Lifting my head, I kissed the top of hers and patted her backside. "Gonna go get a towel to clean you up, okay?"

"Mmm." She shifted her hips, allowing my spent dick to slide from her warmth.

A sense of loss rushed through my mind, bringing back that sense of aimless floating I'd felt earlier, but I pushed it from my mind and slid from beneath Haley's limp body.

She sprawled on her stomach, maroon hair spread over the comforter, a gorgeous flush on her face.

"Don't go anywhere," I heard myself say rather than the *be right back* I'd planned on.

Needy much?

Frowning at myself, I slid from her bed and left her there in search of the bathroom.

An open doorway lay across the dark hallway, and a night-light plugged in beneath the mirror directly ahead revealed the bathroom.

I cleaned up and wet a hand cloth I found beneath the vanity.

Rather than go straight back to Haley, I headed toward the kitchen in search of bottled water.

My mind didn't take note of the lights being on until I stepped from the hallway in sight of the kitchen/living area.

The fridge door stood open, and a round ass filled out low-slung sweats.

Garrett. The roommate.

And he bent at the waist while searching for something inside.

I enjoyed getting dicked down by men on occasion, but in that moment I couldn't tear my focus off the sight of his backside. I'd just had the cutest ass in my hands, but his?

Meaty. Firm-looking. I imagined sliding my dick between those round cheeks I could grip without fear of bruising while he pleasured Haley.

Fuuuck.

The man was gay and wouldn't ever feast on a pussy, but I'd bet my life he'd get on his knees for cock.

He straightened, allowing me a quick glimpse of a muscled back and wide shoulders.

I slipped back the way I'd come before he turned and saw me naked, sporting a chub from staring at him.

Haley had claimed Garrett was perfect, and from what I'd seen of his backside, I had to agree. But he was also off-limits since I'd set on making something of what Haley and I had found, and the only type of man who would be joining us needed to appreciate the female form as much as he did a man's.

Quietly shutting myself into Haley's bedroom, I found her unmoved. Still sated and lax. The thought I'd done that to her made me grin—but the night wasn't over, and I still owed her a few orgasms.

Without a word, I crawled back onto the bed and shifted one of her knees higher to reveal her pink folds to gently wipe her clean. Taking care of her fulfilled me almost as much as hearing her come. That need to care for someone, to lavish attention on them purred inside me with every stroke of the towel over her flesh.

"You're too good to be true," she murmured into her pillow, and I huffed a laugh.

"Hardly."

"Stay," she said when I rolled to toss the washcloth to the floor.

"Planned on it," I said, stretching out alongside her body and pulling her into my arms where she fit so damn perfectly that my chest ached.

She pressed in close, eyes closed, her nose brushing mine as I rubbed over her back with soothing strokes.

"Garrett's home," I told her rather than spewing out my undying love that was way too soon to be real.

Because, yeah. I was falling fast and too damn hard than was healthy.

"Did he say hi or just salivate over your gorgeous, naked body?" She didn't sound one bit jealous— another check mark on that pro list in my head.

"He was looking for something in the fridge, so I snuck back here without letting him know I was there."

"Was he still in his jeans and a tight T-shirt that showed off his muscular back?" Longing laced her words, so I decided to be honest too and swallowed down the drool flooding my mouth over the memory of his ass.

"Sweats." A hint of a groan escaped with the word.

Haley pulled her face back, a calculated glint in her whiskey-colored eyes that stilled my massaging touch along her spine. "Fine as fuck, isn't he?"

"His backside interested my dick," I stated the truth to see how she would react. No way in hell she didn't feel that evidence for herself where my chub thickened against her thigh.

"Hmm." She wiggled against me.

Both our smirks disappeared, and the desire in her steady, unshuttered gaze roused all sorts of shit in my head. Thoughts of more. Greediness. Happily ever afters.

"What's on your mind, Haley?" I asked, tucking some of her wild mane behind her ear.

"I'm thinking about that second guy we discussed—and don't go getting all insecure, either."

"I'm not." I grinned, but my smile faded a bit when the truth of Garrett's sexual identity slid back into my head.

"So." Haley threaded her fingers though my hair, that glint back in her eyes. "Would it be a Haley sandwich, or would you prefer being in the middle?"

I narrowed my gaze and palmed her ass, holding her tight against my groin as the images of both flitted through my mind. Two of us taking her at the same time. Him burying inside my body with a throaty groan while I loved on her...

"Is that your way of asking if I'd let a guy top me?" I murmured.

She smirked and attempted a shrug, her fingernails scratching at my scalp. "Maybe."

Another laugh left me at her sassiness. "Does the thought of some sexy guy with a divine dick fucking my ass turn you on?"

Haley grabbed my hand off her lower back and shoved it between her thighs. "You tell me."

Arousal once more coated her folds, and I rubbed my fingertips through her slickness, teasing up over her clit.

"Mmm." A breathy moan parted her lips, and she gasped when I slid two fingers deep inside her.

"I owe you a few more orgasms." I ghosted my mouth over hers, wanting to focus on her rather than my fantasies.

"Then you'd best get busy and take care of me."

Chuckling at the truth of how much I wanted to do just that, I rolled Haley onto her back and shifted my way down her body, kissing and licking.

Feasting—and giving what I'd promised.

Chapter 15

Garrett

When I arrived at the apartment, I went straight to my bedroom, jaw clenched against the sounds coming from behind Haley's door that perked my dick right the fuck up. At least their going-ons had taken my mind off all things Alec.

Ignoring the desire to join Haley and her guest without an invite wasn't easy, but at least they finished fucking while I'd yanked on some sweats over my erection.

Teeth still grinding, I stalked back to the kitchen, needing...something. I'd had too much alcohol, not enough food, and not nearly the amount of loving I was desperate for.

At least I hadn't stumbled through the hallway from being buzzed, banging against walls and announcing my presence to the two who'd grown quiet behind her bedroom door.

A rifle through the fridge to see what we had left over from meals I'd cooked that week didn't offer many options. Haley tended to devour whatever I didn't eat.

The hairs on my nape lifted, and I straightened, unsure if I wanted to turn around or not.

Haley or Wyatt?

Having no clue how much of a hostess she was with her hookups—or otherwise—I didn't know if she'd offer him water or if he'd come looking for it himself. Had they been aware I'd gotten home?

They must since I'd flicked on the lights.

A glance over my shoulder didn't give me a glimpse of muscle or flushed skin.

Muttering at myself, I opted for a sandwich since we had the makings for a turkey club.

I sat at the kitchen table, my late-night snack in hand when it started again.

Low, feminine moans had my dick back to aching in a blink.

Hands fisted beside my plate, I stared across the open space at the TV, my mind creating a movie on the black screen.

It was my head clasped tight by her thighs, sucking on her pussy lips and clit while she tried to fuck herself on my face.

"Goddamnit." I pressed against my dick, silently reminding myself that I couldn't have Haley, that I would never have the pleasure of her cum on my chin.

But I could get off on listening to her while some other lucky bastard got to have her hands pulling on his hair.

"Fuck it." I left my sandwich on the table and sprawled on the couch, sweats shoved to my thighs.

It wasn't like either of them were going to walk in on me jerking off. They were too damn wrapped up in each other—and I was too ramped and ready to release to *not* finish before they did.

Pre-cum oozed from my slit, and I smeared it down my length. A few good tugs over the swollen head had me hissing.

"Oh, fuck." Teeth clenched, I thrust upward through my hand, imagining Haley's lips wrapped around my cock.

I squeezed the base of my dick, needing a breather. Didn't want to paint my abs with sticky white too quickly. It was my first time hearing Haley make noises like she was getting eaten out within an inch of her sanity—and I had to enjoy that shit while I could.

At the first thump of her headboard against the wall, I groaned, my fantasy once more morphing.

It was my dick shoving into her tight heat, it was my name she groaned rather than Wyatt's. But I took it further, thinking about his dick inside me, every sharp thrust from him pounding me into her.

Yes...fuck yes.

I spit on my fingers, lifted my bound legs, and reached around to my desperate hole, my other hand still gripped around my aching length.

The puckered skin twitched at my touch, and I bit down on my lip to keep quiet as I slid two fingers inside me.

Curses spilled from my mouth that had dropped open to pant. My hand worked over my dick on instinct. I contorted my body to have better access to my ass, reaching deep through the sting until I hit my prostate.

"Fuuuck." More pre-cum leaked from my slit, creating for one hell of a messy jack-off session, the schlicking sounds of me fucking my fist as loud as the noises coming through the wall.

Continued thumps.

Haley's curses.

The goddamn deep rumbled groan of a man.

I went off, shooting spunk up over my abs and chin, my entire body twitching with every wave of release. Even through the ringing in my ears, I heard both Haley and Wyatt climax, pulling one last dribble of cum from me.

"Fuck." I choked on the word while trying to fill my lungs. "Fucking hell." I allowed myself about five seconds of satiated bliss before dragging my ass from the couch for a quick cleanup at the kitchen sink.

God forbid Haley slipped out of her room for the bathroom and took note of me being home and fresh off masturbating to the music the two of them had created.

I sat at the table a minute later but found my appetite had disappeared. Wrapping up my snack for the next day's lunch, I considered the silence in our apartment.

Would Wyatt sleep over or leave after Haley passed out?

From what Haley had told me about him, I knew he was a business owner who was proud of his work. I doubted he was the type to go in late on a Monday morning, but if I'd been in his shoes, I sure as fuck would just for the chance to snuggle with a naked Haley as the sun rose.

Sleepy, she was beautiful. Add in sated, and I couldn't imagine the sight.

Dick on board for another go, I headed to my bedroom, ready to shut myself away and bury my head under the pillow.

Murmurs easily reached through her door, and I hesitated.

Fuck it.

I pressed my ear to the door.

"Will you stay with me tonight?" Need laced Haley's voice, and I closed my eyes with a sigh.

"I have to leave by five."

Fuck, did that low tone of his make my blood race.

"Then I'll wake you up at four-thirty with my lips wrapped around your dick."

Jealousy coursed through me at her breathy promise. I strode into my bedroom, not bothering to be quiet about shutting my door.

Wyatt had satisfied her physical needs, but her question told me all I needed to know.

He was no hookup, and that connection she'd told me she felt with him had only strengthened from their having sex. I foresaw a couple in the near future. They were both looking for more than a fuck buddy, which meant they'd eventually live together if things continued down a good path.

How long until I was once more homeless and destitute?

I crashed onto my bed, face-first into my pillow, my heart breaking over the possibilities—and none of them good.

I'd gone from a high off realizing Alec and his shit no longer had power to make me feel like an idiot to a low even deeper than when he'd kicked me out of our house.

My desire for Haley far surpassed anything I'd felt for my ex though.

She was my person, my safe place.

And Wyatt was going to steal her from me.

I dreamed about it. The grin on his face, the laughter as he hauled her away, leaving me bruised and battered on the ground, empty hands reaching out for my Hal.

A scowl etched on my face when I woke to the toilet flushing.

Five-ten, my clock read.

Had she blown him? Was he cleaning up in the bathroom, endorphins in his bloodstream keeping that grin on his face I'd had a nightmare about?

Pulse thrumming and hand shaking, I hopped out of bed and cracked open my bedroom door.

He stepped into the hallway, allowing me a brief look of his profile. My glower dissolved in an instant.

Dark mussed hair, strong nose and chin—fully dressed and ready to leave, he strode away from me. A fine as fuck ass encased in jeans, every flex of muscle woke my saliva glands. Shoulders stretched out the black shirt he wore.

He disappeared into the kitchen, and I quietly closed my bedroom door, resting my forehead on the wooden panel with a heavy sigh.

Hardly more than a glimpse, but I saw all I needed to.

Wyatt was Haley's type to a T—and mine as well.

Maybe it was time for me to head back to the sticks of Pennsylvania and my grandparents, since nothing but heartache lay in my future.

Chapter 16

Haley

I never got to wrap my lips around Wyatt's delicious dick in the morning. In fact, I didn't even hear him leave my bed.

Blinking my eyes open revealed sunlight around my blinds and Wyatt's absence. I stretched beneath my warm blankets, achy in the best way. Last I'd remembered, I'd been wrapped up in his arms, my face against his hard chest, his heartbeat in my ear.

He'd felt heavenly...and I missed his scent, his warm hands on my skin, and the sweet nothings about being a good girl he'd whispered in my ear as I'd drifted off.

Flying high as a soaring eagle, I grabbed my cell from my bedside table where I'd plugged it in the night before after he'd fucked me a second time into my mattress, giving me those promised climaxes.

A text already waited for me, and I quietly squealed like a crushing high schooler, depression as far from me as it had ever been.

Mr. Hot Stuff: **Hope I didn't wake you when I forced myself to leave your bed. Can't wait to see you again.**

Warm fuzzies filled me, and I messaged Wyatt back, letting him know I'd slept like the dead until six-thirty and that I felt the same.

I changed his name in my cell to Mr. Perfect.

Grinning and excited to get out of bed for the second time in my life, I hopped off my mattress and grabbed a pair of panties and one of my long sleep shirts.

The scent of coffee hit me when I opened my bedroom door.

Garrett sat on the couch with his back to me, his dark hair a mess my fingers itched to smooth down.

"Morning!" I chirped at him, still smiling like the morning person I definitely was *not* while grabbing a mug from the cabinet.

He grumbled something under his breath.

On cloud nine, I poured the steaming brew, my mouth watering and belly fluttering. One sip, and I hummed my approval before smacking my lips.

"Thanks for making the coffee," I said, walking on air while rounding the couch. "You always do a better job than I do."

A grunt was all he gave for my praise over one of his many talents rather the usual slow smirk that curled my toes.

He didn't even have a lollipop stick between his lips.

A pang of...something I couldn't name hit my heart. Far from regret but definitely unpleasant.

Needing him as happy as I was, I sat beside him, curling my legs beneath me.

"Someone didn't get dick last night," I teased in the hopes of making him give me shit as usual.

Garrett let out another noise I couldn't decipher while I sipped again, my smile fading.

I elbowed him, ready to rib him like he always did to me, but he beat me to it. "I was home early enough to hear you getting enough dick for *both* of us."

My jaw dropped at his grumpiness and the jealousy in his voice. He actually sounded…mad, like I'd done him wrong. That cloud beneath my feet dissipated completely, and I blinked myself back into the moment, studying his profile.

Slouched shoulders, lowered head. Deep furrow on his forehead and downturned lips.

I hated seeing Garrett like that—couldn't have it.

"Did you at least get yourself off while listening to us, you kinky bastard?" I asked with a grin, my tone still light to snap him out of whatever bothered him.

"Yep, and it was the hottest goddamn thing I've ever heard," he muttered without a hint of happiness or joking in his tone.

Heat rushed through me at the thought of him stroking himself while Wyatt had made me lose my damn mind.

No.

Garrett would have been focused on the noises coming from the man fucking me into my mattress. His deep voice. His harsh curses while finding release inside me.

Arousal coated my panties even though I felt bad for my best friend.

I drank my coffee for something to do, giving myself time to think of what to say next. Telling Garrett he should have joined us wouldn't go over well since he definitely wasn't in a teasing mood.

There were other excellent ways of distracting him—Wyatt had assured me that was one of my many talents—but anything I offered would cause Garret's nose to lift in disgust.

Why did he have to be gay? I asked in my head for the thousandth time since meeting him. Why not bi or at least bi-curious? I would gladly let him experiment on me if he would show just one ounce of interest in the female body.

He released a heavy exhale and tipped his head back, eyes closing, and I opened my mouth to tell him to unload his burdens on me. Again, he beat me to it. "Alec was at the club, and I didn't sleep last night."

"Shit." I frowned too, my happiness over Wyatt flitting away as I focused my thoughts on Garrett's downtrodden appearance.

Slight shadows beneath his eyes, he *did* look like he hadn't gotten any rest.

"Yeah. He was grinding all up on some twink's ass."

He didn't sound jealous but definitely hurt.

"So, I did the same just to show the fucker that I wasn't some submissive bottom like he'd demanded of me the whole time we were together," Garrett continued before I could spew off some shit about his ex being an ass.

I stretched out my legs and tugged Garrett's arm until he sprawled out on his side, his scruffy cheek on my bare thigh. He snaked a hand beneath my knee, and between his light touch and the scratch of his whiskers on my skin, I needed new panties.

Guess the whole finally getting dick hadn't lessened my desire for him.

"Give it to me," I demanded, my tone not allowing argument or a brush off. I ran my fingers through his hair with my free hand, loving how soft the strands were.

"I felt powerful in that moment, watching Alec's smile dissolve. Seeing the jealousy in his eyes while I turned another guy to putty in my hands."

"Go you," I said with a snicker and enjoyed another swallow of my coffee, glad he'd gotten back even a little bit the confidence he'd told me Alec had stripped from him.

"Yeah. It felt awesome, but then I got here and heard a bunch of moaning and headboard slamming."

I'd taken his high away.

Shit.

"Sorry about that," I whispered, truly meaning every word. If I had known Garrett had come home, I would have stopped Wyatt, shut down our noisy fucking—no matter how close to release we might have been.

Okay, so maybe I'd have bit my tongue or made sure his mouth swallowed my cries and vice versa.

There wasn't anything I wouldn't do for Garrett, but Wyatt was able to take me to the edge where not much else mattered.

"I hope he makes you happy, Hal. He better not ensnare you and then drop you at the first rocking of the boat."

"I know he's not *really* a mythical creature with a spiraled horn," I stated quietly, scratching at Garrett's scalp like I'd done with Wyatt. An image flashed in my mind of both men using me as their pillows, my fingers tangling in their hair. They would prop up on their elbows to lean into one another and kiss while I cradled their heads.

My throat tightened.

Could I share Wyatt with him? Would Garrett even be interested in a threesome with me if he and Wyatt hit it off? Would having a woman in the room while they loved on one another be a dick deflator for my best friend?

I chewed on the inside of my lip, my heart torn when moments earlier I thought I'd been on a good path. Not sure what to say, I kept silent and finished my coffee while Garrett began to breathe heavily as though I'd comforted him enough that he finally found sleep.

* * *

I talked to Wyatt every night that week, sometimes a video chat while we snuggled in our beds.

Sure, we'd fucked each other's brains out, but neither of us wanted sex to be our focus, so we made a pact—no dates on weeknights. Just hour-long conversations to deepen our connection.

Besides, Wyatt still had a shit ton of things on his brain, and I'd agreed to give him physical space so he could focus on his emotions about the whole situation of his adoption. He and River spoke every day too, and from everything he told me about her, I knew she would be my kind of girl.

Forthright and honest, a little bit wild, a lot of independent, and I wanted to be her new bestie.

My heart ached for the two of them, and every time Wyatt's eyes filled with tears while we pillow-talked on FaceTime, mine hazed over too. Who knew empathy could be so earth-shattering and heart-wrenching?

He hadn't reached out to his adoptive parents, hadn't answered either of their calls. He'd skipped their weekly family dinner on Tuesday night. They had text messaged him a bunch of times, begging to talk to him, assuring him of their love, their best intentions.

But Wyatt's hurt dug in stubbornly, and I felt it. I'd lived it. I ached to hold him like I did Garrett every night that week, the two of us all koala bear on each other as usual.

I couldn't erase the frown on my best friend's face, couldn't seem to break through the heaviness on his shoulders no matter how much I told him I loved him or built him up. If anything, it only seemed to make matters worse for Garrett—and he clung to me harder.

Wyatt struggled to identify himself.

Garrett couldn't decide where he belonged.

"You are not going back there," I stated firmly when he mentioned returning to Pennsylvania for the second time because the thought of him moving away twisted my insides up.

We laid on the couch watching a movie Thursday night, me the big spoon, my arm wrapped around his thick chest. With my head propped up on a pillow, I could see over his to watch the TV, but I couldn't make out his face.

He squeezed my fingers laced together with his over his heart. "I don't want to leave you, but I...I can't stay, Hal."

My breath seized at the idea of living without him. I couldn't. Wouldn't.

"Fuck Hollywood and fuck washing dishes," I gasped out, my guts clenched. "Get a new job if you're done chasing your dream of the big screen. Hell, you love working out and sweating—Wyatt is always looking for good help. You're faithful as fuck, never call in sick... he'd hire you in a heartbeat." I continued to spew out ideas, anything to keep him close. "Imagine how tan you would be, the extra muscle you don't need but would gain from real labor. It would be a lot more satisfying that cleaning dirty dishes."

A heavy sigh deflated him a bit further.

"Oh, Garrett." I pressed in tight against his back, kissing his hair, my eyes closing to keep tears from welling. Even though he hurt, the clean scent of him, the feel of his body against mine tightened my nipples.

In that moment of my heart breaking, I didn't even give a shit he might notice the hardened tips through my thin shirt separating our skin. "I'm sorry for being so pushy. I just want you happy."

He lifted my hand and kissed my knuckles. "*You* make me happy, Hal."

"Then stay," I whispered past the thickness in my throat. "Please don't leave me."

"And when Wyatt becomes your person and you no longer need your gay best friend?" He sounded miserable as hell.

"I won't ever *not* need you, Garrett Moore," I argued, determined to keep him from the depression I wished like fuck I didn't understand and feel in the deepest parts of me. "You'll always be my person."

But fuck, how my heart and body burned for more.

Chapter 17

Wyatt

Talking to Haley every night and texting throughout the day helped me work through my identity crisis. Chatting with my sister on a daily basis proved almost as beneficial to setting my mind right too.

I expected I would have to sit down with Lionel and Tina at some point, but I wasn't yet ready to face that emotional hurdle. Too much hurt burrowed deep inside me even though I understood their reasons for wanting to keep the truth from me.

As for my and River's birth parents, I couldn't contain the negative thoughts I had whenever wondering why they had abandoned us to the system.

By the time Friday night rolled around and I readied for my second date with Haley, I decided it was time to make a move. Once the weekend ended, I would look for a private investigator to assist in getting answers even though River didn't feel the need for them like I did.

When Haley suggested we dine in at her apartment, I'd guessed her roommate would be gone again for the night but didn't ask. It didn't matter to me if he joined us to eat takeout and watch a movie.

I'd thought about his ass a time or three throughout the week but hadn't pushed for information or even told Haley I'd been wanting Garrett's fine backside. I knew I would meet him eventually and wasn't about to rush something that might make waves.

One hell of a swell crashed into me when Haley's apartment door swung inward at my light knock.

Garrett stood almost eye to eye with me, his eyes like dark chocolate framed by thick and curly lashes. High cheekbones like a model's dragged my focus down to full lips wrapped around a lollipop stick.

Haley had mentioned his oral fixation, and lust surged through me with an undertow enough to damn near knock my feet from beneath me.

"Wyatt." I stuck out my hand on instinct, and as expected, a jolt ripped through me at his touch.

Neither of us squeezed to show dominance, but we sure as fuck studied each other in the suddenly tense silence hovering over the threshold we spanned. His pupils dilated just enough to ping my gaydar even if I hadn't been aware he preferred dick over pussy.

"Garrett," he finally spoke around his lollipop stick, pulling his hand from mine with seeming reluctance. "Come on in. Haley's in the bathroom."

I stepped past him, filling my lungs with the scent of his soap and a hint of the woods.

My mouth watered.

"Want something to drink?" he offered, turning away for the fridge.

He wore sweats, same as the first time I'd seen him, but he'd also pulled on a T-shirt that clung to his back muscles I'd already gotten a peek at the weekend before.

"I'm good with water for now."

He took out a chilled bottle of chardonnay and poured two glasses before clinking ice into a third and filling it with water.

The candy bulged his cheek. "You hurt her, I'll bury you so goddamn deep that the earth's core will burn you to cinders." The warning came low and quiet as he held my drink out to me.

Biting back a smirk at his intensity, I grasped his hand around the glass he offered, not allowing him to let go. "If I hurt her," I whispered, "I hope you do."

Lips tight, he nodded.

I let him move away.

"Garrett!" Haley hollered from the bathroom.

He pulled the lollipop from his mouth. "What?" he yelled back, his lips glistening. Probably sticky. Sweet.

Goddamnit.

"When Wyatt gets here, you better be on your best behavior! He doesn't know you're going to be home tonight, and I won't have any testosterone-charged air making shit weird!"

Garrett huffed, a smirk curling his lips before he took a sip of wine, eyes moving back to mine.

A definite spark hung in the air between us, interest in his gaze even though the promise of his threat lingered.

"And no drooling all over him, either!" Haley added.

Her roommate slid his gaze down over me, intentionally slow while tonguing over what was left of his candy before crunching it between his teeth. Considering the intentionally flirtatious move, I wondered how faithful he was to their friendship. She adored him, no question, but would he keep from sexual advances with the guy she hoped to create something real with?

She'd told me Garrett knew her feelings for me, that there wasn't anything she didn't share with him.

I narrowed my eyes when his finally returned to my face. "If *you* hurt her…" I trailed off, laying down the law about flirting or making a pass at me like his slowly tenting sweats suggested he might do.

He tossed the stick into the trash, a grin flashing over his features that ripped the oxygen from my lungs.

Garrett was hot while broody and protective, but the happier side of him?

Stunning.

Dick-swellingly delicious.

I wanted to grab hold of his chin and bite on his candy-sweet lips before soothing the sting with my tongue.

"Don't worry, big boy." He stepped close to pat my chest, his palm burning through my shirt. "You aren't my type."

"Glad to hear it," I bit out the words even though he lied through his teeth. Had Haley not been in the picture, he and I would have ended up fucking against the closest wall or one of us bent over the back of the couch.

No. Fucking. Doubt.

I'd never felt such instant lust in my life.

"Garrett!" Haley hollered again.

"What?" he barked back over his shoulder with sarcasm as though she annoyed the hell out of him.

"Let me know when he knocks! I want to answer the door!"

"Too late!"

Haley's footfalls hurried toward the kitchen, and she skidded to a stop at the sight of me and Garrett less than two feet apart, both of us with drinks in our hands. Her gaze narrowed as her focus flitted between us.

"Did I miss the dick measuring contest?"

Garrett barked a laugh and turned away from me to get her wine, and I grinned like an idiot, unable to tear my eyes off her.

She hadn't straightened her hair—a darker shade of red than it had been last I'd FaceTimed with her hung in waves over her shoulders, and she hadn't put on a stitch of makeup.

No less beautiful, and hot as fucking hell in whatever the long T-shirt draped over her petite form was. Not a dress...

"Are you wearing a nightie?" I asked, my focus snagging on the hem which fell to mid-thigh.

Bare thigh. Golden skin. Satiny smooth, I remembered well.

"I decided I liked you enough for you to see me in all my non-dolled up glory. This is the real me poor Garrett has to live with," she stated, waving a hand down over herself. "Not some painted version to get you to fall for me."

"I would have fallen even if this was how you showed up at the Lounge last weekend."

"Gag," Garrett muttered.

Ignoring him, Haley went heart-eyed on me and hurried across the kitchen, throwing herself at me.

Water sloshed from my glass as I caught her one-armed.

"My eyes!" Garrett mocked, heading for the couch with both of their wine glasses as she planted a kiss firmly on my lips. "Either tone it the fuck down or take it to the bedroom. And please, for the love of *God*, keep quieter this time."

"Shit." Haley muttered quietly and pulled away from me, the smile in her eyes fading a bit.

"He heard, hmm?" I whispered, and she bit her lip, nodding, her gaze so damn needy.

Why did that make my dick hard?

Garrett sat with his back toward us, turning the TV on, Haley's drink waiting for her on the coffee table.

I cradled her cheek with my free hand, wanting to give her what I could. I kissed Haley's lip from between her teeth, sliding my tongue in for a little taste since her roommate didn't watch us.

She moaned quietly, her hands finding my hair. "As much as I really want to drag you into my bedroom and have my filthy way with you," she murmured with barely a hint of tone to her voice, "I'm hungry, and Garrett needs company. Long story, but he's struggling with some shit that isn't my place to talk about."

"Not a problem. I don't mind sharing you."

Her eyes widened slightly, but I released her face before she could question if my words carried a double meaning.

Which they definitely did.

Sucks he's not into women like that.

"So, what are we ordering?" I asked rather than giving further thought to Garrett's sexuality. I needed to set that shit aside and focus on what Haley wanted.

She padded into the living room on bare feet to grab her cell off the coffee table.

Garrett's gaze tracked her as she ambled past him, swiping the phone to life.

"Pizza?" she suggested while slowly walking back toward me. She scrolled her finger over the screen, but I didn't take my gaze off the roommate who watched her like a lion stalking his prey.

"I'm good with pizza. Garrett?" I asked.

"Doesn't matter to me," he finally said, turning his attention onto the TV. "I'm not hungry."

"You're eating more than those damn lollipops that are going to rot your teeth," Haley barked while glaring at the back of his head. Her mommy-like tone made me snicker.

The guy was depressed, but I wondered what else went on in that mind of his.

I joined him in the living area while Haley put through a call to order for us. A worn recliner sat adjacent the couch, and I settled onto it. Garrett didn't track my footsteps like he had Haley. He didn't give me a second glance.

But his knee bounced. A muscle ticked in his jaw.

He was attracted to me, no question, and I couldn't decide if he hated that fact or me because he'd have to fight for his best friend's attention.

Haley came back into the living room, but I watched Garrett.

His head swiveled the second she showed up in his periphery, and his eyes stayed on her as she bypassed him, the wine he'd poured for her, and the couch.

For me.

Way more than longing rested in his gaze. He gave off major adrift vibes, ones I recently gained personal knowledge of—the type of neediness that drew me in like a moth to flame.

Haley curled up on my lap, and the look on Garrett's face said it all.

He was jealous of me—and not because he only saw her as a friend.

Gay, my ass.

Haley had told me a few times that he was only into guys. Lamented it, even, when saying how perfect of a man he was in all ways except not wanting pussy.

He'd bullshitted her, and he had to know he'd fucked up in doing so. Being aware of her hatred for lies, I expected confessing to his feelings for her would tear apart their friendship.

But why hadn't he told her the truth from the start?

I didn't know his story, Haley had said it wasn't hers to share, but I couldn't keep from wondering, even when she slid her hand beneath my shirt to caress my abs.

Maybe I could poke the bear and learn some answers. "My Haley here tells me you're a dishwasher," I said, placing emphasis on the *my* to see if I could get a rise out of him.

That muscle ticked in Garrett's jaw again, and he tore his attention off her hand for the TV.

Bingo.

"Yeah," he muttered.

"Do you enjoy it?"

"Fuck no."

I took my time checking out his broad shoulders and the obvious muscles beneath. Clearly the guy was in great shape and needed some help gaining direction in his life. "I'm hiring and could use someone like you."

He shifted his focus my way, his dark eyes hardened, more closed off than I'd seen since arriving. "Someone like me."

"She says you're a hard worker, and I can see for myself you're fit as fuck."

A hint of heat flashed in his eyes and disappeared just as quickly. "What kind of work?"

"Landscaping. One of my foremen over at Sunrise Condos just had a guy quit, and I need—"

"Wait." Haley sat up, staring at me wide-eyed. "You're the owner of Lionel's Landscaping?"

I didn't remember giving her the name of my company before and nodded.

"No fucking way." She let out a huff of laughter and glanced over at Garrett. "He's Blaine's boss! You're Blaine's boss!" She repeated, turning toward me again. "Lily's Blaine."

The dots connected in my head.

"What are the chances?" I said with a laugh. She'd told me briefly about her other best friend—but not that she was in a triad. On the rare occasion I labored alongside Blaine, he sometimes talked about his Lily and Grey. I'd just never put two and two together.

"She is going to die!" Haley hopped off my lap and grabbed up her phone again, giggling. "Oh my God! I can't even right now!"

The yearning on Garrett's face as he watched her, that lost puppy impression I'd felt from him, hit me like a punch to my gut.

I barely heard the conversation Haley had with her girlfriend while standing there in front of her roommate, oblivious to how he looked at her.

My mind had focused on the fact she was between us.

And I wanted more of the same—preferably in a bed where I could get my hands on Garrett's bi, needy ass too.

Chapter 18

Garrett

I could feel Wyatt watching me, but I couldn't look at him or he would see how much I wanted a piece of him. Haley had hit the damn jackpot and then some. The man was beyond fine, his front just as sexy as the back I'd seen the weekend before.

She'd called him luscious, and even though it had killed me to listen to her go on and on about his mouth and dick and how he knew what to do with both, I wanted firsthand knowledge.

Some friend I was.

And Wyatt had picked up on that shit within seconds of meeting me.

I'd felt the spark of interest—no...fuck that...out of control *flame*—between us, same as him, but at least he'd laid down the law about flirting. I'd refrained but hadn't wanted to.

Haley was my person, and even though I hated the idea of sharing her with him, knowing he got all the benefits I couldn't ever have, I had to let her go.

All week, I'd agonized over heading back to my grandparent's house, but the thought of all those miles between me and my cuddle bug made me feel like someone knifed at my chest with the intention of carving out my heart.

I had to make things work in California.

I tore my focus off Haley standing in one of her sleep shirts, without a bra, damn her for being so perfect.

As expected, Wyatt stared at me, his face an unreadable mask.

"So tell me more about that job," I said, needing a mind redirect.

Grounds upkeep for the extensive property including mowing, weed whacking, mulching, and two old patio areas scheduled to be ripped up and replaced with new pavers. A stone retaining wall and water garden—enough to keep Blaine and two guys busy in the months to come.

"I helped run our neighbor's farm stand back in Pennsylvania," I said once he finished. "But other than that, I have no experience dealing with gardening, not that *that* even counts."

"If you're willing and able—which you appear to be," he stated, glancing down at my torso and the tight shirt I'd worn in hopes of making Haley's new love interest jealous, "then I would hire you on my Haley's word alone."

His Haley.

My teeth clenched, same as it had the first time he'd called her that. I wanted to clock him in the jaw—then suck on the bruised skin.

Fuck.

I stretched my neck side to side, turning back toward the TV. "I'll think about it."

Which I couldn't—not really. Seeing him day in and out all sweaty from work would only cause heightened desire, and I wasn't about to cross that line and possibly fuck things up for the woman I loved.

I'd already made enough mistakes in my life.

Haley snuggled on his lap while we ate pizza, well, they ate, and I attempted to. With how she clung to him, I knew my days were numbered. Wyatt had become her koala bear, and it was only a matter of time before she no longer needed me.

I would lose my person, my pillow, the ear I unloaded my shit to every damn day. That sense of having no direction intensified with every ticking second, and depression hung over me like a wool blanket in the heat of summer. I struggled to breathe let alone watch the movie we'd started after eating our dinner.

While heading to my bedroom and shutting myself away for the night would have been best, I'd turned into a masochist, desperate for every second of Haley's presence I could get before I lost her.

From the corner of my eyes, I couldn't help but watch their interactions. Their whispers reached my ears. Haley's giggles. Wyatt's hand sliding up the inside of her thigh.

Seriously? They would get it on right there in front of me when her bedroom was mere feet away?

Haley knew what I'd been going through, and had Wyatt not been there, she would have had her fingers in my hair, giving *me* her attention.

But had I been her, I'd have been wrapped up in Wyatt too.

Conflicting emotions from lust to jealousy wound tight around me until I sat like a tensed sprinter, ready to explode into motion at the first crack of the starter's gun.

My Blow Pop clacked on my teeth as I moved it side to side.

Haley's cell rang, but I was the only one to jolt at the ringer she'd forgotten to turn down. Neither of them paid any attention. She was enamored with Wyatt while he played with her hair, murmuring in her ear while she flushed and smiled.

I turned my scowl back to the TV, unseeing, uncaring of the action movie with the dark-haired actor that usually would give me a raging boner. The lollipop in my mouth crunched to pieces beneath my attempts to ease the tension in my body.

Her cell rang again.

I grabbed it off the coffee table when she didn't, needing a break from the two of them. "It's Lily," I said after glancing at the screen.

Wyatt held out his hand, and I tossed the phone their way. He snagged it from the air like he'd been a hockey goalie his whole fucking life.

"I'm busy, bitch," Haley said by way of greeting, but her grin faded. "What?" She hopped off Wyatt's lap and grabbed the clicker from the coffee table, pointing it at the TV.

The news station ran a breaking story.

Abraham Quell had been murdered while in prison, his penis sliced from his body and shoved up his backside. He'd been left to bleed out.

One of the guards had supposedly leaked the gruesome details of the story, and although it hadn't been verified by law enforcement, I believed the reporter. Even though Quell had been held in solitary confinement away from general population, a man who'd sexually abused children wouldn't last long among other inmates. One slipup on anyone's part that would leave Quell open for attack was all it would take —it was all that it *had* taken.

The fucker had met his end, rightfully so.

"It wasn't his tongue severed from his body," I mused out loud what Haley had hoped for, "but this is ten times better if you ask me."

"Damn right." Haley perched on the couch beside me—fucking *finally*—riveted by the TV.

"That's the fucker Blaine told me about," Wyatt stated quietly.

Haley glanced over at him. "You know he grew up on that compound?"

"Yeah." Disgust showed on Wyatt's face as he pursed his lips, his head shaking. "His boyfriend Greyson is the one who helped put that Quell guy away, right?" He asked the question, but quietly as though more musing rather than looking for an answer.

"Yeah," Haley said, her focus still on the TV. "His father's private investigator dug up the shit the FBI hadn't been able to."

Wyatt made a noise in his throat as though intrigued, pulling Haley's attention toward him. "What?" she asked.

"That's what I have to do."

"What?" Haley repeated while I glanced between the two of them, just as baffled as her.

"Hire a PI to find them."

Without a word, Haley dropped the clicker onto the cushion beside me and left the couch for Wyatt's lap once more, dropping my heart back to its new place of shitty low. Straddling his legs, she held his face in her hands. The intimacy between their locked gazes was almost too much for me to bear, but I couldn't tear my focus off them as they existed in their own little world.

I lusted for another goddamn piece of candy to crush between my teeth. My hands fisted at my sides, my jaw clenched tight.

"So, you've decided, then?" she finally broke the silence between them, her voice low and full of concern.

"I need answers," he replied, nuzzling into her palm like I did whenever she comforted me.

I shifted to ease the tension coiling inside me, knocking the clicker onto the floor and inadvertently muting the TV. Both of them glanced over at me. While I might have considered myself to be an actor, I wasn't sure I schooled my features enough to keep from revealing my feelings. But fuck, how I tried as the seconds ticked past in a strange, quiet moment between the three of us as they continued to stare at me.

"I found out last Sunday that I was adopted," Wyatt explained, having at least picked up on the question in my mind about their exchange.

The guy didn't know me from Adam and had just given me what had to be his greatest vulnerability if his open expression was any indication. That bit of news had shattered him—and I'd experienced that feeling far too deeply myself.

"From your expression, I'm taking it the news knocked your world off its axis," I murmured, my empathy rising and making me want to wrap him up in my arms and cuddle the hell out of him. "I'm sorry."

Wyatt blew out a heavy exhale. "Yeah."

All his confidence had melted away, and strangely, I didn't get pissed as Haley threaded her fingers through his hair like she did whenever I needed her.

"I was adopted too," I spewed out what very few people knew. "Well...kind of."

Haley glanced at me, and the tenderness in her eyes sent an ache through my chest. I couldn't say why I had shared that part of me with a near stranger, but it had felt right.

Necessary, even.

Wyatt held my gaze without heat, without suspicion for the first time since we'd faced off in the doorway. It was like we *saw* each other beyond the surface. He and I experienced the same hurt, the life-altering kind that had made me feel like I stood on shaky ground.

Warmth spread through me as we stared at one another—not lust, but something...more.

"I'm a product of rape," I blurted out the rest of my shit truth because I wanted—needed him to understand that I felt his pain on a deep level.

Wyatt blinked at my blunt statement, but I went on before he could decide what he should say if anything at all.

"My mom killed herself when I was six months old, and my grandparents raised me. They never hid the truth from me, and when I turned thirteen, they allowed me to read her suicide note."

"Fuck," Wyatt muttered, shaking his head, his blue eyes full of empathy like he wanted to drag me into his arms and hold me like he did Haley.

Even though somberness had flooded the living room, my heart beat a little bit faster.

"Yeah. She couldn't handle the sight of me. I was a daily reminder of her pain and emotional suffering."

"Christ—I don't even know what to say."

There wasn't anything good anyone could reply with to that sort of a truth bomb, but talking about my origins didn't bring on the pain it used to.

"Do whatever you need to get answers to your questions, Wyatt," I said, still holding his stare, wishing I could reach out and touch him. Connect physically like I was sure we'd done emotionally with just a few shared words. "What you find might suck, but I've come to terms with my past, and I'm just thankful to be alive. Never existing, never having a chance to see the beauty of this earth and making friends..." I shrugged, since my tightening throat over losing Haley to him—no matter how fucking phenomenal he seemed —didn't allow for more expressed thoughts.

As though attached to my soul and feeling my pain, Haley left his lap and came to me, sliding in against my side to wrap her arms around me.

Wyatt watched his woman comfort me without a hint of jealousy in his eyes.

For the first time since hearing Haley go on about the guy, a sliver of hope rose inside me. Did he understand our platonic relationship? Would he really be okay with her and I continuing on in our friendship?

"Do you think Greyson would help me out?" he asked, and I told myself he must have been too lost in thought to really see how Haley held me. Nurturing. *Possessive.*

"I know he would," she answered, her voice muffled from where she'd shoved her face against my chest.

"I'll talk to Blaine tomorrow." Wyatt lifted his focus off her for my face. "I appreciate you telling me your story, Garrett. Thank you."

I nodded, and he got up to head to the bathroom, leaving us alone.

He trusted her. Trusted me even though she'd wrapped around me like a python.

That hope came back ten fucking fold, and I swallowed hard, not wanting to hope only to have my heart crushed.

"Garrett," Haley whispered and hugged me tighter.

"He really is one of a kind, Hal," I choked out.

She sighed long and heavy.

"Just be careful, okay?" I fought to keep my voice steady. "You fall quick and hard with every guy who gets your attention like this," I reminded her what she'd told me countless times.

"Yeah, but this is different. I—I just know it could be something special."

"I hope you're right," I half-lied, hating myself for loving her so much. She deserved my honesty. Even if it ripped us apart, at least I could clear the air—and she would have Wyatt to comfort her. He seemed the type I could entrust her care to.

I leaned down and kissed the top of her head, finally ready to tell her the truth of how deep my love for her went. She deserved my honesty no matter the outcome.

Eyes closed, I breathed in the scent of lavender, but it didn't soothe as usual. "Hal—"

The bathroom door opened, and she pulled away, the moment between us ruined. Or perhaps fate had decided the timing wasn't right.

I stood, moving past Wyatt as he joined us once more. "I'm heading to bed," I said over my shoulder, putting space between us since I'd had all I could take of their affection. "It was nice meeting you, Wyatt—and good luck."

"Thanks."

I nodded and left them alone.

But I was the lonely one who had already decided he wouldn't turn on music or bury his head beneath a pillow. I would appreciate from afar that another man might be able to make her happy—give her all the things she craved.

Haley's bedroom door shut a short time later, and I stared in the dark, listening to him love her since I couldn't.

Chapter 19

Haley

We didn't thump the headboard.

Wyatt swallowed my cries while I erupted around his dick and he moaned his pleasure over how much I pleased him.

He kept the vocal evidence of his climax to whispered groans, smothering his face against my neck while coming.

While we hadn't spoken about Garrett being on the other side of the hallway with only two doors separating us, we were both considerate of his presence.

I couldn't believe Garrett had told Wyatt about his mom. It had taken me months of being vulnerable with him before he'd opened up to me.

Lots of shit had gotten dragged into the evening, but I wasn't upset or felt like the date had been ruined. Far from it. My best friend and...whatever Wyatt was to me had connected in those few minutes of revelation between the two men.

But there had been more than sharing of painful pasts.

Attraction had been thick between them the second I'd hurried into the kitchen, but I wasn't surprised. Both men were beautiful and irresistible. How could they not be drawn to one another like magnets?

Throughout the rest of the night, I'd seen the them checking each other out—but I'd also noticed Garrett's jealousy over Wyatt occupying my physical space.

And I'd been a selfish bitch staying on Wyatt's lap even if I hadn't meant to flaunt what I'd found right after Garrett had a reminder of Alec and his crushed heart.

"Your thoughts are loud." Wyatt's words murmured against the back of my head before he kissed my hair.

He big-spooned me, one arm wrapped around my waist, his legs entangled with mine.

"Thinking about Garrett."

"What about him?" Wyatt didn't sound upset that my mind wasn't on the slow, toe-curling sex we'd had or the hard body still wrapped around me like a warm cocoon in my bed.

"It was selfish of me to hang all over you when he's hurting."

"He has to know you weren't rubbing in your happiness," he replied, winding his fingers through mine atop my belly. "You don't seem the type."

A shuddered exhale sank me further into the mattress, and I closed my eyes against the dim streetlight sneaking around the edges of my blinds as Wyatt's thumb absently massaging beneath my breast.

"I can't believe he was so vulnerable with you tonight. He's pretty private."

When Wyatt didn't respond, I rolled to face him, snuggling against him, rubbing my face against his hard chest like a needy kitty.

"Yeah," he finally said, his hand on my lower back to hold me tight. "That was definitely...a moment."

"I loved that the two of you connected."

"He was jealous." A hint of cautious curiosity laced his voice, and I pulled back to better see his face.

I couldn't make out the color of his eyes other than paler than mine, but I could see enough to read facial expressions. He didn't smile, but Wyatt wasn't the arrogant type or possessive. He'd left the living room when I'd all but climbed onto Garrett's lap to offer him comfort. I'd done so on instinct, not even thinking about how my date would react.

He'd given us time alone, and I'd never been so grateful.

"Garrett means a lot to me."

"As you do to him."

Fuck, how I wished for more...

"He's hot, isn't he?" I asked while running my fingertip over Wyatt's lower lip. An image flashed in my head of that mouth around Garrett's dick, and I swallowed a moan as my pussy pulsed.

"He is."

"Told you he would snag your attention."

Wyatt nipped the pad of my finger then licked it. "I'm not going to leave you on the side of the road, even if Garrett is interested in me."

"Oh, he's interested alright," I said with a smirk. "He couldn't keep his eyes off you."

Wyatt didn't respond, just trailed his fingers up and down my spine with tender caresses like he seemed fond of doing.

"What?" I pushed when I couldn't stand not knowing what went through his head.

"I liked how you went to him. Comforted him—like you couldn't help yourself."

"It's instinct."

"You love him."

I nodded but couldn't expand or deny being *in* love with him. What would Wyatt think about the two of us sharing him? Biting the inside of my lip didn't offer me any answers, and without talking to Garrett first, I didn't want to approach the subject.

"I'll be honest since I'm aware you hate liars." Wyatt brushed his lips over my forehead, his warm breath tickling my hair above his mouth. "I wouldn't be able to keep my hands off him if I were you either."

"He's so fucking fine," I muttered, loving how Wyatt didn't care that I was attracted to my roommate—and he knew how much I appreciated hearing truth.

"If I hadn't met you first, I'd be all over his ass given the chance."

"Oh my God," I moaned at the thought of the two of them together. Maybe I ought to suggest—

"You look good on him."

Fuck. I swallowed hard.

"But even better, I love how you comfort him—the same way you do me. Gives me hope, you could say…"

"Are you fishing?" I asked with a huff of laughter.

"Yep."

"I like you," I admitted to what he was looking for. "A whole fucking lot."

Wyatt rolled me beneath him, his mouth stealing my breath and fucking with my sanity. The man could kiss. Fuck, could he ever. Arousal leaked from me, from his lips and tongue on mine, his hands tangled up in my hair to hold my head where he wanted me.

"You taste like wine and pizza," he whispered and nipped my lower lip.

"Sorry."

"Don't be." He nipped again and turned his attention to my neck. "You're so goddamn delicious." More kisses, slow drags of his tongue over my clavicle, between my breasts...

Wyatt slid down my body, taking his time tasting me from mouth to hip bones, bypassing where I throbbed.

"You're a tease," I whisper-moaned, my fingers fighting for purchase in his hair.

"Mmm," he hummed over the top of my pelvis.

I lifted my hips and shoved his face southward. "Take care of me."

"Always, sweet Haley," he said, his tone warm and promising—as though he planned on more than just pleasing me in bed. He latched onto my clit and suckled, pulling a dozen curses from my lips and keeping my thoughts firmly focused on the chemistry between us.

I spread my legs wider as he settled between them, grabbing hold of my ass cheeks.

Wyatt nosed me from asshole to clit, a rumbled groan of appreciation making me tingle clear through to my toes. "So." He kissed the bundle of nerves. "Damn." He licked it. "Delicious." Wyatt latched on, and I bit the inside of my lip to keep from crying out.

God of Pussy Eating.

He had me so fucking turned on I couldn't snicker at the new nickname that shot to my brain.

"Yes," I moaned instead, trying to fuck myself on his face.

Another low rumbled noise of appreciation against my core caused goosebumps to ripple over my skin. He'd already made me come three times, but my body definitely wasn't done for the night.

Arousal and saliva slid down my ass crack, and I couldn't keep from whimpering out my need for more.

Two fingers slid into my sopping pussy, curling exactly right.

"Oh *God*," I groaned and clenched my teeth, but Wyatt wrapped his free arm around my hips to hold me from fucking myself against his hand.

"Let me eat you, baby," he murmured against my clit while stroking deep inside me. "Want to make you come again."

"Oh fuck, yes." I grabbed hold of his hair and held him in place while he went to town, devouring me like a starved man until I creamed all over his fingers, biting my tongue to keep quiet.

He slid slickened fingertips over my asshole while lapping at my cum.

I lifted my knees to give him better access, still high as a damn kite.

Wyatt teased and toyed with my hole, pressing but not breaching.

"You can fuck me there if you want," I whispered, eyes closed and ready to pass out.

"Christ, woman." Wyatt groaned, removed his finger from my crack, and pressed a lingering kiss on the puckered skin. "Someday…"

He dragged his lips all the way back up my body, and I licked the taste of myself off his tongue he slid along mine in languid strokes.

"Your *mouth*," I groaned against his, arousal wanting to spring back to life between my thighs.

"Your *everything*," Wyatt answered and rubbed his nose over mine. He let out a heavy exhale and rolled off me.

"Where are you going?" I whined—didn't even give a shit I was obvious as fuck.

"Going to clean you up, make sure you're comfortable, then head home."

My chest tightened. "No."

"Yes." He chuckled and yanked on his boxers and jeans he'd left in the middle of my bedroom floor. "You have to open the shop in the morning, and I want you to sleep. Be right back."

Huffing an annoyed exhale, I pressed my lips tight, telling myself that his wanting to take care of me meant more than waking up to sleepy kisses in the morning. My eyelids fluttered shut as he left me alone for the bathroom.

Darkness rained down over me—but warm wetness pressed between my legs, jolting my eyelids open.

"Sorry," Wyatt whispered with a chuckle but went about thoroughly wiping me up with gentle caresses like he'd done the weekend before.

"Holy fuck did you wreck me," I moaned, batting at his hand when his caretaking went on too damn long. I rolled over onto my belly and smooshed my face into my pillow.

A kiss lingered on the back of my head as my comforter settled over my back. He tucked it tenderly around my shoulders. "I'll see myself out and call you tomorrow."

I grunted some sort of agreement but didn't even hear the bedroom door close before sleep claimed me fully.

Chapter 20

Garrett

I ignored my stone-like dick and lay on my back, listening to the woman I loved being pleasured by a sex-on-a-stick man. Pre-cum oozed from my slit, but I didn't bother with that either.

Even though Haley and Wyatt tried to be quiet, my ears strained for every gasp and groan, soaking that shit up like a cactus in the dead of summer. It would have to be enough.

My chest ached but with more than pain, almost… sweet. Sickeningly enjoyable. I guessed that truly made me a masochist.

They quieted. Someone went into the bathroom.

And I needed to move, since I wouldn't find contentment in jerking off.

Bottles of water sat in the fridge and seemed the best bet to cool my blood.

I stood in front of the appliance, the door open and refrigerated air wafting over my heated skin while I sucked down an iced water until the empty plastic crinkled in my hand. Thinking about Alec helped to deflate the tent in my mesh shorts I'd tugged up before heading to the kitchen.

The hairs on the back of my neck rose, and not from goosebumps.

I grabbed another water, shut the fridge door, and turned.

Sure enough, Wyatt stood at the end of the hallway watching me. I tossed him the cold bottle.

"Did you play hockey or something?" I asked when he caught it without fumbling.

"Lacrosse."

"Mmm." I shot the crumpled plastic of my bottle toward the trash can.

"Basketball?" he asked when I hit the mark.

"Yep."

We eyed one another in silence that grew tenser with each passing tick of the clock above the sink. He'd dressed, shoes and all.

He was leaving, and I wondered if Haley had put up a fight. She had to work early—

"You're in love with her." Wyatt didn't ask a question.

I expected I'd been too damn obvious even though I'd tried to hide my feelings for her. I kept my lips sealed, simply waiting to see what else he had to say on the topic.

He tore his attention off my face to open the water and drink the same as I'd done. My focus fell to his throat as he swallowed down every damn drop, and my tongue salivated to lick his skin.

He probably tasted like Hal…

Fuck.

I clenched my jaw, fighting off the erection the cool fridge and water had helped me deal with.

"Are you living in denial or what?" he asked when he finished.

Still, I kept silent.

"If Haley initiated more than comfort, you would be hard as fuck. Aching. Leaking. Salivating for a taste of her."

My dick loved the images he painted in my head, and the tightening in my groin continued.

"Yeah, that's what I figured. You need to be honest with her."

A snort huffed from my nostrils. "If you've learned anything about *my* Hal, you know how she despises liars."

Wyatt's gaze narrowed. "You think she'll be pissed, that her anger will wreck the bond between you?"

"She'll hate me."

"Haley could never hate you, Garrett. She's madly in love with you." He recapped his empty bottle.

A barked laugh escaped me. "Yeah, okay."

"I'm serious. Not telling her the truth could be one of the biggest mistakes of your life."

Mistake.

Fuck, I hated that word. Hearing it on Wyatt's lips hit me like a kick to the gut.

I eyed him, wondering what the fuck he was up to. Did he really believe she loved me beyond platonic, that being honest with how I felt wouldn't rip us apart? If Hal ever would forgive me—which I doubted fully—why the *fuck* would he want that? He had to realize she *would* be my Hal afterward.

But she wouldn't.

People who lied and manipulated her to get what they wanted ended up in the shit bin where her own damn mother sat. Sharing the truth of my desire for Haley would be a mistake I couldn't bear the consequences of.

So many fucking regrets rattled in my brain, knowing I could never cradle her in my arms in the way I truly wanted. The weight in my chest pulled my mind toward emptiness and depression, but I clung to how I could have her in my life. I needed my Hal in whatever capacity available.

Thank fuck Wyatt had walked back into the living room when I'd been ready to spill my guts to her.

"What are you playing at?" I asked, crossing my arms and leaning against the counter at my back.

He tossed his water bottle toward the trash and scored.

Of course he did.

His blue eyes returned to mine, piercing and intense. "I want to see her happy. If it's me...you..."

Both of us.

Did my mind fill in the gap or was that what I read in his eyes?

"Fuck." I scrubbed a hand down over my face, my dick thickening fully.

"Think about it." Wyatt strode past me toward the door, and I wanted to ask what he'd meant—what he hoped I would consider. "Oh..." He turned, grabbing his keys and cell from the kitchen table. "I was serious about that job offer."

Swiping the screen to life, he once more met my stare. "Phone number?"

I mumbled what he'd asked for even though I wasn't sure about working for him.

A ding sounded from back the hallway, alerting me to his text.

"Think about it," he repeated, and I fucking knew he meant more than the job.

"I will," I agreed—but only to the job offer, not the other shit because I was a selfish son of a bitch and couldn't lose what she and I had.

"Get some sleep." Wyatt glanced down at my tented shorts. "After you take care of that gorgeous hard-on."

Heat flushed through me, and he chuckled over my face going red.

"Asshole," I muttered.

"Masochist."

Chin lifted, I stared him down.

"Tell me I'm wrong," Wyatt pushed.

He wasn't wrong on that point.

The door snicked shut behind him, and I exhaled until I sagged. Fucking hell did that man twist my mind and body.

When I finally fucked my fist, it wasn't just to thoughts of Haley like usual. Wyatt was there with us. Fucking her. Fucking me—while I sucked on her pussy.

Stripes of white lay over my contracted abs and heaving chest, and still I ached. I'd had one hell of a fantasy jerk-off session, but it didn't satisfy what I craved more than the act itself.

Intimacy.

Connection.

Passion.

Things I'd craved with one woman for months...but a newfound desire had lit inside me.

I wanted Wyatt too. Lusted for his hard body and more of the tying together of minds I'd felt earlier that night when we'd both allowed ourselves to be vulnerable. While I hardly knew the man, I felt like my soul had found a missing link...a piece that fit with mine.

Hal was my fantasy Cinderella—but I wouldn't mind a Prince Charming as well.

Especially one who had his shit together and would help me traverse through life, seeing as how I had zero direction.

Sleep was a long time in coming as my mind warred over what I needed to do rather than what I wanted.

And in the morning, Haley kept that war going on.

She wrapped her arms around me from behind, her sleep-warmed cheek against my bare back as I stood waiting for the coffeepot to finish.

I slid my fingers through hers atop my abs, squeezing, thankful I'd emptied my balls before getting out of bed.

"Morning," she whispered with her husky half-asleep tone. If I hadn't recently given myself relief, it would have turned me on like a goddamn light switch. Still, tingles raced through my groin.

I grunted a reply as usual, grabbing mugs from the cabinet overhead.

"Did we keep you up last night?"

I barely bit back my snort. "I put the pillow over my head."

Liar.

My jaw clenched, and I untangled my fingers from hers to pour our coffee.

Her hand stayed put, thumb absently rubbing over my abs while her exhales heated my back. "I'm sorry."

"What for?" I moved off to the side, making her release her possessive hold over my body. If only I could do the same with my heart as easily.

She took the coffee I held out to her and closed her eyes while sniffing the rising steam. "For flaunting what I have with him while you're depressed over Alec."

"I'm hardly depressed over that fucker."

Haley lifted her sleepy focus off her coffee. Hair rumpled from sleep and a good romp between the sheets the night before...she'd never looked so hot. No makeup. Flushed cheeks.

"What?" she asked.

"Hmm?" I tore my focus off her mouth—and the lingering redness from scruff. I hated that it hadn't been mine that had marked her up.

But...I think I'd have been as equally content watching it happen too.

The fuck is wrong with me? I should be jealous—

"You're staring at me really funny."

Forcing a grin, I lifted my coffee and sipped. "Yeah, seeing what the two of you have found makes me envious as fuck. What red-blooded man wouldn't be? But I'm happy for you, Hal. Really. Hang onto that man and ride the fuck out of him."

She laughed lightly, her entire face lighting up.

"Don't even," I bit out, having realized what I'd said. "I don't want details."

Fuck, did I ever.

"TMI from my lips would tent those shorts and make your hole ache to be filled."

"Bitch," I grumbled while she laughed.

"Sorry—"

"No." I cut her off, my chest squeezing tight. "Don't be. You won't hurt my feelings."

Just my balls.

"I want you thoroughly content and satisfied with your life, Hal, and if that's Wyatt, then I'll share."

"Share, huh?"

Heat rushed to my face. "You know what I mean."

Haley moved in, clasped the back of my neck, and pulled my head down.

I bent low, giving her my forehead like she usually went for, but she dipped and pressed her lips firmly on mine.

My heart seized, but she stepped away before my brain could respond.

"I love you, Garrett. So damn much. I just want you to be happy too."

"Love you, Hal," I croaked out—and turned away fast as fuck before she saw the thickening in my shorts. "Gotta...do some shit," I lied, heading back the hallway.

I didn't have a goddamn thing to do all day but sit and pine for what I couldn't have.

"I'm hopping in the shower," she called after me.

As if I needed yet another image in my head.

I shut and locked my bedroom door behind me and didn't bother with prolonging my agony.

That time, it was a fantasy of Haley and her alone, her small hands sudsing her petite body with soap, that filled my mind while I shot spunk over my torso.

Emptiness overshadowed me as I listened to her get ready for work and eventually walk out the door, but I didn't know how to fill the void inside me.

Cum would replenish, but my heart would remain uninhabited by anything but longing.

What a bleak fucking future.

Chapter 21

Wyatt

I went to Sunrise Condos on Monday since that guy who had been working with Blaine quit the week before.

Blaine grinned when I showed up with a bag of muffins and coffee. The haunted look in his eyes I was used to seeing, the rounded shoulders, had disappeared the summer before. He'd found the type of love romantics read about in novels, the passion that only came about in fairytales, the connections every goddamn human on the planet yearned for.

Blaine was one lucky bastard, and we shared a good laugh over the smallness of the world as we discussed Lily and Haley being friends.

"Lily says she can be a handful."

I nodded at Blaine's statement while we lounged beneath a tree for our coffee break. "She's fiery, has no filter, is needy for affection...can't get her out of my mind."

"You know she's in love with her roommate, right?" he asked, his tone wary. "I mean, I don't want to fuck things up for you, but Lily told us that awhile ago, and I thought I should say something to keep you from getting hurt."

"Yeah. I've seen it." I swallowed down the last of my coffee and shoved the cup in the bag we'd emptied of muffins.

"What do you mean you've seen it?"

"The three of us got pizza and watched a movie last night. She looks at him with more than fondness, and he can't keep his eyes off her."

"Wait. What?"

"Garrett's in love with her too."

"But I thought he was gay."

I glanced over at Blaine and raised an eyebrow.

"Shit. Seriously?"

"Mmm hmm." I crushed the cup/bag together between my palms. "And I'm feeling like shit for taking her from him. They're close as hell. Best friends—I've never seen anything like it. Purely platonic even though there's hidden longing."

"Sounds familiar."

I once more eyed Blaine, well aware of his recent past. "Were you upset with Grey when you found out he was in love with you that whole time? That he'd lied to you for ten plus years?"

"He didn't really lie to me. I just never saw his feelings for what they were."

"Kept the truth from you...whatever you want to call it. You seriously weren't mad?"

"No."

Nodding, I glanced out over the lawn Blaine had cut not long after the sun rose. "I really like Haley," I admitted, "and I want her to find the person she's looking for to fill that void in her life. I thought it might be me, but Garrett will always hold a piece of her heart."

"Is he hot?"

"As fuck." I grinned and cast Blaine a glance. "The second I saw him, I wanted to drop to my knees or bend him over a couch. All thoughts of Haley had flashed out of my head for a few seconds like she didn't even exist."

"Shit."

"Yeah. Talk about fucked up. I told him to tell her the truth about how he feels. Even planted a seed in his mind about the both of us loving on her. Not sure he got the hint or if he would ever consider sharing her with me if she forgave him for lying to her."

"Keep your options open," Blain suggested. "Don't delete the app yet—just in case."

His reminder of Missing Link turned my mind toward the other woman I'd met and the idea I'd had the night before.

"Hey...any chance you could get me Grey's PI's number?"

Blaine's head whipped my way as he brushed crumbs off his lap.

Being the non-prying type, Blaine didn't ask, but I explained to him what had gone down the weekend before. Finding out I had a twin sister, that we'd been separated as infants, and that my adoptive parents hadn't ever shared that truth.

"Talk about fate fucking with you," he muttered.

"I know, right?" I shook my head. "My sister and I are in touch with each other a lot—she wants to come visit me soon—but I...I'm not there yet. Without seeing her in person, I can kinda keep it from being real." I shrugged, expecting that didn't make sense to him. "There's just so many unanswered questions."

"You want Grey's guy to find your birth parents?"

"Yeah. My sister didn't bother with trying, but I realized I'm going to need it when I'm ready to move on."

"I'll send along your name and number. I'm sure he'd help you out. I...I don't think he's cheap though."

"I don't give a shit." I pushed up to my feet, arching my back to stretch out.

"Do your adoptive parents know anything?"

My brow furrowed, lips thinning for a few seconds. "I confronted them about their betrayal, but I'm not ready to talk shit through. The grudge still feels good," I admitted.

"It probably doesn't to them."

I scowled at Blaine as he stood and held out his hand. Giving him the trash, I forced my face to relax.

He was right—I was thinking selfishly, but who wouldn't in my shoes?

Withholding the truth hadn't done anything but hurt me in so many goddamn ways…

"Fuck." I clenched my jaw while rolling my head to lessen the tension in my neck. I'd told Garrett to talk to Haley, lay it all out there to hopefully clear the air and make them both feel better.

I needed to take my own damn advice.

I ended up putting it off for two days as my guts churned over the confrontation. And I called rather than showing up since I couldn't handle the thought of seeing Tina cry and Lionel consoling her while I stood on the outside of their emotional bond looking in.

"Tell me everything," I demanded with a tight voice the second Tina breathed my name as a hello.

Her inhale came over clear through the line. "Let me put you on speaker."

The cell clicked, and muffled noises rose in my ear.

I'd showered and settled in for the night—after devouring some frozen lasagna. Perched on the edge of the couch, I waited, my stomach in knots and shoulders up near my ears. My shallow breaths sounded loud in the stillness around me, reminding me how alone I was. Lost and needing answers—assurance of who I was and where I'd come from.

"Wyatt," Lionel greeted me.

I inhaled deeply, hoping to calm my racing heart. "You knew I had a twin," I said, ignoring his greeting, too desperate for small talk. "What else have you kept from me?"

"Not much at all," he said, and I could imagine him entwining his fingers with Tina's. My throat tightened. "We never met your birth mother. Everything was done through the adoption agency."

"Why did you tear us apart?" My voice waivered. "Why not adopt both me and River?"

"We couldn't afford it."

I closed my eyes and slouched, my stare falling to the hardwood floor. "And you figured just withholding the truth would make things okay? Did you ever consider I might find out? That I would want answers? That I would feel betrayed by the two people I trusted the most?"

"We thought we were doing what was best for an abandoned little boy," Tina said, her voice as wobbly and unsettled as my insides.

They had meant to do good, and they had. Lionel and Tina had provided me with a decent life. One filled with affection and plenty of fond memories. I just struggled with what felt like disloyalty.

I rubbed at the ache in my chest.

"I really wish you'd told me." My voice sounded resigned rather than pissed off like I'd forced during my first confrontation in order to hide my hurt.

"I'm sorry," Lionel said. "More than you could possibly imagine. We're so sorry for not being honest with you from the start, son."

I wanted to be a complete asshole and correct what he'd called me but couldn't hurt him.

He and Tina had raised me. Loved me. Sacrificed shit in order to give me a better life than I'd have had in the system or with the woman who'd carried me but didn't want me.

"It—might take me some time to process this," I finally said, my voice low and finally cracking beneath the pressure of my reality.

"Take all that you need, Wyatt," Tina said quietly. "We love you and will always be here for you."

"Thank you," I whispered, tears welling in my eyes.

Although our short talk eased some of the weight on my chest, I still felt that damn sense of floundering.

Within seconds of hanging up with my parents, an incoming call ended up making me hopeful for eventual answers.

Dan Higgins, PI, had reached out to me and agreed to help me find my birth mom.

Like Blaine had warned, the man's services weren't cheap, but I knew how he'd come through for Grey in helping to bring the case against the cult leader who'd fucked with Blaine's childhood.

I gave him all the facts I had, which weren't much. Everything River had told me, all the information she'd emailed me, I forwarded to Higgins.

He said he'd be in touch.

Anxiety had me on my feet and pacing. I needed distraction...

Haley and I had a date lined up for Friday night, which I expected would last the weekend unless Garrett got his head out of his ass and opened his damn mouth, but I couldn't wait to tell her the steps I'd taken toward getting some answers and eventual closure.

We'd been texting, talking on the phone every night before going to bed, and although that wouldn't happen for another couple of hours, I grew impatient with every minute that passed.

She sounded breathless when she answered, giddy with laughter.

"What's so funny?" I asked, unable to help my own grin.

"Garrett's an asshole."

I heard him holler something in the background.

"And I said to go suck a dick, you brat," she yelled back, giggling her ass off.

He hadn't told her—or maybe he had, and they were incandescently happy.

"Bad time?" I asked, steeling myself for rejection.

"Not at all. Just let me escape to my room so we have some privacy. Garrett's been up my ass since you were here, all needy and shit. Whining like a little bitch and clinging to me like a koala."

My breath left in a rush.

She didn't sound annoyed by his actions, and the thought of him being up her ass...

My dick liked the image her words had put into my head. A whole fucking lot.

"I wouldn't mind being up your ass," I tossed out, my grin coming back full force.

"I said you could have it," Haley shot right back.

I groaned. "You turn me on like a goddamn light switch, woman."

"Mmm. Tell me more." Her tone went all husky, and I sprawled back on my couch to give my choking cock some room to breathe even though I wore thin sweats.

"Just the thought of your tight little body makes me hard as fuck."

"Sounds painful."

"Ignoring it is painful," I told her, eying the tent beneath the cotton.

"Then do something about it."

Christ, did she tempt me like no other.

"I'd rather if *you* did something about it," I said, letting a bit of a growly groan leak through my voice while tugging down on my balls.

"Shit. Seriously, Wyatt...how are you so damn fine?"

I chuckled and slid my finger beneath the waistband. "So, what's it gonna be?"

"I just got home from work. I stink and need a shower."

"Don't give a fuck."

"Fine. I'll shower, and you get your fine ass over here so you can have mine."

"Fucking hell." I groaned and tugged on my balls again.

Haley was going to be the death of me—if Garrett didn't beat her to it.

Chapter 22

Haley

I replayed my conversation with Lily from over my lunch break while showering and shaving my legs.

As usual, I had spilled my guts, and she gave me the advice I'd expected from her mouth.

You only live once.

Go for it.

Ride the wave.

Meaning enticing Garrett to join me and Wyatt over the weekend even if I only got to see the two of them together. But it was a chance I was willing to take. I needed answers, goddamnit, and I couldn't find the words to explain or ask Garrett about the situation my heart found itself in.

But Wyatt had opened my mind before I was prepared. I thought I'd had two more days before I would face the two of them again...but no.

He headed toward our apartment with every intent of fucking.

Did I have the balls to put something else into motion?

I prepped myself inside and out, just in case Wyatt did end up taking me in the way we'd teased each other about. I'd had dicks up my backside a few times, and while I found it enjoyable, it felt best when another sank deep inside my pussy too.

The thought of having both men made for one slick mess between my thighs, but I didn't masturbate. When I came—be it around Wyatt, Garrett, or both, I wanted the climax to rob me of sanity.

I edged myself for a few extra minutes beneath the hot spray to ensure I eventually went off like a rocket ship blasting into oblivion.

Garrett laid on the couch, hugging a pillow rather than me when I finally went out to the living room. I'd warned him Wyatt was coming over, and he'd simply nodded before getting comfortable.

"Are you sure you don't mind?" I asked him for at least the fourth time since I'd hung up the phone with Wyatt.

"You know I don't. As long as he treats you good and you give me plenty of warning before kicking my ass out of this apartment..."

Frowning, I took the pillow from him, stretched out on the couch in front of him, and snuggled into his warmth, my face on his bare chest.

Why the hell I tormented myself, I didn't know.

He smelled divine, like the deep forest and dappled sunlight, and the feel of his hard arms tugging me closer dampened the panties I'd tugged on minutes earlier. Heat rushed over my skin, and a shuddered sigh shook through me.

I wanted to press in closer, feel his groin against mine, but didn't want the disappointment. Keeping our bodies apart from the waist down would be best, unfortunately.

His lips brushed against my wet hair. "Okay?" he asked, his low tone rumbling beneath my ear along with his heart that thrummed faster than normal.

Was he looking forward to Wyatt coming over? I knew the sexy man turned my roommate on.

"Yeah," I breathed an answer and bit my lower lip to keep from spilling all the longing and desires I had in my heart.

I'd kissed his mouth on Monday morning without thought. It had seemed natural, instinctive, and while there hadn't been any tongue and our lips were dry, I'd been shocked clear through to my tingling toes.

Thank fuck he'd turned away when he had, or I might have climbed him like a tree and took things way beyond platonic. Which would have sickened him.

Fuck. Why gay? Why not bi?

Garrett rubbed my back absently, his hand low enough that his fingertips brushed the band of my panties beneath my long sleep shirt.

Being with him felt so damn right. Real. Arousing...yet comfortable.

A knock sounded, and both our heartbeats sped up, thumping against each other's.

I pulled back and met his gaze.

His pupils had swelled, and he had that funny look in his eye again...almost like...he wanted me?

Biting my lower lip, I shifted my hips toward his, brushing against his groin.

Holy fuck, he was hard as hell.

I swallowed audibly, frozen as he let out a slow hiss, his gaze darkening. Garrett didn't move, didn't take his focus off my eyes.

"Garrett—"

Wyatt knocked again.

"Answer the door, Hal." He choked the words out, shifting away, pressing against the back of the couch to get his lower body as far from me as possible.

I forced myself to stand on shaking legs, immediately glancing at the bulge tenting my gay roommate's sweats.

Is any *of that because of me?*

I bit my lip to keep from asking.

"Hal—the door." Garrett rolled onto his stomach and grabbed the pillow from the floor where I'd tossed it to hug beneath his head.

Holy fucking shit...

My core spasmed. Arousal leaked from my pussy. I couldn't catch my breath.

Legs trembling, I stumbled through the kitchen. I pulled open the door, and one glance at my face faded the happiness in Wyatt's eyes into pure predatory need.

I was no actor. He had to see the stark lust wracking my body through my eyes.

He moved into the apartment without a word. Kicked the door shut behind him.

And grabbed me up into his arms, his mouth smashing against mine.

I wrapped my legs around his waist, clinging to his back as his hands found my ass cheeks beneath the sleep shirt.

He tasted like mint and home, and my pulse pounded between my ears, same as it did in my core.

"So fucking good," he whispered against my mouth and stroked his tongue back inside, stealing my thoughts. Everything but the taste of him, how well I fit against his body, faded from my mind.

His lips, his breath, his hunger…God, Wyatt was addictive as hell. I filled my lungs with his exhales, swallowed down the low rumbled groan rising from his chest.

A bubble wrapped around us, a moment of pure perfection and complete comfort—

Someone cleared his throat, and I tore my mouth from Wyatt's.

Fuck, fuck, fuck…

Our gazes clashed while we panted for breath, our mouths inches from one another.

A quick glance toward the living room let me know Garrett hadn't sat up to watch. Obviously, we hadn't been quiet enough though.

I grimaced but couldn't tear my hands from Wyatt's back to rub at the sudden pain in my chest.

"Bedroom?" Wyatt asked quietly, and I nibbled my lower lip, torn over what to do.

I couldn't focus, couldn't find clarity of what I'd felt, seen in Garrett's eyes and beneath his shorts. But luscious Wyatt held me in his strong arms, and my body ached for his.

Desire for both swelled inside me, tearing my mind, my heart, in two. How could such equal need exist? Why the fuck couldn't I choose one over the other?

"Haley?" Wyatt pushed for an answer.

I nodded an agreement at the bedroom suggestion because I couldn't voice an explanation of what I burned for.

"Garrett," Wyatt called out in greeting while carrying me toward my room.

"Wyatt," Garrett replied, his tone still haggard.

Was he jealous of me?

Or Wyatt?

Thoughts flew through my mind like a speeding train, and I couldn't focus on anything more than the need coursing through every cell of my body.

Static electricity or perhaps dueling lust raised the hairs on my arms as we passed behind the couch toward the hallway. An equal drawing toward both men seemed to rip me in half the more distance Wyatt's strides took me from Garrett's presence.

I wanted them both in whatever capacity I could have with a desperation that bordered on madness.

Wyatt tossed me onto my bed and turned to shut the door.

"Don't," I whispered, my pulse pounding in my throat and hindering my voice.

He glanced over his shoulder, his palm on the door. One eyebrow raised, he studied me while I fought to calm my racing heart. I still couldn't come out and say it, damnit. Me, the one with no filter.

"You want him to hear me fuck you?" Wyatt asked, searching my face.

I sat up to pull my sleep shirt off overhead, giving myself time to form words. "I...I think he likes to listen?"

I'd gone with a matching bra and panties set—virginal white even though I was far from innocent, and Wyatt let out a low groan.

"Fuck, Haley." He turned toward me, leaving the door open, and prowled across my room. He ripped off his shirt. Shoved down his jeans.

The lack of boxers or briefs left him gloriously naked, and goddamn, the man looked fine as fuck. All tanned muscles and tattoos, and that leaking cock...

Wyatt wrapped his hand around his length, slowly jacking as he neared the bed. "Think he'd like to watch rather than just listen?"

I jerked my focus upward to find heat in his blue eyes. "Why? Are you an exhibitionist?"

He stood beside the mattress, still lazing his hand up and over his erection. Sexual energy rippled between us, but I waited for him to make a move.

"I could be," he finally said glancing down over my sprawled form, "if he's interested." His pale eyes returned to my face. "Why don't you take your sexy little ass out there and ask? Bet you an orgasm he'll go straight for you the second he sees you in that lace."

For once, I didn't snort at the suggestion Garrett might have more than platonic feelings for me. The memory of his hard length pressing against me kept questions of his sexuality flitting through my brain, but I couldn't make sense of it. That hard-on *had* to be for Wyatt—there's no way my koala would lie to me.

Sharing would mean watching.

And I lusted for that almost as much as I did Wyatt's dick deep inside my throbbing core.

Fuck. Okay. I can do this.

My insides quaked like a magnitude 8 on the Richter scale, but my legs held me up when I slid off the bed to stand in front of Wyatt. I rested my hand on his bare chest, the heat of him searing my palm.

"Is this what you want?" I asked, my head tipped back to search his eyes. We hadn't discussed a relationship or exclusivity, but I checked-in to make sure we were on the same page because I felt too drawn to him as a person to fuck things up between us.

His slow smirk shifted all the feels inside me, pulsing need through my core. "Yes—but only if you do too."

Any capacity…

I needed Garrett happy. Craved it as much as I did his hands on me.

At least I could have one of those.

I blew out a heavy exhale and headed toward my bedroom door.

The TV's screen flashed with an action movie, and I neared the back of the couch, knowing Garrett laid there hugging that damn pillow. Was he still hard thinking about Wyatt? If he agreed to even be in the same room with us, I knew my insides would burn to a crisp from his eyes alone.

But given the chance to maybe have his hands on Wyatt…

God, yes.

I lusted to see the two of them together almost as much as I dreamed of both their bodies bracketing mine.

Sure enough, Garrett laid right where I'd left him.

Pulse thrumming, I leaned over the back of the couch, my boobs a nipple shy of spilling from the white bra I'd wrapped them in, my damp hair spilling down to caress his face.

Garrett shifted onto his back. His gaze caught on my tits, and he jerked his focus to my eyes. The black of his pupils still ate at the chocolate brown...and the tent in his sweats hadn't wilted one goddamn bit.

"Want to watch?" I barely whispered the words.

He blinked. Swallowed—and hopped off that couch so damn fast he stumbled.

Giggles erupted from me, and I couldn't stop them from the adrenaline rushing through my bloodstream.

"Shut up," he muttered, rounding the couch—and holding out his hand.

That stopped the noises leaking from my lips.

I met his stare. Longing rested in his eyes, something I'd seen countless times in the past but hadn't been able to put a name to. Garrett loved me wholeheartedly, but was it more than just friendship?

Could straight for you really be a thing?

Hope welled up inside me so damn fast and pure, my knees trembled.

Sliding my fingers through his, I let him lead me back to the hallway. I traversed the edge of a chasm, its deep reaches hidden from my sight.

But I trusted the hand firmly holding mine—and I trusted the man who waited for us like a beacon in the night, a true north to guide us into the light.

Chapter 23

Garrett

Did I want to watch.

What the fuck kind of question was that? She knew I thought Wyatt was hot as hell, that I lusted to see every inch of his damn body. Every time she talked about him and all that muscle she'd gotten to touch and lick, she'd seen me go hard.

Just like I'd done when she had snuggled me on the couch.

There had been no escaping that telling situation, but I wondered if she assumed it had simply been because I was anxious to see her man.

Wyatt sat against her headboard in all his naked, tattooed, fucking deliciousness. Having no shame, he stroked his thick cock, and I swallowed a rush of saliva while pulling to a stop inside the bedroom door.

Our gazes locked, my heart pounding in my chest.

What the fuck were we doing? What did he—

Haley placed her palm on my lower back and gently pushed. I stumbled over the threshold. "Sit beside him," she whispered.

Oh shit.

I was going to watch him fuck her—like up *fucking* close and personal rather than from a chair or something?

Wyatt patted the bed, and swallowing hard, I forced my shaking legs to take me toward him. Black springy hair covered his legs, thinning on his upper thighs. He trimmed around his dick and balls, both of which made my mouth water for a taste. Pre-cum beaded at the slit of his cock, and he smeared it down and back up again.

"Garrett," he stated my name quietly, and I realized I stood beside the bed staring at his dick like a starved freak. "Get your fine ass up here." He patted the mattress beside him.

"O-Okay." I did as told, leaning against the headboard, my hands finding the sheets at my hips and holding on tight. My sweats did nothing to hide my raging hard-on, and I didn't know where to look.

Haley's moan from the foot of the bed decided for me.

She watched the two of us, her chest heaving, eyes wide, and lips parted. A shudder rippled through her as she took us in.

"Strip for us," Wyatt told her, and I stared, not about to correct the *us* that slipped from his lips.

He knew what I desired. No way I could fucking hide it. Was he forcing me to face the truth so she would hate me? Kick me out of her place? Did he hope that by revealing my lies he'd get what I'd wanted for months?

Haley lifted her hands and unhooked the front clasp of the lacy bra that had barely covered the dark pink nipples beneath. They furled tight as the lace fell away, causing all thoughts to fade from my mind but *her*.

Holy fucking shit...she's perfection.

"Fuck, Haley." Wyatt grabbed my hand, putting it atop my tented sweats. He squeezed, silently telling me to touch myself, and removed his touch from me to take up stroking himself again.

Groaning, I adjusted myself and pressed against the base, knowing I was going to blow in my sweats in a matter of seconds.

"Panties," he told Haley, and she shivered, her gaze flitting between us.

I tried like fuck to keep from looking like a ravenous animal, tongue salivating, panting for what lay beneath that lace.

She shimmied them down.

Fucking bare, glistening pussy lips filled my vision. Another groan escaped me, and I had to squeeze my dick.

"Garrett?" she murmured my name like a prayer—a question. With longing.

Fuck my life, did I want her. Badly.

"Sit on him, Hal," I croaked out, rather than begging for her to touch me. Kiss me. Love me. "Let me watch you ride him."

It would have to be enough.

"Fuck yes," Wyatt murmured, grabbed a condom from her bed stand, and settled back in beside me to roll it over his length. "Be a good girl and give him what he wants, sweet Haley."

My Hal climbed onto the bed, her breasts swaying slightly as she moved up over Wyatt's legs.

"Lose the sweats, Garrett," Wyatt demanded, his low tone rumbling through my groin. "Jerk yourself off while you watch your best friend fuck herself on my dick."

Christ, this man.

"Fucking hell, Wyatt." Haley moaned her own arousal over Wyatt's words and rested on her knees above him.

Scrambling out of my sweats, I couldn't look in her eyes—couldn't handle seeing her desire for him. I couldn't watch him—didn't want jealousy to rip my insides to shreds.

Instead, I peered at his hand as he gripped his base and held his sheathed length straight up in invitation.

Haley's knee brushed against my thigh as she settled into place, and I pressed toward her, keeping the connection between us. "Do it, Hal," I whispered through clenched teeth.

She lowered, the swollen head of Wyatt's cock slipping inside her.

They both groaned, and I squeezed the base of my dick, watching as she slowly settled down over him, stuffing her pussy full.

Wyatt slid his hands around her hips, gasping when she bottomed out. "So fucking hot...goddamn are you tight."

My dick pulsed in my hand, and I clenched my jaw while staring at her spread thighs, her swollen clit, and the wet, pink lips stretched around Wyatt's girth.

Alec. Think about Alec and that twink. His bitch sister. The assholes who'd kicked the shit out of my guts.

Mission accomplished, I managed to draw breath, the tingles in the base of my spine subsiding to a dull ache.

No jealousy spiked through me when Haley began to lift and lower. The lewd sounds of her sopping pussy clutching at Wyatt's length made my mouth water. Her creamy arousal coated the condom with every upward stroke, and I imagined it was my cock she rode.

My hands grasping her hips.

I wanted to lay on my belly between Wyatt's legs and suck on his balls while she fucked herself on his length. I lusted to push her forward onto his chest and work my throbbing length into her tight ass.

"Fuck," I groaned at the image in my head.

"You like watching her?"

"Fuck yeah," I answered without thought, pre-cum oozing from my slit. I smeared it over my palm, slickening my strokes over my rigid length.

"You feel so fucking good, Haley," Wyatt growled out. He started moving, thrusting upward into her body, intensifying the wet, schlicking sounds of their fucking.

She panted for breath, running her hands up her taut belly toward her tits. My mouth watered to taste her nipples, and my focus caught on her fingers tugging and flicking them. "G-gonna come," she moaned, her back arching. "Fuck I'm going to come so hard."

I bit down on my tongue and strangled my dick as her voice broke on a cry.

A shudder ripped through her, and Wyatt murmured something about her being a good girl.

Wind rushed through my ears, and I swallowed repeatedly, staring enraptured as she lost herself in pleasure.

Pink flushed her face. Her eyes glazed over with passion until her eyelids fell shut. Lips parted, she released two more heady cries that made both me and Wyatt groan. Haley was beautiful, but the woman coming all over Wyatt's cock with shudders and whimpers...a gorgeous goddess. A siren set on devouring my soul. Shattering my mind.

I bit the inside of my lip to keep from erupting along with her—wanted the moment to last for a goddamn eternity. A metallic taste hit my tongue. I'd bitten too hard.

"Fuck, Haley," I heard myself moan through the ringing in my ears.

Wyatt lifted her off his cock when she came down and flipped them so she was on her belly. He lifted her onto her knees and slid back into her body in one forceful thrust. He and I grunted at the same time.

"Oh fuck...Wyatt...shit you feel so *fucking* good," she groaned into the mattress, her back arching like a cat in heat.

He stroked in and out of her, his abs rippling in sexy as fuck movements that shifted my hips along with his even though I didn't touch either of them.

I fucked my hand while he fucked her pussy, and goddamn what a sight she made.

Chest to the bed, she sprawled as though spent, her hair a riotous maroon mess across white sheets. Pale, curved back, the swell of her hips...Wyatt's firm grip on her waist.

That fucking torso of his I wanted to mark up with my mouth.

Soft mewling noises left Haley as he continued to move in and out of her body, the scent of her arousal thick and tangy reaching my nose. My mouth watered, and I swallowed repeatedly while thinking about getting my tongue on her—on him.

"Come here," Wyatt said, his voice low and rumbly.

I pulled my attention from where he fucked into her but couldn't find it in myself to lift my focus any higher than his parted lips.

"Give me your mouth, Garrett."

Oh fucking hell.

Haley shifted, turning her head.

Our gazes collided as though seeking out answers. Glazed over, her dark eyes seemed to sink straight into my soul and root around, desperate for truth.

Did she want me to do what he'd said?

She didn't argue with what he'd demanded of me, but—

"Hal?" I asked, hesitant to cross lines and upset her, but goddamn, the chance to put my mouth on Wyatt...

"Kiss him."

Fuuuuck.

I pushed up onto my knees, so damn hungry I couldn't think straight. There were no warning bells in my head once she'd offered me the green light, and there was no hesitancy on my part at her command.

Leaning right the fuck in, I grabbed hold of his neck and slammed my mouth against his. It had been too long since butterflies attacked my insides. Too long since I'd parted my lips to let another man invade my body. Wyatt moved in as though he belonged there.

Mint—

That thought fled as Wyatt obliterated my mind with his tongue stroking inside my mouth in time with his thrusts into my best friend.

She moaned and arched her back deeper in my periphery when I peeked, brushing her side against my thighs.

Wyatt ate at my mouth with luscious strokes of his tongue, and I continued to fuck my hand, my knuckles moving over Haley's back.

"Oh my God." Haley let out a low moan, shifting closer to me. "You two…"

I tore my mouth from Wyatt's owning, desperate to see her.

Haley watched us over her shoulder. Gorgeous dark eyes overrun by black pupils, she peered at us with lust in her eyes.

My gorgeous Hal…

"Would you let a woman suck you off, Garrett?"

Wyatt's question sent a shockwave through my groin, but my focus slipped down to Haley's mouth rather than jerk toward him.

She released a soft moan—and licked her lower lip.

Fucking hell.

I swallowed hard, my mind torn, battling with the throbbing need in my groin.

Wyatt pulled out and shoved his face between her thighs, pushing a moan from Haley's throat.

Her eyelids fluttered shut.

Maybe she would just think I was too far gone in my lust for Wyatt to care it was a woman rather than a man's mouth on my cock…

In that moment, the tightening of my balls decided for me.

I moved on my knees until I knelt in front of her. Grasping her chin with a shaking hand, I lifted her head, and she peeled open her eyelids.

Dark eyes collided with mine, cloudy from arousal as Wyatt ate at her ass.

There was no playing this off as mere lust.

She knew I was well fucking aware it was her mouth opening for me—because I groaned her name as her lips closed over me.

Chapter 24

Haley

"Oh fuck, fuck…fucking…Jesus Christ." Garrett gasped and whimpered curses as I leaned forward to suck him down further.

He grabbed hold of my face. "Jesus," he repeated and backed out, leaving a smear of pre-cum over my tongue.

I probed at his slit for more, his eyes on mine. Unwavering. Not a hint of disgust that it was a woman sucking his dick and moaning over his salty flavor. Hope tingled in my chest, and I clung to the feeling, wanting him—both of them—so badly that wetness stung my eyes.

Garrett pushed back in with a deep groan, blinking as though trying to keep my face in focus.

My love for him swelled inside my chest, expanding and reaching to my extremities. There wasn't anything I wouldn't do for him. Nothing I wouldn't give him.

"You're driving him insane," Wyatt murmured against my core before licking me from my sopping pussy to my asshole and making me desperate to feel him deeply seated in either hole.

"Mmm," I agreed, relaxing my throat as Garrett pushed in once more.

"God, Hal." Garrett gulped, pulled from my mouth as though needing a break, and held my face, his thumbs caressing me in time with Wyatt's lips.

Tingles raced over me at their dual touch, pebbling every inch of my skin. Lust raced through my blood, a desperate need to have them both inside me.

I stuck out my tongue in invitation, impatient for more. My eyes pleading, my heart aching.

Garrett cursed and slid back in, hitting the back of my throat again.

Wyatt kneaded my ass cheeks in time with Garrett's slow fucking of my mouth. It was like the sure tsunami wave we'd been riding had slowed its crash toward shore—the calm before the storm. And I was caught the fuck up, my senses on overload.

The scent of sex, man, and sweat filled my lungs. Garrett's saltiness on my tongue made my taste buds weep with pleasure. My nerve endings from both their hands on my body lit my insides like lightning across a dark sky.

Wyatt ate at my hole, nibbling and sucking, and my eyelids fluttered shut. He'd come over for my ass, and I ended up filling myself with his dick, but I don't think either of us truly cared how we got off as long as it was together. He licked and probed at me with his tongue, breaching the ring of muscle hiding my deepest, darkest parts.

I groaned around Garrett's dick, arching my back, wanting Wyatt there.

His finger replaced his tongue, rimming. Teasing.

A whimper leaked from my lips wrapped around Garret's girth, but Wyatt didn't give me what I lusted for.

He crowded in close, pushing his dick balls deep into my aching pussy instead.

I moaned over having them both inside me. Shuddered at the sensory overload of being spit-roasted.

The men began moving in tandem, invading and retreating with the same slow, agonizing thrusts that raced my blood and pebbled my skin.

"She likes it when you pinch her nipples."

A shiver licked over my heated skin at Wyatt's seemingly offhanded suggestion.

Would Garrett—

He did.

Ah, fuck…

I lost my breath, my shiver turning into a shudder as his warm palms squeezed my swaying tits.

Garrett didn't fumble around like a gay man would—he touched my flesh with warm, sure hands. No hesitancy. He knew how to pluck, roll, and pinch with his fingertips.

Beginner's luck, I told myself, or maybe his ex had liked nipple play. Either way, I brushed aside the thoughts and focused on *feeling*.

Four needy hands grasping at my flesh. Two gorgeous dicks stuffing inside my body.

I wished I could have their mouths too.

Wyatt planked over my back, releasing one hand from my hip to slide around my belly. At the first feathered touch over my clit, a full-on body shudder wracked through me. "Need to come?" he asked against my ear with his rumbled tone that fluttered my insides.

I moaned around my mouthful of cock, too damn desperate for thought.

"I'll take care of you, sweet Haley," he promised.

Wyatt's heat left my back, and I opened my eyes, straining to look up at my best friend.

His pupil-blown dark eyes stared down at me like I sprinkled the stars in the night sky, binding my heart even tighter to his.

Was there such a thing as straight for you? Or did he just love me enough, care for me, sense that connection between us as deeply as I did, that it didn't matter what wasn't between my legs?

Wyatt toyed with my clit, smeared his fingers along where he thrust into me. "Such a good girl, sweet Haley...fuck you're taking us both so well—like you were made for us."

His praise rose goosebumps over my skin, pushing me toward the edge...and Garrett's burning stare...

He slid deeper into my throat I kept open and relaxed even though I wanted to beg him to come. I needed to taste him, listen to the noises he made while finding his release—something I'd never had the privilege of hearing.

Wyatt slammed into me, his fingertips closing over my clit.

Strangled denials leaked from my lungs but couldn't make it into the air. I didn't want to lose myself to the climax of the century until Garrett did. I needed to see his face, watch him come undone.

For me.

"Mmm." I whined around my mouthful of dick as Wyatt began rubbing over my clit with a firm, circular motion.

"Hmmhmm!" I begged Garrett with my eyes, pleaded for him to give it to me.

"Tell me you're close, Garrett," Wyatt's husky voice floated over my ears, "'cause I can't hold back. She's too tight...too hot. Fuck."

"So fucking close." Garrett groaned his agreement. "Can I—"

I wrapped my lips around him tight as I could and sucked.

Wyatt pinched my clit and slammed in deep. "Oh fuck... Haley." His dick jerked inside me, and I panted through my nostrils, holding on, clinging to the edge... fucking hell it hurt...

Garrett.

Wyatt's sharp thrusts hit my cervix, and his groans while coming were heady and sexy as hell.

"Fuck, Hal...Jesus, your mouth...fuck." A muscle ticked in Garrett's jaw, his eyes glazed over—and he erupted with a deep groan, flooding my mouth with hot spurts.

I released my hold on my own climax, swallowing his cum rather than shrieking my release as the two men throbbed inside my body.

"Fuck." Garrett grunted as another spurt hit my tonsils. "Christ." Another and another—I swallowed it all down, enraptured by the look of wonder, of complete euphoria, on his gorgeous face as the three of us fell together.

The same goddamn feels in his eyes rushed through me, robbing me of breath.

"Hal." Garrett croaked my name as one last shudder rippled over him, and he backed away, leaving me gasping. "Goddamn."

Wyatt eased from my body and slid onto his side, taking me with him, pulling Garrett's palms from my face. One of Wyatt's hands cupped a possessive hold over my pussy, the other rubbing up and down my thigh.

Garrett had slouched to sit on his heels, his cock spent and resting on the bed between his thighs.

I slid my gaze over his heaving chest, his rounded shoulders, while coming down from the most glorious high *ever*.

Our gazes caught, tingles racing through my blood stream.

No disgust shone in his eyes. He still appeared stunned, as drunk off his climax as I felt. Would he let me snuggle him after the line we'd crossed?

"Come here," I whispered, holding out a shaking hand, my chest tight.

Garrett snuggled in against my front like we often did on the couch, his face tucked into my neck, and I released a heavy sigh, my eyelids fluttering shut. He didn't keep his groin away from me but pressed in close, the damp flesh of his cock against my thigh as though he recognized we belonged together.

Wyatt's heat against my back seeped through my core, meeting Garrett's in the middle—a perfect fucking fit.

The three of us lay in silence, and I let myself float, completely relaxed.

Fully sated.

Incandescently happy.

Sure, a shit ton of words needed to be said, but I didn't have the energy.

It could wait.

Snuggles couldn't.

Chapter 25

Wyatt

Except for that first time when Garrett had entered Haley's bedroom, he didn't meet my eyes. His focus stayed on Haley the whole time she fucked herself on my dick, while I ate out her ass and she swallowed his cock like the goddess she was.

And hearts shone from those dark orbs of his the entire fucking time.

For her. All for his Haley.

I'd seen their connection before, but it became a tangible thing once I took the lead and removed those barriers between them. A goddamn living entity brought to life by crossing barriers they'd both erected for different reasons.

She'd held back from coming, needing his first.

And I'd been so fucking caught up in what I'd done for them that I'd blown my load before either of them, filling the condom before he let go—and she followed. The sounds they'd made, the feminine whimpers, the masculine grunts…

Christ, I'd never heard such a mouthwatering harmony. Music I could lose myself in. Crave. Become addicted to.

But they would have been fine without me—and that truth hit my chest like a goddamn sledgehammer, cracking through bone and making me bleed internally.

Yes, Haley enjoyed my dick, and Garrett definitely got off on watching me slide my length into her tight pussy, but he easily could have taken my place.

I imagined them face to face, him owning her body while she sucked on his delicious tongue. They would be wrapped up in their own little world…

It was like the two of them had crossed over the platonic line I'd led them to without any effort.

As though it had been meant to be.

They were meant to be and certainly didn't need me.

Unease rose alongside the pain inside me like thick smoke, choking my lungs. Garrett hadn't looked at me, even before kissing me like I'd told him to do. He'd been hyperaware of the woman below us, his groans against my mouth coming in response to every noise she made rather than the strokes of my tongue along his.

Was the guy even bi? Or had I imagined the draw between us when we'd first met? He kissed me, fuck, even seemed to like it, but Garrett wasn't open to me. Haley had been his sole focus.

I'd come over with the intent of sex—eventually—but had wanted to share with Haley about the two phone conversations I'd had earlier that evening. But one look at her flushed face, those pupil-blown eyes of hers when she answered the door, and all I could think about was losing myself in her body. Burrowing in deep. Forgetting reality for a while.

Well, real life lay in stark color before me. I could feel the warmth of her flesh, hear his heavy breaths…his abdomen pressed against my hand still on Haley's pubis.

But I was an outsider regardless of my opening their eyes, a door neither had considered before beyond their fantasies or dreams.

Long, silent moments dragged out while my stomach continued to knot itself. The goddamn condom still clung to my softened dick, Haley's cum dried on my fingers.

Perhaps they rested in comfortable silence, but I sure as fuck couldn't.

I gently pulled away when the unease grew to be too much, and neither said a word or twitched a damn muscle to insist I stay. There was no lazy stretching with satisfied smiles, no questions of where I was going when I made for the bathroom.

Throat tight, I cleaned myself up and got two wet, warm towels for Haley and Garrett—but they still hadn't moved. Both had passed out cold, I realized by their steady breaths. In slumber, she clung to him with a possessive hold, and he clutched at her like she was his whole world.

Tears hazed the beautiful sight of them, at how perfectly they fit together. My heart lay like a cement block in my chest, heavier than it had been after talking to Lionel and Tina.

Would I ever find my place outside my business?

I placed the towels on Haley bedstand, quietly retrieved my clothes off the floor, and left them sated.

Sleeping in her bed, entwined as lovers ought to be.

While my chest ached, I didn't regret what we'd done. I cared deeply for Haley, wanted her happy. And although I didn't know Garrett all that well, he felt that same lack of belonging from being abandoned as a kid. He drew me in as strongly as Haley had done, but they completed their puzzle of two.

Allowing myself one last fill of their tangled, gorgeous bodies, I silently wished them well.

Then I did the right thing.

I turned and walked away.

* * *

I clutched my steering wheel, driving aimlessly up the coast. Too many emotions bottled up inside me, begging for release, but I had no fucking clue what to do with them. A few hours in the gym would exhaust my body, but not my mind.

Spilling the shit inside my head would be the best bet to quiet it down, but I didn't have anyone to listen.

I had a couple drinking buddies but wasn't in the mood for too-loud music and hops. Sure, I had a newfound twin sister, but we hardly knew each other. If I told her my situation, she'd think I was off my damn rocker. Falling for two people and having to watch their love outwardly express—fucking explode into existence. Even worse, the happiness inside me for both of them was as persistent and palatable as the deep disappointment of being unable to share in that dep connection they shared.

Blaine was the only man I was aware of who had insight into a polyamorous relationship, but with his woman being Haley's best friend, there was only so much I could tell him. And while I trusted Blaine as one of my best employees, could I do the same with my thoughts and emotions?

I found myself in familiar territory, hadn't even realized where I'd driven my car.

Rhett and Ashton's house lay around the bend.

Going with my gut, I pulled into their driveway and cut the engine. It was just after eleven, but lights still shone around the blinds in their front sitting room.

"Fuck it." I pushed open my door and strode up their walkway. I worked for the couple, and we were more acquaintances than friends, but it had been their app that had put me in my current position.

I pressed the doorbell and shoved my hand into my pockets, praying like hell they hadn't left the light on downstairs and were already in bed. What if they were wrapped up in each other like Garrett and Haley? Maybe post-climax buzzed...or panting in their foreplay.

"Shit." I spun on my heel—and the door pulled open.

Rhett still wore dress slacks and a button-down as though he'd just gotten home from the office, but the bare feet and tumbler of amber liquid over ice in his hand suggested otherwise.

"Wyatt." He rarely grinned, but a hint of a smile rested on his face until he took a good look at me in the light spilling from his foyer. "Come on in." He stepped back, giving me room, but I hesitated.

"I'm sorry for stopping by like this." My voice sounded like gravel.

"We had a dinner party that broke up less than an hour ago, so no worries. Come on in," he repeated but more as a demand than suggestion.

I stepped into the foyer.

Ash lounged on the couch in the sitting room on my right, and I forced a grin. "Hey, Ash."

"Wyatt." He smiled, his glazed eyes revealing he'd already had more than the glass of wine in his hand. "What are you doing here?" His question held jollity rather than annoyance, his thickly lashed hazel eyes full of kindness as always. "Want a drink? Scotch? Wine? Beer?"

"I'm good. Thanks."

Rhett shut the door behind me and motioned toward a chair. "Sit and spill your guts."

"I'm that obvious?" I asked, a huffed chuckle that didn't contain an ounce of happiness pushing from my lungs.

"You look like shit and ready to puke," Rhett said while settling next to Ash, "and not from alcohol."

Thankful for his blunt honesty, I heaved a heavy exhale and perched on one of the chairs, my elbows on my knees.

Rhett stretched his arm across the back of the couch, reaching to run his fingers through Ash's blond-tipped wavy brown hair. Ash moved in close against his side, laying his head on Rhett's shoulder.

"So that app of yours, that whole *why choose* conversation we had a couple weeks ago? I fell down a deep rabbit hole and now…" I closed my eyes and filled my lungs, wishing I could rid the tumbling emotions from my head as easily as an exhale. "I'm not saying it's your fault, just…fuck, I don't know what."

"Tell us what happened," Rhett said, his commanding presence and tone not allowing any other option.

As if I had gone to their place for any other reason.

I scrubbed a hand down over my face, sat back, and launched into the shit tale of my life since learning the woman I'd met on Missing Link was secretly in love with her roommate who just happened to lie about his sexuality—and his repressed feelings for her. Add in how I'd found a lost twin I hadn't known about, the whole adoption thing, and I was even more depressed rather than relieved once finished with the tale.

"Shit," Ash murmured, empathy radiating from his gaze.

"Yeah," I agreed.

Rhett stayed silent, simply peering at me with his dark eyes.

"So, what are you going to do?" Ash asked.

"That's the problem," I muttered. "I have no fucking clue. I did the right thing by leaving the two of them alone to work things out once they wake up, but I carved out a piece of my heart and left it there between them where it isn't needed—or wanted."

"How do you know it isn't wanted?" Rhett asked.

I shrugged. "It's just a feeling."

"One your recent life-changing circumstances could be suggesting," Rhett stated. "That sense of abandonment, of not knowing where you belong—

maybe it's projecting onto the connection you'd made with Haley and Garrett."

"Yes," Ash agreed, nodding and giving his partner the eyes that Garrett had done with Haley. "You need to tell them," he said, returning his wavering focus back on me.

Rhett continued to study me with steadiness regardless of the liquor he sipped. "Maybe wait until later tomorrow," he said. "Allow them time to talk about the walls you helped bring down first. Let them get things set straight between them before dumping more emotional upheaval atop what they'll be dealing with."

"*Emotional upheaval*," Ash muttered an echo while elbowing him. "You sound like an ass."

"Because I am." Rhett didn't take his focus off me. "Wyatt isn't selfish—I'm suggesting exactly as he would do even if he hadn't spoken with us."

Rhett was right. I was the type to let them work through the situation out without interference. It was the interjecting my thoughts and desires into whatever they might find that bothered me. Especially seeing as how I felt my presence hadn't been needed once things had started to progress in Haley's bedroom.

"Do you want them?" Rhett asked, and I didn't hesitate to nod because I couldn't imagine going forward without them in my life. "Both?"

"Yeah," I whispered, my throat tight at that truth as well.

"Then go home and get some sleep, put in a good day's worth of sweating tomorrow, then head over there after they've had time to settle their own shit and spill your guts. They'll either welcome you with open arms, or you'll walk away brokenhearted. At least you'll have an answer and can move on."

The problem with Rhett's advice?

I didn't want to move on.

Chapter 26

Garrett

Soft warmth pressed against me, and I knew I dreamed. Keeping my eyes closed to prolong the heaven my imagination awarded me, I snuggled in closer. The scent of lavender and sleepy Haley filled my lungs.

My lips twitched—and so did my morning wood.

Small hands ran over my back, hot breath on my neck...

Haley.

I blinked my eyes open, my breath held.

A gorgeous spill of maroon hair lay across the pillow we shared. One of my hands fisted in her tresses. The other clutched at her round ass cheek, keeping her tight against my groin.

Aching groin.

"Holy shit," I croaked out a whisper, and Haley released out a throaty sigh.

Adrenaline rushed through me, and I held still, barely breathing as the night replayed in my head—and I grinned like a damn dork, thankful as fuck Wyatt had initiated what I'd been dying for.

Wyatt.

I lifted up enough to see he didn't cradle Haley's backside like I'd wanted him to be doing.

"He left us," I said, dropping my head back down, my smile fading. Why the hell had he taken off?

Haley rolled onto her back, and I let her go. She sat up, glancing around the room, her hair a riotous mess, the pale globes of her breasts rising with her inhale. A quick swipe over her cell phone's screen, and she muttered, "What the hell?"

"No message?"

"No," she whispered.

I glanced at the clock, taking note of the time. "He's probably at work."

"Why didn't he say goodbye?" Haley whispered and flopped back onto the bed as though as bummed as I was over his absence.

A sleep line went from the corner of her eye down to her jaw. She rolled her head toward me, and our gazes caught, her furrowed brow smoothing out.

So many barriers had been crossed the night before. I'd touched her breasts. She'd sucked my dick. And I'd blown almost a week's worth of cum down her throat.

She'd swallowed like she'd been hungry for me.

My pulse kicked up as desire thick and potent rushed through my blood.

"Hal?" I whispered, and she moved in, snuggling like we did on the couch.

No clothing lay between us. Warm flesh pressed close, hard against soft.

I bit back a groan.

Haley touched my eyebrows. My cheekbones. Slid a finger down over my nose to outline my lips.

Hers parted as I attempted to fill my lungs.

She cradled my cheeks in her hands and moved in, her intent clear as the desire in her dark eyes.

I met her halfway, our mouths touching in a soft brush that lingered longer than the peck she'd given me a few days earlier. My groan escaped, and she whimpered a reply. Another gentle caress sent a shudder through both of us.

What the fuck was happening? I had my lips on Haley's. Her tongue flicked over my lower one, and I parted to let her in.

Overwhelming need rose up inside me, and I clutched her small body closer. Tighter. Stroking over her tongue with mine, swallowing down the sweet taste of her mouth, every sigh leaking between our lips.

"Taste so damn good," I murmured and sucked on her bottom lip, wishing Wyatt reached over her body to grip my ass.

Haley shifted, sliding her knee up over my thigh, and I clutched at her leg, bringing it higher.

"Garrett..." Another sigh, another shudder, and I rocked my pelvis against her on instinct, desperate to invade another part of her body as she allowed me to do with my tongue.

"Always wanted this," she whispered, grinding her wet core against the back of my dick. "Wanted your kiss. Your hands on me even though you're gay."

Fuck.

I kept her plastered to my front but pressed my forehead against hers, fighting for calm. My heart thundered in my chest, my breaths coming in pants. "What are we doing, Hal?"

"You're about to slide that gorgeous cock deep inside my body and kill me with every slow thrust of your hips."

I groaned, clenching my eyes shut. Pre-cum oozed from my slit, smearing onto her lower belly.

"Can I have you?" she whispered against my lips, a sexy siren's tone rather than an insecure request.

One shift of my hips would lead to the heaven I'd dreamed about since first laying eyes on Haley, but I couldn't have her like that if barriers still laid between us.

My goddamn lie.

Swallowing hard, I pulled back so I could see her face.

Swelled pupils overran the whiskey brown of her eyes. Pink flushed her cheeks and swollen lips. Her satiny skin rested beneath my fingertips, but I kept them still while drawing breath.

Perhaps this was why Wyatt had taken off. To miss the shit storm about to rain down on me. Or maybe he'd bowed out to let us figure shit out and move forward.

Either way, I fucking hated him in that moment, the unwanted climax he'd forced on Haley's and my relationship.

"I'm not gay."

Haley blinked.

"I mean, I do like guys but women too," I hastened to add, hoping to lessen the blow.

Her brow furrowed again—deeper—her body stiffening slightly against mine.

"You," I tacked on, needing her to understand—and accept.

"As in straight for me, or…" Her tone was guarded as fuck, so goddamn telling that I wanted to curl up in a ball and die.

"I'm bi," I whispered what I should have told her months earlier, even while knowing I doomed myself to heartache.

She blinked again, her lips going into a thin line. "You lied to me."

"I was desperate, Hal. Alec kicked me out, and I was living in my car."

I didn't stop her as she pulled away from me, rolling off the bed. Pulse racing and hands clenched, I swallowed hard.

"Hal, please. Let me explain—I didn't have any other choice." My voice cracked along with my heart.

She snatched her sleep shirt up off the floor and yanked it over her gorgeous body.

"And it was really only a half-lie—"

Haley spun to face me, fire in her eyes. "There's no such thing!"

Disappointment in myself, for the hurt I'd caused the woman I loved more than anything on earth, settled over my shoulders, weighing me down. Tears stung my eyes. "Hal—"

"You lied! Manipulated me into giving you what you needed. End of. I—I can't fucking believe this." Her voice broke, and she wrapped her arms around herself, shutting me out—ripping my goddamn soul in two. "I allowed you inside my head, Garrett. My heart...you... Fuck."

Shit.

I hopped off the bed, desperate to drag her against me and make everything better, but she stepped back, hand held up like a big fucking stop sign glaring red in the darkness settling over my mind.

"You need to leave," she rasped the words as though her heart broke, but I saw the wall she thrust between us, the anger rising to shroud her hurt.

"Hal, please." I swallowed against the sob wanting to rip from my chest. "Let me explain—"

"Feed me more lies?" She snorted a harsh, sarcastic laugh, her eyes glinting with the prickliness I adored.

"You know me better than that, Garrett Moore. I can't fucking believe you did this to me."

"Hal—"

"Pack your shit and get the fuck out of my apartment." She spun and headed into the hallway. "I'm hopping in the shower. You better be gone before I'm done."

The bathroom door slammed shut behind her, the lock clicking harshly in the sudden silence.

Sinking onto the edge of her bed, I clutched my head in my hands. Agony ripped through my core.

"Fuck, fuck, *fuck*!" I pulled at my hair, teeth clenched against hollering my frustration and hurt. Pain I'd caused both of us.

I knew it would come to this. Fucking knew! Goddamnit!

Swallowing hard, I tipped my head back, the wetness of my eyes hazing the sight of her bedroom ceiling. What the fuck was I going to do?

I couldn't gather up all my things in twenty minutes. Our lives were intertwined throughout the entire apartment. And where the fuck would I *go*? Back east?

"Fuck that." I stood, snatched up my sweats, blinking away tears.

Every cell in my body ached to force my way into the bathroom, fall to my knees, and beg forgiveness.

But I knew her limits, her hatred for liars and manipulators. All we'd had, the closeness we shared, and I'd landed myself in the shit house alongside her mom, exactly as I'd feared.

There would be no forgiveness, only lingering, bitter disappointment and possible depression I wouldn't be able to find my way through.

Swallowing hard, I left her bedroom, intent on doing what she wanted.

Rather than waste gas driving around to think, I sat on a bench by the ocean and ignored the minutes, hours passing by. I was supposed to head into work at ten for the lunch hour but forgot. When I finally called in to lie about being sick, I got canned.

No point in arguing to keep a job I loathed, I hung up and slouched even farther onto the wooden plank beneath my ass.

I'd woken up in heaven and landed in hell.

The path in front of me didn't fork—there was no goddamn road leading beyond where my feet pressed into the ground. I had no options other than returning east to live a miserable lie of a life.

Wyatt had opened the door between us, and while shit was bad, I couldn't blame him for what had gone down that morning.

That was all me.

Or was it?

Again, I wondered what he'd had played at by instigating our fallout. If he'd planned for Haley to kick my ass to the curb so he could have her all to himself, he'd succeeded.

But he'd abandoned us without a note or message, something else he and I both knew she hated.

I straightened, rubbing my hands down my jeans as an idea flitted through my brain. Giving it further thought put weight onto my feet, and I stood. A plan formed as I returned to my car, and determination set in when I turned the key.

Teeth clenched, I drove the twenty minutes to the address Google provided me.

Wyatt's work truck sat in his driveway, his car in the opened garage in front of it.

I parked him in, grabbed my stuffed gym bag off the back seat, and strode up the front walk like I owned the damn place. Adrenaline crashed through me, but I held steady and knocked, once more desperate and grasping at straws.

My heart pounded in my chest as my stomach twisted into knots.

I knocked again, curses rolling through my head.

He was home...had he checked out the peephole? Saw the scowl on my face? Had he spoken to Haley, patched shit up with her, and she demanded he ignore me?

"Fuck." I clenched my free hand into a fist, clutching my bag's strap tighter. I had nowhere else to go, didn't even have fucking money for gas to get me back to my grandparents—

The door pulled inward.

Shirtless, shorts slung low on his hips, and water droplets over his ripped torso, Wyatt stood before me.

Regardless of my anger and anxiety, my dick took interest.

My scowl deepened.

He glanced at my bag before meeting my eyes again.

"You should have left well enough alone," I bit out, wishing I could cast all the blame on him. "She knows I lied, and now I'm staying here until I can find another place to live."

Rather than waiting for an invite, I moved forward, forcing him to make way unless he wanted to get bowled over.

"Oh," I said casually while moving into the foyer, "and I'm going to need a couple of Lionel Landscaping work shirts, *boss*."

Chapter 27

Haley

I stood in the shower until the water ran cold, my tongue between my teeth to keep from sobbing to relieve the absolute fucking agony gripping my head and heart. The fight or flight had kicked in, and I'd needed time to process what had gone down in less than twelve hours.

The bathroom gave me the privacy to set this straight in my head.

Even though Garrett had lied to me *before* knowing about my past, my triggers with that shit, I still felt betrayed. He should have spoken up sooner. Should have just told the damn truth from the very beginning.

I'd have let him stay since I'd been desperate too.

Goddamn him for ruining one of the best things in my life.

Longing to call out to him tugged on my heartstrings more than once while I fought off tears and the heavy blackness in the back of my mind.

I hoped he would be gone when I exited the bathroom.

I prayed he would be on the couch waiting to beg forgiveness and help me push against the depression attempting to swallow me whole.

I wanted to slap his face and kiss his lips.

Curl up against his body and let his arms take my sadness away as they always did.

The apartment sat empty, silent as a tomb when I pulled the bathroom door open. I finally allowed the tears to fall and collapsed onto my bed to wallow in my misery.

My pillow smelled like him.

Like Wyatt.

And I clutched that motherfucking feather bag to my tight chest as the sobs broke loose.

How could the most glorious night of my life morph into such tragic pain? Wyatt had walked out without a goodbye. Garrett had left because I'd told him to.

I went from two lovers to zero in one night.

Same as I'd gone from two parents—even if they had both been assholes—to zero within hours.

The wounds of my childhood rose up with choking force, heaping atop the shit I'd learned since opening my eyes. From the highest high to the darkest depths… depression's glee cackled in my head like a living voice, flooding me with fear.

I won't be like Mom.

"Goddamnit!" I shrieked and tossed the pillow onto the floor, feeling like I was going to lose my mind. "Fucking hell!"

Anger lit in my guts, and I grabbed hold of it in my helplessness, clutching to it as a barrier against the claws of darkness trying to pull me under, determined to take my mind like it had done to my mother.

My cell still sat on the bedstand, and I grabbed it up, heading toward the living room where I wouldn't have a visual reminder of the night before.

Lily answered, thank fuck.

"He lied to me," I whispered past the tightness choking off my air and broke into tears again.

"What's going on? Are you okay?"

"No!" I gulped a breath, just the sound of her voice weakening my defenses to keep from sobbing. "He's n-not gay. He l-lied so I would rent him your old room."

"Garrett."

I nodded even though she couldn't see, a whine building in my throat. Curling up on the couch, I clenched my eyelids tight, tears coursing down my cheeks. Even though I'd dreamed of him being straight, wished he'd wanted me for all those months, I couldn't stop the sense of absolute betrayal that made my stomach twist into a tangled knot of pain that wouldn't unravel.

"Tell me what happened," Lily stated quietly, empathy in her voice.

It took me a long fucking time, choking on words and sobs, but I explained to her what had gone down since the afternoon before.

The phone call.

The sure sex on a stick headed to my place.

His suggestion to ask Garrett to watch.

His instigating the two of us putting our hands on each other.

The mind-blowing sex.

Soft, delicious as fuck kisses in the early morning light when I'd thought for sure it had been our connection, our closeness, that had made Garrett want more with me.

Wyatt's abandoning us that left me unsettled and on edge.

Then the earth-shattering truth that sliced my heart the rest of the way in two.

I'm not gay.

Lily didn't have much to say when I finished with those words that had ripped apart my heart, just a few muttered curses.

"I'm dying inside, Lily," I whispered, wetness still on my cheeks even though sharing the shit allowed me to breathe without choking.

"I know why you hate liars," Lily said and let out a heavy exhale, "but not everyone tells them with bad intentions."

"There's never an excuse to lie," I bit out as the anger rekindled. Once more, I reached for it, strained out desperate imaginary fingers to clamp hold like a lifeline to sanity.

"Sometimes they're necessary, but in this case," Lily said, "I think he should have told you the truth from the very beginning. Yeah, I get he had minimal choices and needed a place to live, but once the two of you got to know one another, he should have opened up."

I scrubbed a hand over my face, swiping away my tears. "I still would have been pissed."

"But you wouldn't feel this betrayed."

Our lives had become so intertwined emotionally, and too much time had passed to lessen the fallout.

"Do you think you could ever forgive him?"

"Ask my mom and dad how I feel about forgiveness," I snipped in response to Lily's question while glowering at the wall.

"Garrett's sins against you are far from similar to your mother's, Haley." Lily's chiding tone irked me, but she continued on before I could curse her out. "He's madly in love with you—anyone with eyes can see that."

"I thought it was platonic. I *thought* we were on the same page."

Lily snorted a laugh. "Oh, please. You *were*! You wanted his dick the first time you saw him. Those chocolate brown eyes and black lashes. The lickable V and abs you drooled over that first night as roommates. You lied to him too, Haley Foster."

"I hate you," I muttered over her truth bomb even if the silence of my desires toward him didn't feel the same as his manipulation.

"You love me, bitch. Now, dry your damn tears, call that sexy brat up, and tell him to get his ass home so you can begin the rest of your life together."

My stomach tightened. Couldn't do it. No. Fucking. Way.

"Don't forget about what Wyatt did." I reminded her rather than reiterating my inability to forgive the shit Garrett had pulled. "He abandoned me. Us. Just like my dad had done."

"Do you want Wyatt?"

I remembered his kiss, his warmth wrapped around my back when we'd finished what he had started. The sense of belonging, being cherished and cared for, settling over my mind while drifting off to sleep in absolute peace of having found my place in life.

Fresh pain lanced through my heart at the memory of sitting up to find him gone without a goddamn word.

"Yeah," I whispered. "I did."

"You didn't text him to find out why he took a walk of shame?"

I swallowed against more tears. "No. He left us without a kiss goodbye or a text—it was like he'd gotten what he wanted from both of us and had no need to stick around."

Same as Dad who'd had his fill of being a family man to a psychotic cunt of a wife and needy daughter who wouldn't leave him alone in her desperation for affection.

"You've always been the aggressor, so text the man. I think you're reading into this too damn much, Hal."

My chest hurt to the point I couldn't focus on much else than shielding from deep-seated wounds I thought I'd moved on from.

Mom's lies and her bullshit crowded the back of my mind, taunting me toward the darkness I feared would land me into the psych ward alongside her.

I'd been weak letting Garrett burrow so deeply into my heart. I'd shared too much with him *and* Wyatt. I'd forgotten how easily people chose to look out for number one.

Anger, sweet righteous indignation, wrapped me up tight in her arms, protecting as the hours slid past— and I clung to the bitterness to keep my focus on taking the next breath. Ignoring the whispers in my head came easier with every passing hour.

I went into work at ten and stayed until closing. The hours moved in slow-motion, a never-ending river of shit—but I stubbornly sludged through the day without complaint. Gretchen the Toxic Twat was in bitch mode, and no display met her standards. Not a single fold of clothing I'd done turned out correct.

By the time my shift ended, I wanted to scrape my fingernails down her painted cheeks and gouge out her goddamn eyes. Scream in her face and tell her all the opinions I held bottled up inside my simmering guts.

But I walked out of Pieces with my shoulders back and chin lifted. I'd gotten through the day all on my own.

Neither Garrett nor Wyatt reached out to me.

Disappointment battled for attention in my brain, but I told myself I was thankful they didn't call or text offering excuses. Reasons for their wrong decisions.

I remembered that form of manipulation from my emotional abuser as well.

I'm so sorry.

I promise I'll do better.

Please forgive me.

Fucking bullshit, all meant to keep me close so she could do the same thing over and over again.

Well, I didn't need anyone, and I clung to that truth like a raft in a tumultuous ocean even though I didn't have stars to guide my way.

Since no one else had my back other than Lily, it was up to me to protect my heart. That meant no more letting my guard down. Period.

Being the aggressor sometimes meant looking out for me, myself, and I, like a goddamn Tasmanian devil— same as the other assholes walking the earth.

Crowning myself Badass Bitch with thick as fuck anger armor, I curled up on the couch to sleep since I refused to allow the scent of both men to haunt my dreams.

I would launder my sheets in the morning, keep my goddamn chin high, and finally prove to the world that Haley Foster could stand on her own two feet and find her own way through life. No more codependency, she would manage her depression like a boss.

And never become like the one who'd beaten her down.

Chapter 28

Wyatt

I thought I'd been doing the right thing, stepping aside so Haley and Garrett could be happy together.

I'd fucked up. Big time.

I gained a roommate I didn't want—but liked too fucking much for my own comfort.

While I didn't have a spare bed, I had a pullout couch in the room I'd set up as an office.

Garrett had made himself at home while I stewed over what to do.

He'd told me what had happened after he and Haley had woken up, the anguish in his tone, the misery in his eyes hitting my chest like another sledgehammer, stealing my breath.

I had caused his hurt.

Dragged up torment for Haley that I knew she'd fought hard to overcome.

I wanted to text her to tell her why I'd left, but she would blame me as much as she was pissed with Garrett. She would cling to that anger to see her through—same as she'd done years earlier like she'd told me.

I had expected a negative outcome, considering Haley's stance on lying but had felt sure their obvious love for each other would be enough to carry them through.

And now he's all up in my space, and I don't know if I should reach out to her or not.

Garrett sat on the other side of my couch, his focus on the TV, but I doubted he watched the ball game. Cotton sweatpants covered him from waist to ankles, but ripples of muscle and skin lay bare to my hungry eyes that traveled over his torso regardless of how my heart ached for Haley.

It was no wonder she had fallen for him. The man was fit and fine as fuck.

Add in that air of neediness to him, and I got caught up in the same thirst trap she had. Wanting to soothe, hold, and tell him he had meaning. That he was loved and appreciated.

Having new, similar insecurities thanks to finding out about my adoption, I knew it was what he longed for. Even though I suffered in the same way, I'd had a lifetime full of hugs and affection. Hair ruffles and a mother's warm embrace—

I closed my eyes.

Tina.

It had just been over twenty-four hours, but I couldn't help hoping for an update from Higgins sooner than later. The anxiety had been set aside easily when I'd been in Haley's bed, but with the adrenaline crash, the long hours at work in the sun, then Garrett's unexpected arrival while I'd readied to head over to their place...

Exhaustion beat me the fuck up—physically and emotionally.

"Did you talk to her at all today?"

I lifted my head up from where I'd rested it against the back of the couch. Garrett still stared at the TV.

"No."

His lips pressed tight for a few minutes. "Was it intentional? Hoping she'd get pissed at me, kick me out, so you could take my place in her life?"

"Is that really what you believe I wanted to do?" I asked, my voice raised in surprise.

"I hardly know you—what the fuck else am I supposed to think?"

Shit. How badly had I fucked up?

"If that were the case, you know I'd be over there balls-deep in her tight pussy rather than sitting here with your broody ass."

His glower did funny shit to my insides...twisted me up *and* turned me on.

"Do you regret what happened last night?" I asked when Garrett once more focused on the game.

He wasn't quick to answer. "I should," he finally said, "but I can't."

"Honest to God, I thought I was doing the right thing for both of you—that's why I left last night after you fell asleep."

Garrett finally gave me his eyes for longer than the span of a heartbeat, and the pain in their depths hit my chest like a goddamn fist. "If you had been there this morning rather than rushing out like a know-it-all, things probably would have gone differently."

"That's bullshit and you know it."

"I looked for you within seconds of waking. Haley even pulled away from me to check when I said you'd taken off."

His words swirled through my brain, but I couldn't make sense of them. "You both finally had each other where you wanted the other and you worried over *my* absence?"

"Yeah, you stupid fuck." Garrett's focus returned to the TV while I stared at him.

Fucking hell.

Haley had kicked him out of their home, leaving Garrett desolate—how much more would she do to me for having caused their breakup, never mind taking off without a word. She would see it as abandonment—the woman had to hate me.

I cleared my throat, but it didn't ease the tightness trying to stop my lungs from inflating. "Want a beer?"

"Yeah, sure," he muttered.

I grabbed two cold ones from the fridge, unsure and feeling utterly helpless.

My fingers brushed against Garrett's when I handed him his beer, and both of us lifted our gazes to each other's eyes. Sexual energy zapped between us, a magnetic draw, regardless of the heaviness on our minds and hearts.

I looked away first and settled on the other end of the couch again.

We watched the game in silence, as though of the same mind—wanting to escape our hurt.

Eventually, we fell into typical fandom headspace, complaining about bullshit calls and high-fiving when

Garcia hit a two-run homer in the bottom of the eighth to take the lead.

"So did you learn anything about your real parents?" Garrett asked when the game went to commercial break.

On my third beer, I felt a shit ton more relaxed, wondering at my lack of anger over the reminder.

I told Garrett about my getting in touch with and hiring Higgins and my call to my adoptive parents the day before, everything that had led up to me heading to their apartment.

"You okay?" he asked quietly, those dark eyes of his on my face and full of empathy.

Blowing out a heavy breath, I nodded. "I just really need answers, you know? Maybe then I won't feel unwanted and misplaced. Fucking *betrayed*."

He scrubbed a hand down over his face and stubble, and I inwardly cringed, hating that I caused him more pain by not thinking my word choice through.

"From what Haley told me, it sounds like Tina and Lionel definitely love you," he said rather than focusing on the lies that had torn him and Haley apart. "They wanted you, Wyatt. And from what you've told me about their texts, they still do."

I nodded again, reluctantly, my heart and thoughts torn in two—same as they were for him and Haley. "It just... doesn't feel the same as when I was an ignorant kid."

"I know what you mean."

Our gazes held for a few seconds, far from uncomfortable, the heat from earlier on the back burner as that connection I'd felt with him on our first meeting fixed firmly into place once more between us.

"Even though the results of last night's little...affair sucked," Garrett finally said, "I'm glad I'm here. With you. Not driving my miserable ass back to grandparents who took on the burden of raising me."

I wanted to haul him into my arms but held out my bottle instead. "Me too."

We clinked the glass necks together and sat back to watch the rest of the game.

Garrett went into the office to sleep before I hauled my ass up off the couch, and I listened as he settled in for the night.

Having accepted his presence in my home, the attraction and want I still had for him, and the fact he started working for me bright and early the next morning, I decided to reach out to Haley.

It was close to eleven, but I texted anyway, hoping to bring some sort of closure to the situation between us as well.

Me: **I'm sorry for what went down with you and Garrett this morning. He's here at my house btw. I'm also sorry for leaving like I did. I know you hate liars and being abandoned. We both failed you. I could say I wanted to go back and do things differently, but that would be a lie. If that makes me a bad person, then I'm the worst because I can't regret our night together. I'll understand if you can't forgive me, if the shit I pulled is too much to overcome.**

Out of words, I dropped my cell to my lap, my stomach in knots over knowing I had yet another answer to wait for.

My chest tightened, and I rubbed at it, powerless to make shit right for any of us. There were a million more things I wanted to say to her, to beg for another chance, the opportunity to set things straight, but I decided to give her time to work shit out and respond on her own volition.

Two agonizing days later, I was still checking my cell every five minutes, the pain fresh as ever in my heart.

"Nothing?" Garrett asked as I eyed my cell and rubbed over my pecs.

"No."

He leaned forward to grab another slice of pizza from the box we'd brought home with us. "I enjoyed laying the last of the block today," he said, and I decided to follow his lead and take my mind off Haley and all the things I'd fucked up.

We'd been working on a patio the previous couple of days. I'd shown Garrett on Tuesday morning how to measure out the area and set the dry lines that would keep our progress straight to create something beautiful when we finished.

"You're settling into the landscaping business like you were born for it," I told him, more thankful than he knew for having him as an employee.

"It's rewarding as fuck."

I actually grinned while helping myself to another piece of pizza.

"Never thought working with my hands like this would be so satisfying."

"What about having your name in lights?" I had to ask since he'd told me all his reasons for moving to California. He had even shared about his asshole ex and the mistake he'd made that landed him on Haley's steps.

The reasons for his lying to her.

"I've come to realize that I don't give a shit about being an actor," Garrett said around a mouthful of food. "If Hollywood is anything like Alec—and it sure as fuck seems like it considering all the shade I got tossed my way just from his word alone—I'm fucking done with that shit."

"I can't say I'm sorry to hear that, because their loss is totally my gain. I'm thankful as fuck to have you by my side."

Garrett shot me a grin, the first one that seemed relaxed. Happy even.

And my heart swelled in my chest.

Garrett had turned out to be one hell of a workhorse, sweat soaking his shirts and never seeming to grow tired beneath the hot California sun. The flex of his forearms and bulging biceps while laboring alongside me to lay all those pavers had proved fucking impossible to ignore. I drooled almost as much as I dripped sweat from my brow.

Sexual tension had slipped into place the first day we'd shared coffee in the kitchen before work, both of us attempting to ignore the reappearance of morning wood at the sight of the other. And that shit had lingered all through the day.

And the next.

Right up through the devouring of our pizza.

He had showered first, taking longer than necessary.

I'd taken my time cleaning the day's grime from my body but didn't jerk off.

And within seconds of finishing our dinner and sitting back on the couch beside him, I wished like fuck I had.

The scent of my bodywash on him made my mouth water, and I wondered how long it would be before one of us snapped, breaking to the obvious lust between us regardless of Haley's absence.

"I love how that patio turned out," Garrett said, his gaze on the TV. "We did that. Our hands. Our sweat." Pride laced his words, but I couldn't help rib him a bit.

"It turned out gorgeous because you have a kickass foreman telling you what to do," I teased—and fished just a little bit.

"*You're* a good dry line. I like it when you boss me around."

His low-toned declaration hit me like a fist to the solar plexus, reminding me of our time with Haley when I'd had to take the reins because he'd been like a deer in the headlights. Unsure and needing guidance.

Goddamnit...if he knew how much that shit swelled my heart and dick up—

My phone rang, putting those thoughts on hold.

"It's the PI," I muttered, my insides coming alive with butterflies even though I'd hoped to hear from our Haley first.

Garrett's gaze shifted my way, and I answered. "Higgins. How's it going?"

"Better than I'd hoped for," he said, his tone level and at odds with his choice of words. "I found her, but it's not good."

Her.

My birth mom.

I found my hand lowering, my finger tapping my cell's screen to put him on speaker because I needed to share that moment with Garrett. "What did you learn?" I asked, my voice haggard.

Garrett scooted closer as though feeling my need for emotional support.

"I won't pull any punches."

"Don't want you to," I assured him even though my voice waivered.

"Dahlia Angel was a crack addict. In and out of rehab and jail for possession and dealing."

I fisted my hand. "Was?"

"Past tense on the addiction shit," Higgins answered, "not that her life has gotten much better."

Garrett grabbed my shoulder and squeezed.

She's still alive...

"Her last known address is up in Fresno. She just finished her latest stint in jail for aggravated assault, lives in government housing, and is collecting unemployment."

What the fuck kind of woman had given birth to me and River?

"Any *good* news?" I asked with a sarcastic huffed exhale.

"I'm afraid not."

"Fucking hell." I rubbed at my face, and Garrett squeezed my shoulder again.

"Will you email me everything you found?" I asked. "I need to forward it to my sister."

"Will do."

I hung up a minute later, tossing my cell onto the coffee table, out a couple grand but with the exact information I'd hoped for—minus the shit of her actual life.

Grey's PI was worth every goddamn penny even if his findings sucked ass.

"Come here." Garrett grabbed my upper body and pulled me into him.

I went willingly, twisting toward him for an awkward hug so my cheek rested on his bare shoulder.

Fuck, his arms felt good. Solid. Steadying.

He didn't bother with useless words or questions, just let me relax and soak in his comfort until I breathed easier. A heavy exhale completely relaxed me against his toned torso.

"Confronting her will give you closure." Garrett spoke as if he'd heard the thoughts in my head.

I didn't want a goddamn thing to do with the crackhead who'd given birth to River and me—but I needed to know why she'd abandoned us. Even though my sister didn't seem to care one way or the other, having answers would be healing for her too.

"Thanks for this," I murmured, my cheek still against his warm skin that smelled like me. The angle of our hug kept our groins away from one another, thank fuck, because being near to him, having his arms around me, thickened me to the point of pain regardless of the shit Higgins had just dropped on me.

"You're my newest best friend," Garrett said with a light chuckle, the first I'd heard from his lips since he'd moved in with his meager belongings. "Not much I wouldn't do for you."

There were a million and one things I would have loved to ask him for, but shit needed settling first.

I pulled away from his warmth when I'd rather have dived in deeper. Closer. "Call Haley."

He had yet to reach out to her since nothing he could say would earn him forgiveness.

Garrett settled back into the couch but didn't put distance between us. "And if she doesn't want to talk to me?"

"Then it'll be my turn to hold you."

Chapter 29

Garrett

Wyatt's statement came out with a little more suggestion in his tone than I think he intended. Or maybe I was hearing what I wanted rather than the truth. There was no denying the desire between us, a potent craving to console each other's hurting hearts with aching dicks.

My hands shook while I swiped my cell to life, and the second I lifted the ringing phone to my ear, Wyatt grabbed my free hand. My groin woke the fuck up even though anxiety quivered my insides.

His direction over the previous couple of days had led me down a new path, one I thoroughly enjoyed and hoped to travel for a long time to come. Hopefully, his nudge to reach out to Haley would result in more positive results.

I closed my eyes and tried to slow my breathing, every shrill ring in my ear jolting adrenaline through me.

Haley didn't answer.

"Hey," I started to leave a voicemail, scrambling for things to say. "I'm...um...just calling to check in on you. See if you're okay. I'm at Wyatt's." A grimace twisted my face as I swallowed hard. "Yeah. He already told you. Anyway, um... I fucked up, and I'm sorry, Hal. I know I don't deserve it, but I hope someday you'll forgive me. Maybe even give me another chance to show you I can be a better friend. I miss you. Miss you telling me to go suck a dick. Miss your cuddles and laughter."

Having run out of steam, I hung up and dropped my phone. "She's not working, so she would have answered if she wanted to talk to me." I rubbed my hands over my face, cursing. "Lily and her men took off yesterday for some resort in Mexico for a couple weeks, so she's not with her and too busy to answer either."

"My turn then." Wyatt manhandled me, pulling me sideways onto his lap.

And I koala-ed the fuck out of the man when he wrapped his arms around me. Throat tight, I clung to the hard muscles on his back, my face against his neck. We fit together too fucking well for being similar in height and build.

The scent of his soap smelled different on his skin than mine—ten times more delicious. Intoxicating. Ball-tingling, mouthwatering...

Fuck.

My dick thickened, but I stayed put, soaking in the comfort he offered.

"I'm trying really...er...hard to keep this shit platonic, but yeah." Wyatt shifted, his erection brushing against my thigh. "Sorry."

Lust raced over my skin, and my brain stem went on autopilot, lifting my body and resettling on to his lap.

Straddled.

Groins pressed tight.

Wyatt's hands found my ass at the same time I wrapped mine around his neck.

Our gazes clashed as heat, searing and consuming, flickered between us.

We both rocked into each other as though of the same mind, lips parting to whisper—or suck in oxygen to suddenly starved lungs.

His focus slipped to my mouth, and I remembered his kiss, the way he'd moved his lips over mine, the slow fuck of his tongue… Need raced through me, for release, for escape from the ache in my chest.

"Give me your mouth, Garrett."

His command shot lust through my blood, and I dove in, sagging at the taste of him once more on my tongue. We didn't kiss. We ate at each other's mouths like we hovered on the verge of starvation, ruled by instinct to survive. We fought for breath, swallowed moans, hands needy and grasping. Rough and bruising.

Sucking on his lips and tongue satisfied me better than any damn lollipop, and I couldn't get enough of his taste.

"Off," Wyatt demanded against my mouth, yanking at my sweats. "I want to feel all of you."

I tore my lips from his long enough for us to shove the fucking things to the floor as he did the same, and I climbed back aboard, skin to skin. Cocks hard and leaking, rubbing against each other.

He held my face and kissed me like I was a glass of iced water after a long day's work. I wrapped my hands around our dicks and smeared the slickness of our pre-cum together.

"Ah fuck," he groaned into my mouth before ripping away to watch. "Fuck, yeah. Christ, that feels so good."

Our foreheads pressed together, and his palms slid down my back to once more grab my ass. We stared at my fists wrapped around our lengths. We rutted. Cursed. Panted. A mess painted my hands, and we made crude schlicking noises while we fucked up into my fists.

"Never felt hands like yours," Wyatt said, his voice nothing more than a rumble of need. "So good, Garrett. Fuck."

Wyatt's hands kneaded my cheeks with bruising force, and I ached for him, my heart cracking wide open from all the praise he rained down on me.

"Touch me," I begged on a moan. "Please."

He claimed my mouth in a bruising kiss.

My ass—

His fingertips trailed down my crack, and I whimpered like a dick-needy whore. Featherlight touches over my puckered skin teased rather than satisfied, so I released one hand from our dicks and reached back to give him what I needed.

Pre-cum smeared over my hole.

Not quite lube, but enough that he easily teased the tip of his finger past my ring while I took over fucking our dicks with my hands again.

"You're so fucking hot," he whispered against my mouth, and our kiss went still, lips touching but unmoving as he dipped into me. "Goddamn, Garrett. You're driving me mad."

I squeezed around his finger, and he cursed, thrusting harder into my hand as though imagining shoving into my ass.

"More," I demanded, and he pulled his finger out—and pushed back in, clear to the knuckle.

The burn drew up my balls rather than deflating my dick, and I hissed at the sting. It'd been a long fucking time. More wetness oozed from my slit, and I rode his finger, fucking against his cock, my heart racing.

"Are you close, Garrett?"

"Yeah," I breathed against his mouth, my balls and spine tingling.

"Paint my abs with your spunk," he ordered, a goddamn bossy fucker I couldn't get enough of. "Want to feel your desperate ass clench around me."

"Oh shit." I gasped—and came in an eruption, shooting off like a geyser all over his torso like he'd told me to. "Fuck…" I thrust, moaning and shivering. "Wyatt—"

He let out a deep groan, releasing into my hand. On my stomach, dripping into my pubes.

His finger slid from my ass, and our mouths met before either of us finished ejaculating. Twitches and shudders rolled over us as we clung to one another. The kiss turned languid but far from finished. Tongues took up where our groins let off, slowly fucking in an erotic dance I never wanted to end.

Cum covered my hands, but I ran them up through the mess on Wyatt's torso, over his pecs, mapping out his upper body, then behind his head. Our chests stuck together, hard muscle grinding even though our cocks lay spent between us.

We were filthy. Fucking perfect.

He tasted so damn delicious too. Hops and spice… I sucked on his tongue, hungrily swallowing the sweetness of him. I crowded in close, a whimper for more escaping me.

Wyatt chuckled lightly and grabbed hold of my chin to keep me still. Sated baby blues met my eyes. "The fuck, Garrett?"

"I could suck on your tongue for hours," I breathed the truth out on a groan.

"Fuck." Wyatt squeezed my ass cheek he still clutched. "You're going to make me hard again."

"Good. I'll have something *else* to suck on."

Wyatt growled, leaned in, and bit my lower lip.

Fucking bit me.

My dick wanted another round. "Wyatt…"

He tipped our foreheads together again. "Haley told me you had an oral fixation, but goddamn."

At her name, I went completely still.

What the fuck had I done? Wyatt had been Haley's first…and I'd climbed aboard the fuck train without a second thought. It didn't feel like a mistake, but fuck if I could tell my conscience that.

I pulled away from his hold.

"Fuck," I muttered as drying cum and stickiness attempting to keep us together.

Wyatt chuckled again. "We're a goddamn mess. You smeared spunk all the fuck over me…even on my neck. Shit." He outright laughed, and my insides fluttered through the guilt.

Had I made another mistake? Let Haley down?

My stomach felt like a rock.

"Where are you going?"

I hadn't moved beyond shifting so spunk no longer stuck us together. "N-nowhere."

"Up here, baby." Wyatt tapped my temple, and I closed my eyes against his inquisitive stare.

Baby. Fuck, did I enjoy hearing that word on his lips.

"I'm fucking everything up. You're Haley's—not mine. She was with you first, and here I am salivating after you. I smeared my cum all over you like a goddamn caveman and yet I'm ready to be your bitch, roll over, and obey your every command. What kind of fucking friend am I?"

"Haley and I don't have an understanding, Garrett." He once more held my chin, making me feel young and controllable.

Something I shouldn't have loved—but did.

Fuck knew I only ever managed to mess shit up on my own.

"We never discussed exclusivity." He studied me with that same vulnerable look we'd shared after learning about each other's adoptions. Warmth spread into my limbs and back again, settling in my chest, easing the ache from missing my Hal.

"Yes, I wanted to pursue what she and I had started, but she cut me off," Wyatt continued when I couldn't find my voice. "Cut you off. Things are up in the air, and we have no direction, but that's not going to stop me from touching you. Tasting you. Having you if she wants to rob herself of everything we desire to give her."

His words made sense but didn't stop the grief in my heart over our actions. The choices I'd made—the goddamn mistake—had caused me to lose her. Possibly forever.

"Shower?" I strangled out the suggestion, needing to escape the heaviness, the heartache for a while.

"Yeah. You made a mess out of me."

If Haley hadn't been in the picture, I'd have made a joke about using my tongue to clean him up then sucking him until he made another mess, but I kept my lips closed—and my tongue to myself.

Chapter 30

Haley

Both Wyatt and Garrett had reached out to me within days of the shit hitting the fan to offer apologies with words I'd heard dozens of times. Their promises meant jack shit, same as my parents' had over the years.

My anger, while protective, exhausted me, and I struggled to stay afloat from the sea of depression wanting to rise up and swallow me whole.

I craved them both to the point I couldn't eat. Couldn't sleep.

But my goddamn stubbornness had kept me from responding even though my heart urged me to answer when Garrett had called.

In his voicemail, he'd asked for a second chance, wanting to be a better friend.

Those familiar excuses rolled off my back like water, but it was the rest of his message that had choked me up. The memories of our friendship and hearing his voice breaking every time I hit replay throughout the following days brought tears to my eyes and created another slivered crack through my already bleeding heart.

Add in that Lily had left for vacation the same Saturday morning I thought I'd found my place in life, and loneliness piled atop the mess in my head. I refused to call her and moan the blues while she was enjoying her time away with Blaine and Greyson.

Gretchen's continued bitchiness like she'd had PMS for a damn month straight didn't help matters *at all*.

By Friday afternoon, I'd managed to keep my head above water, but she was an hour late for our monthly meeting. She breezed into the back room with her big-assed sunglasses, Coach bag on her arm, Jimmy Choo heels clacking on the tile.

"Where is everyone?" she asked, breathless, while glancing around.

I guessed she'd noticed the lack of the rest of her employees out on the floor other than Darren who was scheduled along with me for closing that night.

"Gone," I told her while ripping into another box of stock that she'd ordered—that we didn't need.

"What do you mean they're gone? We have a meeting!" She tossed her purse onto the table with an annoyed snort.

"Had," I muttered under my breath. "Two hours ago."

"What?"

"Your employees have a life outside this shop, Gretchen," I surprised myself by saying since I never created waves. "You can't expect them to just sit here and wait on you. Especially if you don't send word you're running late."

"Of course I can!" She sniffed, hands on her hips, checking out my messy bun and lack of makeup.

"Jenny's son had an orthodontist appointment at four-thirty," I informed her. "Sharon's son was home sick with the neighbor, and she couldn't stay any longer."

"I don't give a shit!"

Fucking selfish cunt. My jaw clenched.

"If I call a meeting, then they need to be here!"

My insides tightened, and I finally shot her a glare I'd been holding in for too fucking long. I imagined Garrett cheering me on to finally open my damn mouth. "You scheduled the meeting at three—*you* needed to be here."

"What the hell happened to you, Haley? I can't have you looking like..." Gretchen waved her hand down over the mess of me, totally ignoring the fact I'd just called her out. Her nose wrinkled as though I smelled as bad as I appeared. "Like a damn homeless person. You represent my shop. *Me.* Everything you say or do reflects back on me, and lately, you've been a real Debbie Downer. You're affecting the whole atmosphere here. The staff too."

Fucking bullshit. Her employees loved me. Put up with her shit *because* of me.

"And now this." Her hand gestured at my lack of beautification due to barely surviving the darkness, the disgust in her eyes an emotion I was well acquainted with.

I tossed aside the stack of wrapped camisoles I had in hand. "Rather than beat a person down when they're already wallowing in grief, you ought to try to rouse some empathy."

Her nose curled, but I wasn't done.

"Oh, that's right." I snorted, turning to grab my purse from my cubby. "Narcissistic cunts don't know what that word means."

Gretchen sputtered, her eyes blinking wide.

My fingers closed over my keys in my bag's front pocket, and even though my hands shook, I managed to peel the one off I no longer needed. "You can take this goddamn piece of shit job, shove it up your prissy, fake ass, and enjoy riding the hell out of it while you can because twats like you eventually end up alone and miserable."

I slapped the offensive bit of metal onto the table between us.

"Where the fuck do you think you're going?" Her voice raised as I started toward the showroom, slinging my bag over my shoulder.

"Away from your toxic ass!" I shot over my shoulder. "Have fun trying to run this place without me."

I strode past racks of designer clothes.

"See ya," I murmured to Darren who redecorated the bay window since Gretchen had bitched about the job I'd done the day before.

He stared at me. "Shit...don't you dare leave me alone with her!" he hissed.

"I've put up with her manipulation and emotional abuse for long enough. If you're smart, you'll quit too."

"Haley!" Gretchen called after me, her voice bordering on a shriek I'd heard countless times once she'd lost her shit.

I walked out the door. Let the fucking thing slam behind me to I wouldn't have to deal with her tirade.

Although pride for finally standing up for myself and giddiness tickled my stomach, I was ready to buckle. Exhaustion clung to my spine, quickly slowing my steps that had been peppy due to sudden freedom from that bitch.

I had no backup plan. No college education. No rich daddy to provide for me until I found another job.

But I was a survivor—I'd been on my own since the day I'd turned eighteen.

I'd gone on alone before, and I would do it again.

Tomorrow, I promised myself, planning on a night of pretending Lily was there to help me celebrate what I should have done months earlier.

I ate an entire half-gallon of ice cream for dinner while watching Friends reruns. The hottest spray I could handle hit my aching back while I stood in the shower. Bottle of chardonnay in hand, I crashed on the couch again.

Lonely and far from celebratory.

My chest caved in, empty and aching for my koala and Wyatt's delicious distractions that never failed to lighten my mind. I missed them both to the point of tears I refused to shed.

Just to torture myself, I listened to Garrett's message again. Memories of our laughter, our teasing, filled my mind, and I relived every second he, Wyatt, and I had spent together—their hands on my skin, loving on me.

The gasps and groans that had heated me to the point of combustion.

"Fuck." I scrubbed at the wet tracks on my cheeks and sucked down oxygen, determined to keep my shit together even though I'd enjoyed two glasses of wine and was well on my way toward being overly buzzed.

My cell rang, and I grabbed it of the couch cushion beside me, thinking—hoping—Garrett tried to call me again.

A number I didn't recognize flashed on my screen with the same area code as Lily's old cell number. Only one family resided near the city of Philadelphia that I knew of.

Wariness crept up my spine, making my skin shiver and tightening my stomach.

"Hello?" I answered.

"Haley? It's your uncle."

Lily's dad—the only uncle I had.

Unease erupted inside me at the thought of my cousin and best friend having been in some tragic accident, and I bolted upright. "Is Lily okay? She's still in Mexico with Grey and Blaine, right?"

"She's fine, Haley," he stated quietly, and by the tone of his voice, I could tell something else wasn't. "I'm calling about your mom."

How much shit could a woman take in one day?

I sank back, closed my eyes, and listened as my mom's brother filled me in on what had gone down at St. Catherine's Behavioral Hospital where she had been institutionalized for close to a year.

She'd committed suicide, using her bedsheet to hang herself.

No note, no final goodbye.

My heart lay dead in my chest, unmoved toward tears or regrets. Same as always throughout my life, she'd put her own needs above her only child's. Her depression then mental illness had dragged her down to the point she'd chosen to escape reality rather than facing life and attempting to make amends for all the childhood trauma she'd inflicted on me.

Not that I'd have forgiven her even if she'd asked.

Resignation settled inside me without any emotional upheaval. "Did you tell my dad yet?" I asked once my uncle went quiet without a hint of tears in my voice.

"No. I thought perhaps you would want to do that."

"Nope." I hadn't spoken to the sperm donor for years and had no wish to open up doors best left closed. I gave my uncle the last contact number I had for the man while pouring the final drop of chardonnay into my empty glass.

"If you require any—"

"I'm good, Uncle. Thanks."

"Well, we'll be lifting you up before the Throne of God in prayer, Haley. Trust in Him to see you through this tough time."

I rolled my eyes and made a noise of agreement, promising I would call him if I needed anything.

As if.

The last fucking thing I wanted to hear or talk about was how some God in Glory wanted to wrap me in his arms—when he'd allowed sin in the first place, then decided to let souls who didn't love him burn in hell.

Fuck that.

I'd had enough narcissism in my life for real.

Once we hung up, I sat in silence, listening to the sounds of traffic outside my closed windows, a dog barking nearby, and my new neighbors on the left playing some dance techno shit a little too loudly.

Closing my eyes, I allowed myself to feel, searched my heart and mind, expecting some sort of grief over the death of my mother like stinging eyes or a tight throat.

Nothing but bitterness swirled in my guts and bruised heart. Continued pissiness toward the woman who'd lied to and abandoned me clung to my soul.

Mom had lived a selfish life and ended up broken beyond repair, desperate for release from her problems—all of her own doing and exactly as she deserved.

I fought off depression similar to what I remember being the first signs of her psychosis. Dad had tried to talk her into getting help when I'd been a young teen, but knowing better than everyone else, Mom had refused. She'd ended up with psychosis that landed her in the psych ward.

"I won't be like her," I whispered what I often did whenever I felt frail in my emotions.

My declaration continued to chant in my head, solidifying to a fact I felt in every cell of my body. No fear of falling and wallowing rose to choke off my will to live.

I would press onward, rise above my wounds rather than wallow in them and allow negative issues surrounding me to be my focal point.

Making a new life for myself without liars and manipulators was possible. I just needed to set my teeth into that fact and be the pitbull my koala—no, *Garrett*—had claimed me to be.

My goddamn throat choked up over that resettling of my mind, but I reminded myself I didn't need him and Wyatt to find happiness and contentment.

Determined to create both on my own, I opened up my laptop and began the search for a job. One that would provide enough money to keep me afloat and hopefully, offer a chance to make new friends.

Chapter 31

Wyatt

Garrett seemed to need space, so I gave it to him. Quiet introspection on his part became the norm the next couple of days, and the double shutting out of the two I longed for fucked with my brain. I felt emotionally abandoned by the man I craved and the continued silence from Haley...

Something needed to give before I lost my fucking mind.

I wanted to go behind Haley's back, see if she'd gotten in touch with Lily in Mexico who would tell her men everything. Blaine would let me know what was going down—he cared about both of us too much to let shit grow worse between Haley and me.

But same as I required time to deal with my parents and the whole adoption thing, I expected Haley did too.

My patience ran thin, the close proximity of the other half of the duo I longed for in too much of my space to ignore.

Garrett showered.

I sat on the edge of my bed, elbows on my knees, head hanging, already cleaned up from the long day beneath the hot sun.

My balls ached for release—and I wanted to give him the same. Soothe his hurt in the only way I knew how, by offering comfort. But so much more than my arms or an awkward hug and words that would fall on deaf ears.

There was nothing I could say to ease his heartache, but I could help him forget even if only for a while.

I listened as he exited the bathroom. Tracked his footsteps into the second bedroom. Strained my ears for every rustle he made.

Footfalls once more sounded, and I looked up, my gaze on my door I'd left open.

He didn't glance my way, his head down, focus on the hardwood floor.

"Garrett," I called out.

He took a step backward and shifted his attention to me. Dark eyes, expressionless, met mine.

I sat up straighter, my knees spread beneath the towel I hadn't replaced with shorts like he had.

His gaze flicked over me. "Yeah?"

"You okay?"

Garrett shrugged, his shoulders falling right back into the same slumped position as before.

I stood, re-tucking my damp towel, and moved toward him, my pulse kicking up a notch.

"What are you doing?" he whispered as I opened my arms, ready to invade his personal space—but he didn't shy away.

"Taking care of you." I pulled him against my chest, the skin contact immediately settling bits and pieces inside me that had warred for days.

Garrett's stiff body relaxed with a heavy exhale, and he laid his cheek on my shoulder, his arms reaching around me.

Silence descended—but a sweeter sort, one with whispers of breath and beating hearts.

I yearned to pull him in tighter, wrap his soul up with mine, make all the shit go away.

"I wouldn't survive this without you," he whispered. "Losing her…it's like a part of my heart has been ripped out. It's barely beating."

He sighed and pressed in even closer, rubbing his scruffy cheek over my shoulder, his face closing in on my neck. Hot exhales ghosted over my skin, causing goosebumps to ripple down my arms.

"You make it easier to breathe."

His declaration made blood rush into my groin, but I didn't bother trying to stop the awakening of sexual tension between us. I needed him in that moment more than I had with anyone.

"I don't have the connection with Haley that you do, but she owns a piece of me too, Garrett. I ache for her forgiveness." I swallowed audibly, my heart racing. "I ache for you too."

His dick thickened against mine—and he didn't pull away either.

I ran one of my hands up his spine, grabbing hold of his nape and tilting his head back.

Need replaced the emptiness in his chocolate-brown eyes when they landed on mine.

A jolt ripped through my body, settling in my balls, and I exhaled unsteadily.

Garrett's lips parted, drawing my focus toward the mouth I'd been dreaming about.

"Garrett?" I croaked his name, hoping...

"Yes," he whispered, shooting adrenaline through my system.

Our lips slammed together, both of us hungry, driven to fulfill the longing I could feel radiating between us like a living entity.

We stumbled into my room.

He ripped my towel away.

I shoved down his shorts.

Still, our mouths clung, tongues dueled, teeth nipped. Our kiss went beyond comforting, only intensifying the tension coiled between us.

We fell to the bed, and I rolled him beneath me, ready to love on Haley's needy brat—the man I burned for—until he lay spent. Boneless. Mindless.

Garrett grabbed my ass and squeezed, his fingertips digging into my skin before sliding down my crack. Groaning into my mouth, he feathered over my hole, causing my dick to leak over his taut abs.

"Garrett…" I pulled away enough to catch his pupil-blown eyes.

"I know you want to take care of me." He swallowed hard. "But I-I really need…goddamnit."

I grasped his chin to keep his focus on my face. "To be in control."

His breath left in a rush, vulnerability bleeding from his dark orbs. "Please."

I rolled without hesitation, taking him along with me, spreading my thighs to make room for his bulk.

"Whatever you want, Garrett," I told him. "Whatever will ease this torment."

His dick jerked against mine, and he took my mouth, grinding our groins together.

I palmed his ass and held on as he obliterated all thoughts but coming from my head. Pre-cum covered our stomachs in a slick mess to thrust through, and my balls drew up tight.

"Garrett," I warned, knowing I approached the edge of erupting.

He stilled his hips, slid his lips over my jawline, and sucked on my earlobe. Hot breath lifted the hairs on my nape, and I groaned, tilting my head to let him have his way.

Those lips and that tongue trailed lower, over my clavicle. Teeth scraped at my pecs—my nipples. But he bypassed them, settling onto his haunches, his hands finding the backs of my knees and lifting.

I stroked down my cock, watching him devour the sight of my drawn up balls, taint, and asshole. It was on the tip of my tongue to ask him how long it had been since he'd topped, if he wanted help, but I bit my tongue.

More silence, but the wait came easy because there was no stopping what we'd started. I had reminded him the week before that Haley had cut us off, but fuck if I could do the same with her. I lay sprawled out for Garrett's pleasure, but I craved her presence. My mouth watered to taste her, my skin tingling for her soft caresses and demanding requests.

Fucking miserable and yet high off lust for the man studying my body.

Finally—fucking *finally*—Garrett slid his hands down the insides of my thighs, and I took hold where he'd released, pulling my legs higher. Opening myself for him, making myself vulnerable in the final way I could with him.

"Fuck," he whispered, his thumbs rubbing over my taint with teasing strokes.

I bit the inside of my lip, caught up in the fall of dark hair over his brow, his long eyelashes lowered, those plump lips of his red from kissing. He was so damn beautiful he made my throat close up.

At the first brush of his fingertip over my hole, I groaned, contracting on instinct.

"When's the last time you let a man have you here?" Garrett lifted his attention to my face as he continued the light caress.

Pink flushed his cheeks. Black pupils ate at his eyes.

The same lust and longing coursing through me radiated from him, tangling with mine in the space between us.

"A long time," I admitted, my voice ragged, "but I want it. Want *you*."

A slow smirk lifted a corner of his lips, and holding my gaze, he sprawled out below me. He stuck his finger in his mouth, and I cursed, my insides coiling tight in readiness for his touch.

Spit-slickened, the pad of his index smeared over my hole—and the fucking brat shifted forward, taking my cock deep into his throat while breaching my body.

"Fuck!" I jolted upward, fighting to keep from fucking into his face. "Shit—Garrett. Fucking hell, man!"

He moaned, that smirk long gone from his lips stretched around my cock but still simmering in his eyes as he peered up over my torso.

Gorgeous. Absolutely fucking stunning…

A shift of his wrist twisted his finger up inside me, and I cursed again as he pressed against my prostate, shooting sparks, lightning sensations straight through the base of my spine ricocheting upward to short circuit my brain.

My head fell back, and I allowed Garrett to have control. To love on me—take care of me in a way no man had done before.

He held nothing back, sucking on my dick like a damn lollipop, making noises of appreciation over my pre-cum like my length was sweet, cherry flavored candy. Every deep reach of his finger into my body ramped up my need for more.

So. Much. More.

My groin throbbed, balls tight and high. I yanked his hair, pulling him off me before I shot down his tight throat.

He whined, and I chuckled through the haze of lust holding me captive.

"Need you," I begged while holding his stare.

He flicked out his tongue, dragging it up my length.

My dick bobbed, more pre-cum oozing.

"Garrett..." A muscle ticked in my jaw—and he flashed a grin that bottomed my heart into my goddamn toes.

"Yes, Wyatt?" He licked again, suckling on just the head, tongue probing at my slit.

I groaned, searching beneath my pillow for the lube and condom I'd stashed earlier with the intention of having him.

This is better.

I handed them over, and he eyed the items while planting one last kiss on my cockhead.

He took both—and shifted his mouth lower, lathing over my asshole.

We groaned as one.

"Goddamnit, Garrett!" I cursed him out through clenched teeth, grabbing hold of the base of my dick to keep from coming.

He chuckled against my hole and rimmed me some more, not stopping until I writhed, begging for him to put me out of my misery. Too much need coursed through me—I couldn't think. Couldn't fucking breathe.

The snap of the cap and squirting of lube made my mouth dry, and I stared between my splayed thighs, watching Garrett sheath and lube up. He tossed aside the bottle and slid two fingers deep into my hole without preamble.

"Fuck." My jaw clenched, neck arched. A delicious sting spread outward from where he invaded my body, and I panted as he spread his fingers, scissoring to open me up for him.

"You're so fucking hot inside," Garrett moaned the words.

He once more stared at my ass, his fingers probing deep, hitting my prostate and coiling my stomach up tight.

I hissed, and the brat chuckled again. "If you can't handle two fingers, Wyatt, you're in for a heap of discomfort when my dick fills you up."

"I like the pain." I sounded like a hand strangled my throat—like my fingers did the base of my dick.

"Mmm." He lifted his focus—and an eyebrow—and worked in a third finger.

"Ah, fuck."

He shoved in deeper, and I once more lost sight of him as my head tipped back, my brain beyond the ability to do anything but focus on my senses.

The scent of my bodywash and sex filled my nose. Gasps and heavy breaths flooded my ears. Darkness lay behind my closed eyelids, allowing me to better *feel*.

And fuck, did I ever.

Garrett's physical touch, his hot palm on my thigh, fingertips digging into muscle. Those thick fingers of his reaching deep inside my ass. The emotions flooding through me—want. Contentment. Anticipation. Thick desire I could sense like a cord binding us together.

Need...

I forced my eyelids open to find him watching me. "Garrett," I whispered his name as a plea, praying like fuck he knew what I meant because I couldn't find the words to explain the yearning inside me.

His fingers slid from my ass, and he moved forward, our gazes locked as he planked over me, his hands planted by my shoulders. Our pants painted the air between us, the fire of lust combustible between our heaving chests.

The head of his dick smeared lube over my balls, and I grabbed hold of his length, sliding it over my taint until he caught on the rim of my hole.

He sucked his lower lip between his teeth and pressed, stretching my ring far beyond what his fingers had done.

I let out a hiss and bore down, needing him inside me so goddamn badly, I didn't care how much pain awaited me.

He breached, and I clenched my jaw, my nostrils flaring to suck in oxygen.

Garrett lowered his weight onto me, holding my face in his hands. "Okay?" he asked, his voice as wrecked as my soul.

I released a slow exhale, sliding my hands up along the muscles tensed along his spine. "Yeah." Wrapping my legs around his waist shifted his fat cockhead inside my body, and I let out a groan. "More—"

He pushed in before I finished the word, giving all my body was willing to accommodate, which wasn't much. "You feel so fucking good," he groaned the words, his forehead tipping down to mine.

And it would be even better once he filled me up, taking up residence inside my body, same as he'd done in my heart.

Chapter 32

Garrett

Wyatt whispered my name again like I was the god of his universe, his sole source of life-giving energy. And no amount of lingering guilt would allow me to deny him.

I didn't want to walk away.

Couldn't.

A slow drag from the clasp of his hot ass made us both groan, and I stroked back in, burying half my length in his body. Even with the latex between us, his silken heat burned me up from the inside out.

"More."

The needy fucker topped from the bottom, but I didn't give a shit. It had been too fucking long since I'd been offered the gift of an ass.

I backed out—and thrust.

Wyatt grunted and pulled me down, leaving no air between us. Our mouths connected in a consuming kiss, mutual desire for more shared between us without words.

I rocked in and out of him with harsh thrusts, digging my toes into his bed for better traction, trying to dive deeper. Jab into his heat farther. Fill him to the point neither of us would be able to differentiate between our souls.

Never had I felt a connection like I did with him. Ever. Beyond the body...something far more consuming that mere lust.

I sucked on his tongue, swallowed his groans, ate at his mouth like *he* was the life-giving force because he lit me the fuck up.

Sweat and pre-cum smeared between our stomachs. His fingertips dug into the muscles on my back, and his heels clutched at my ass.

I snaked a hand beneath his back to clutch at his shoulder and tangled my other fingers in the hair atop his head.

And still, I couldn't get close enough.

Deep enough.

He came without warning, untouched, coating our abs with hot spurts of cum, his tight ass strangling my dick with steady pulses.

I tore my mouth off his as he grunted his release. "Jesus *fucking* Christ," I choked out, lifting to watch the last of his spunk dribble from his slit.

I drove into him once, twice more, and erupted, my back arching as I tried to split him in half.

"Fuck, Wyatt... God." I convulsed with every jet of spunk into the condom, wishing I painted his insides.

My body collapsed, spent.

We both sucked oxygen, our hearts pounding between our tightly pressed chests.

Wyatt lazed his fingertips up my back, his heels sliding down to hook behind my knees. "That was..."

I couldn't find the words either, simply closed my eyes and soaked in the euphoric sense of rightness. Contentment.

But as our bodies cooled and pulses slowed, that creeping remorse over Haley eased its way back into my mind, and I let out a heavy exhale.

"Okay?" Wyatt asked, his voice nothing more than a rumble and caress of hot air against my cheek.

"I miss her," I murmured, eyelids clenched tight.

"Me too. So goddamn much."

Silence once more settled, and I took the comfort he offered while allowing myself to feel beyond our connection. Heartache still hovered along with the guilt, but I didn't wallow in either.

Haley held control over both our futures, and while I feared I had lost her for eternity, I clung to the hope she would remember all we'd shared, all we'd had.

But given a second chance with her, would I go back without Wyatt?

A few days earlier, before I'd gotten to know the man, it wouldn't have even been a question.

But now…

I kissed his neck, shifting to pull my spent cock from his hot clasp.

He hissed as I slid free, and I lifted enough to study his face.

Crystalline blue eyes, no longer darkened by lust peered up at me. Longing still rested in those depths, the same tug, that magnetic pull I'd felt since the first time I'd seen him.

But now, I realized, finishing my thought, I was deeply invested in him too.

I leaned down and brushed my lips over his, not sure if giving into our lust had made things better…or worse.

* * *

The dam between us had been torn down, and the flood of mutual desire ran over, swamping everything in its path.

We spent the weekend in Wyatt's bed, taking turns memorizing each other's bodies, kissing, licking, and sucking—well, I did more of the latter. Twice more, he offered up his hot ass, and I drilled him until we both erupted and ended up dead to the world Sunday night.

Monday morning, I woke to his mouth around my dick and rolled onto my knees the second he popped off, leaving me leaking and aching.

But he wasn't interested in fucking me without watching me come undone beneath him—he flipped me onto my back.

Clasped tight against one another, he worked his way into my body, our gazes locked.

Wyatt didn't fuck me.

He wrecked me with slow, grinding thrusts, crooning about what a good fucking boy I was.

I didn't correct the term—no, I fucking soaked that shit up, wanting to rub all over him like a goddamn cat.

We stole heated kisses on the job site.

I sucked his dick on the way home from work twice that week, and he repaid the favor in the shower after washing every inch of my skin and lathering my hair with kneading fingertips.

His hard, thick thigh became my pillow, and I told him to pet me, same as I'd done with Haley.

Those were the times I missed her the most. The cuddling on the couch, the shared comfort and sense of belonging.

I spilled my all my guts to Wyatt. Told him about my borderline homophobic grandparents, how awful family gatherings were since I'd refused to hide in a closet. How I felt I didn't belong anywhere, how I longed to find my place in life.

He shared his inner fears, the sense of floundering while trying to decide how to proceed with confronting his birth mom. River dragged her heels, and Wyatt refused to go alone.

I offered, and he brushed it off—but I didn't take offense.

The man wasn't ready for answers he might not want to hear.

And we talked about Haley.

A lot.

Every fucking day, every goddamn night she kept her silence.

The hurt of missing her hadn't faded one fucking bit—Wyatt stated the same—but at least we had each other to draw comfort from. We enjoyed the fuck out of each other but agreed neither of us felt whole.

I feared we never would.

Chapter 33

Haley

Within a matter of days after settling in my heart I could make it on my own, I drifted without course or direction.

Friday night, I lay in my bed, alone. No soft strands of hair beneath my fingers, no clacking of a lollipop in my ear. No sure arms hugged me from behind, keeping my heart firmly anchored in assurance I existed where I ought to.

Rock bottom had always been an imaginary place in my mind, one filled with agonizing pain and hopelessness.

And I'd learned it. Lived it.

But at least I'd managed to shower the stink of the previous couple of days while wallowing in my mind's shit from my body.

Tears clogged my throat, and I struggled to fill my lungs—almost didn't want to. My limbs weighed me down even though my chest felt hollow. Empty. Silence reigned in my ears, but thoughts flooded my mind, loud and persistent.

I'd applied for countless jobs, some way beyond my skills because why the fuck not, listing Lily as my top reference. The three applications I had hope in because of my management history didn't gain me shit. I'd called as a follow up because squeaky wheels always got the grease, and when I stood up for myself, pushed to learn the why of not being chosen, I learned it was the final job listing on my resume that had killed my chances.

Gretchen didn't have anything nice to say about me. I wasn't surprised, but I'd kept my fingers crossed no one would call her.

Should have known better.

I wanted to stab the twat with a pitchfork. Rant and rave, scratch out her eyeballs.

Empathy for what Garrett had gone through with Alec flooded through me, and my stare on my bedroom ceiling went hazy from tears.

I needed Lily, but she was still in Mexico. Lingering resentment and bitterness toward Garrett and Wyatt kept me from reaching out for them too.

Wine.

Groaning, I rolled from my bed and shuffled into the kitchen on weary feet.

My cell rang from my bedroom as I fought with the stubborn cork, but I could barely find the energy to open the damn bottle let alone rush back to answer. Not that it would have been anyone with a job offer. All businesses of interest for my job hunt weren't still open after eleven at night.

The cork gave way, and I cursed in relief, turning for my bedroom, fully planning to drink straight from the bottle.

My cell sat on my bedside table, and I took a long swallow of my wine before lifting my phone to see who had called.

Wyatt.

I choked on a sudden sob, my hand trembling.

He'd left a message.

Slumping onto the edge of my bed, I considered deleting it without listening, but the jagged rocks where my emotions had landed left me bleeding, needy in a way I'd never known. Perhaps I'd overreacted. Perhaps I'd gone Mom's route a little too far in my selfishness, leaving others to bleed out.

Swallowing hard, I pressed play and lifted my phone to my ear.

"Hey."

Wyatt had cleared his throat as though nervous, but that single rumbled word sent a tear down my cheek.

"Blaine called me earlier today and told me about your mom's passing. I know you couldn't give two shits about her, but I wanted to reach out to make sure that you're doing okay. I told Garrett, and even though I know you're holding onto your anger toward him, he's really hurting. He doesn't remember his own mom, but…"

He let out a heavy exhale as fresh pain lanced through my chest over Garrett suffering for me.

"I know you fear becoming your mom, Haley," Wyatt continued while I curled in on myself, wetness coating my cheeks. "You're not her and never will be. You're far from a narcissist, and while you're stubborn as hell, you aren't selfish like she was."

I also wasn't psychotic. Didn't have the same triggers or tendencies when I didn't get my way or make mistakes.

I owned that shit—but I hadn't. Biting back sobs, I listened to Wyatt's voice that flooded me with warmth.

"You're also strong. Resilient. But you shouldn't have to deal with whatever you're feeling right now alone. Garrett needs you—same as you do him."

The northern star I'd turned away from gently pulled on my focus, steering my course toward what would help see me through.

I hoped Wyatt's message would continue on, and he would tell me how much *he* needed me, how desperate he was to hold my hand too.

"Garrett dropped his phone at work today, and it's not turning on, so please call him on my cell," Wyatt whispered—then hung up without saying goodbye.

The suppressed sobs ripped through me as I clutched my cell to my aching chest. Emotions ran through me like a damn tidal wave, attempting to pull me under.

Regret for not standing up for myself to my mom when I was younger—and for never talking to my dad about how much his leaving had hurt me. Keeping feelings and thoughts bottled up didn't resolve issues, and I had no one to blame for my emotional lowest but myself.

Sorrow for turning away from two of the deepest connections I'd ever made in my life, two men who had accepted me for who I was prickliness and all. Talk about a fucking mistake.

Was it too late to make amends? Set shit straight?

Mom had already decided the first choice for me. Although I doubted I would ever be able to forgive her fully in my heart, I had to remember she had been ill. Yes, she'd made her choices and the bed that had offered her a cowardly way to escape her sick mind, but no longer would I tell myself she deserved that lonely death and so much more.

I imagined she'd hit the depths of despair like I'd been wallowing in—but like Wyatt had said, I *was* stronger than her. I didn't have any signs of psychosis or personality disorders.

A sense of lightness spread through my limbs, and I scrubbed a hand over my face, I focused on breathing deeply, ending the tears.

The second issue was my father. I did as Wyatt had once suggested—I put myself in his shoes. Considered his introspection, how he'd dealt with his own emotions living beneath the same reign of terror I had. As an adult, he should have fared better than I did, should have had stability and wisdom enough to know his only child suffered alongside him and needed guidance in how to deal with emotional hurt.

Was it possible he hadn't seen beyond his own pain? Had something in his past made him incapable of empathy? He'd never been affectionate as far back as I could remember. There were no shoulder rides, no bedtime stories, or making blanket forts.

Maybe he'd been robbed of that in his own childhood and didn't think to initiate such things.

I let out a heavy sigh, knowing I would need to talk to him, but that could wait a bit longer.

Wyatt had opened a door inside me I'd been firmly planted behind, and he deserved my thanks—and so much more.

But I needed to take one step at a time in fixing what I'd fucked up.

My fingers shook, but I texted Wyatt three simple words to get the ball rolling: **Send Garrett home.**

I crawled beneath my blankets.

Either Garrett would come back to me or he wouldn't, and curling up under my covers seemed the best place to wait for happiness—or more self-inflicted heartache I would have to find a way to deal with.

Chapter 34

Wyatt

I'd hung up from leaving a voicemail, wishing I'd been able to say more, that I needed her just as much a Garrett did, but I'd been the one to cause their fallout. It had been my selfishness to have the both of them that had broken down the walls between them.

It was up to me to help repair what I'd ruined.

And if there was space left in their hearts for me once they worked things out, I would willingly give both of them everything I had.

Garrett lay passed out in my bed after a long day at work beneath the sun and one-hundred degree sweltering heat, but I hadn't been able to rest.

The news of Haley's mom's suicide had sent Garrett into a funk that had worried me. I'd reached out to Haley since I didn't know how to offer more than the comfort of my arms, which he hadn't seemed to want.

"Fuck." I scrubbed a hand over my face, bleary-eyed and blinking my refrigerator into focus. I'd been sitting at the kitchen table for close to an hour, a half-emptied bottle of warm beer in my hand.

It grew close to midnight—I noted the microwave's glowing green numbers.

A loud as fuck notification tone jerked my attention to my cell laying in front of me. I'd set my volume to its highest since I didn't want to miss a reply—if she would offer one.

Send Garrett home.

Haley's three-worded text hit my chest like a sledgehammer.

She wanted her best friend and nothing more.

There was no acceptance of the apology I'd sent the Monday before. Nothing for me to hinge hope on, nothing to read into even though the message I'd left her hadn't hinted I'd wanted anything more than to fix what I'd broken.

While I told myself that was what I wished for—her to be happy with the man she obviously loved—her text hurt like fuck.

I'd hoped for a call, a chance to talk to her myself before Garrett did.

But no.

Her heart belonged to Garrett, and I swallowed that truth down like a bitter pill. What had started out as a hug offered as comfort ten days earlier had turned in to a shit ton more between Garrett and me. A connection of not just bodies but hearts and minds.

At least for me, anyway.

Having Garrett in my arms, coming undone countless times beneath or on top of him had given me a sense of bonding more than from both of us being adopted. It felt like a part of me entwined with him beyond the physical.

Add in our easy conversation, being all up in each other's space for two weeks straight, and I knew him better than any of my other employees or close friends I used to party with.

Stumbling footsteps entered the kitchen, and like a physical caress, I felt Garrett's eyes on me.

"Couldn't sleep?"

I glanced over my shoulder to find Garrett's stare on me, a furrow in his forehead similar to mine. He scratched his chest, noticing the phone I clutched in my hand.

"Everything okay?" he asked when I didn't answer his first question.

"Haley texted."

He shot forward, grabbing for my phone.

I handed it over willingly, my heart like a rock in my chest.

His shoulders sagged. "Oh fuck." He swallowed audibly and gave me his focus.

The wetness in his eyes twisted my insides, but it was what I saw in those depths that hit me hardest. Excitement, joy... and longing.

"Go home to her," I whispered, wanting to hang onto that last emotion in his gaze more than the others because I knew he felt pulled in two directions, same as I would in his shoes.

"What about you?" He choked out the words.

"She didn't ask for me, Garrett. Haley wants you—she's willing to give you a chance, so if you knew what was best for you, you'd grab your bag and go home."

Garrett chewed on his lower lip, and I reached up for his chin, tugging until the flesh popped free from his teeth. "I…"

My smile felt more sad than happy. "I'll be fine. I'm excited for you. Seriously. Get your ass out of here."

"I thought you liked my ass." His attempts at a joke fell flat.

"You know damn well I do. Fuck, do I ever, but Haley's happiness is what's important here."

Garrett inhaled deeply and slowly let his lungs deflate. "Yeah."

I'd spoken truth, but his agreeing still knifed at me. "Then what are you waiting for?" I forced tone to my voice that wanted to whisper from a shattering heart.

Those dark eyes of his slid over my face, searching, perhaps memorizing in case it was the last time we shared the same space.

I swallowed hard.

He bent down and kissed me gently, no tongue, a simple press of lips that lingered long enough that my heart rate kicked up at the well-learned knowledge of what his mouth was capable of.

"Can I call you?" he asked when he backed away, leaving me cold and empty inside.

"Please," I choked out what I wanted, even though it would be best to do a clean break so we could all move on with our lives.

He got up, and I listened as he tossed his shit into the lone bag he'd brought from their apartment.

Less than five minutes later, he stood in the kitchen once more.

I didn't get up because if I did, I would hug him—and I would have one hell of a time letting him go. In that moment, I thoroughly understood abandonment, and I experienced a tiny bit of the hurt I'd caused Haley by leaving her.

But I wasn't given a chance to make things better like Garrett was.

Our gazes held, and he seemed to understand my feelings and the thoughts rattling my brain. A single nod, and he turned away.

The door snicked shut, and I sat alone in the silence, staring at the chair on my right I'd become accustomed to seeing him occupy. He'd made himself at home in my life in so short a time, and I'd enjoyed having him there. Looked forward to waking up beside him in the morning, sharing kisses between sips of coffee, his gorgeous body on display and available for my caring touch whenever both of us had wanted.

Even more, though, I'd found comfort in having someone all up in my space, having conversations about mundane shit. Sports. The damn lollipops he crunched on.

Garrett wasn't just a guy I'd fucked around with.

He'd become a friend, a good one who seemed to understand me on a level deeper than anyone in my small circle.

"Fuck." Closing my eyes, I tipped my head back and breathed through the ache in my chest.

I was alone.

Again.

"Fuck."

I swiped my cell off the table and put through a call to my sister since she claimed to be a night owl.

"Hey, Rowan."

"Hey, baby sis." We didn't know who'd been born first, but seeing her as younger felt right. "Sorry for calling so damn late—"

"I was awake. What's up?"

"I was thinking we've put this shit off long enough."

"You really want to meet the woman who abandoned us?" she asked, more wariness to her voice than hurt like I felt deep inside my bones.

"Fuck no, but I need to get this shit over with—*after* seeing you. Do you have any plans tomorrow?"

"You mean today?"

I glanced at my clock. It was after twelve. I'd had my weekend plans with Garrett obliterated by a three-worded text, so I needed to keep my head busy. "Yeah...so later this morning?"

"I'm free every Saturday. What did you have in mind?"

"We can have breakfast together then drive up to Fresno." I'd yet to meet the mirror image of me and finally felt ready to figure that part of my life out since all the other issues surrounding me had resolved—just not in the way I'd hoped for.

"That sounds good to me. I've been dying to see you in real life." Her voice teased, same as it had the last couple times she'd begged me to see me. "Do you think we should call her first though?"

"Nope. I want to meet you, confront her together, then see where we go from there."

Because fuck knew I had no plans for my life outside Lionel's Landscaping.

"She didn't want us then, so I doubt she's going to want us now." The assuredly of River's tone and the bluntness of her statement ripped through me. She sounded flippant—she didn't care one way or the other.

But I sure as fuck did.

She hadn't been betrayed by her adoptive parents, lied to by the people who'd paid good money to obtain a kid.

I felt so goddamn *alone*, my heart slugging along to keep beating. My sister was set on having me in her life...why couldn't that be enough?

I should have been ecstatic to finally meet her, maybe connect as twin siblings seemed to, but the deepest part of my soul still ached for more with the two people I'd given my heart to.

And lost.

Garrett

My damn hands shook as I unlocked the apartment door and let myself into the place I'd called home for over eight months. The soothing, familiar scent of lavender filled my nose and made my eyes sting.

I'd been on a goddamn roller coaster of emotions since learning about Hal's mom's death—then reading her text...

Even though I hungered for—*belonged* to Wyatt in some ways, I yearned to do what she wanted. That meant leaving him behind for however long it took to settle things with my cuddle bug. Yet a part of me still stood in the kitchen beside him.

Working alongside him, sharing space and most of our thoughts, had come easily between us. We'd clicked beyond that initial moment of bonding, falling into a comfortable rhythm inside and out of his bed that I'd made myself at home in.

But until I straightened shit out with my Haley, I couldn't move forward with the longing I felt for him that wouldn't fade.

Heart in my throat, I moved through the kitchen Haley and I had shared for the best months of my life, noting the dirty dishes on the counter, the unswept kitchen floor.

A lone lamp lit the living room, the same one she often left on if I stayed out late after she'd gone to bed. Two piles of unfolded of laundry sat on the chair, and the throw blanket we'd used to cuddle beneath lay tossed over the back of the couch.

The toilet flushed, and I stood in the kitchen, listening as feet shuffled across the hallway—but she didn't shut her bedroom door behind her.

I let out a slow exhale of air I hadn't realized I'd held in my lungs. Setting my bag on the kitchen floor, I kicked off my shoes. Put my keys and dead cell phone on the counter.

One last deep inhale in attempts to steady my nerves, and I walked through our apartment on near-silent feet.

The lamp on her bed stand revealed Haley lay wrapped up in her comforter, maroon-red hair still atop her head in a messy bun.

She had her back to me.

Deep longing to just hold her, breathe her in, welled up inside me, and I moved forward without thought, my soul so damn hungry to comfort her I couldn't breathe.

She didn't shift or acknowledge my presence as I pulled back the blankets on the opposite side of her. She didn't make a peep as I slid in behind her warm body.

But a heavy sigh sagged her against me as I wrapped her up in my arms.

Eyes stinging, I buried my face against her neck and breathed in the clean scent of her skin. A sense of rightness rolled over me, thickening my throat.

"I'm sorry," I whispered, not bothering with any excuses.

Haley rolled over to face me. Red-rimmed eyes peered at me, her nose a bright shade like she'd spent too long on the beach without sunscreen.

She'd been crying.

Tears welled in my eyes, and hers responded in kind.

"He told you about my mom." Haley didn't ask a question, but I nodded and hugged her tight, not bothering to offer my condolences. She wouldn't want them, same as I didn't over my teenage mother who'd chosen death rather than her son.

Haley and I had always been close, but that news had made me want to wrap her up inside my arms for eternity.

"Need to talk about it?"

"No."

I brushed my nose over hers, allowing her the space she needed to deal with whatever grief or regrets she might have. "I missed you."

"Same." Her attempted smile wobbled as her eyes once more welled. "I'm sorry for overreacting like I did."

"It's okay, Hal—"

"No it's not." A tear slid down her cheek as her voice cracked. "You're my best friend. My koala. And I almost lost you for being butt hurt over something stupid."

"It wasn't stupid. I made a serious mistake by not being honest with you from the start."

She blew out a heavy exhale. "But I wouldn't have given you Lily's room if I was aware you might attempt to get in my pants."

We studied each other in the dim light, and I knew we both followed the logic from her statement onward.

There wouldn't have been nights spent snuggling on the couch. The traumas of our childhood shared over countless glasses of wine. No teasing, no sexual banter I'd had a love/hate relationship with.

Perhaps...I hadn't chosen wrong after all.

And just maybe, not calling Alec that night to help me with his sister hadn't been the wrong choice too.

Regardless of the heartache, it had gotten me away from him—landed me at Haley's front door.

Something cracked open inside me, a sense of release flooding my soul like I'd never known. The burden I'd carried around on my shoulders for almost a year dissolved, leaving me sagging, my heart lighter than it had been in...well, forever.

Haley clutched at my shirt as though afraid I was pulling away.

"I'm not going anywhere," I promised.

"Good because you're mine."

I studied her serious expression, the determination in her luminous, dark eyes.

How easy it would be to fall back into what we had started that night with Wyatt, but one last bit of honesty needed to be dumped between us.

And I refused to keep shit from her ever again—regardless of the fear over what her reaction might be.

"I slept with Wyatt—and not just as in sharing his bed," I stated quietly and held my breath.

Her face didn't twitch. "I figured you would. The man is hot as hell, and the sexual tension between the two of you is enough to make a woman combust."

My lungs deflated like I'd been punched in the sternum. "You aren't mad?"

"No," she didn't hesitate to answer, a glint in her eyes as she pressed in closer to me. "Wish I'd been there to see it. Who fucked who?"

"Christ, Hal, are you for real?" I chuckled, amazed with how easily things had settled between us. Forgiven and forgotten, just like that.

She punched my arm. "Details. TMI—give it to me."

I groaned, my dick twitching to life from her words and the memory of Wyatt's hands on me. "It started when I straddled his lap and jerked us off together."

"Who came first?" Her breathy tone suggested arousal.

"Me—because he told me to."

"Oh shit." Haley shifted like she needed to ease an ache between her thighs, but she didn't press any closer toward my dick that was more than willing to help her out. "Did you kiss his mouth?"

"Fucking devoured it," I said, my heart and length aching at the memory—and the dozens of times afterwards.

"God, that man can *kiss*." A hint of her moan laced the final word, causing my length to jerk. "And his dick is so. Fucking. Delicious."

I couldn't argue either fact. With Wyatt at my disposal for sexual gratification, I hadn't needed those lollipops, that was for damned sure.

"I smeared our cum all over his abs and chest," I continued on with my tale since my words turned both of us on.

Haley burst into giggles—fucking glorious laughter that filled my heart to bursting.

"I topped him first," I admitted, searching her face for jealousy.

Heat flared in her eyes. "First...meaning you got the dick you've been craving after."

"Yeah. Countless times." My backside twinged at the memory, and my dick thickened fully at her moan.

"Oh. My. Fucking. God." She swallowed hard like the thought of him and I together flooded her mouth with drool.

My relationship with Haley had always been easy, but I no longer felt whole. I wanted Wyatt—missed him even though I hadn't been away from him for an hour. I opened my mouth to try and explain the feelings I had for both, but she spoke first.

"You know he's on Missing Link looking for a long-term poly relationship, right?"

I studied her dark eyes, but I'd never been able to read her like Wyatt had so easily done when she'd wished to hide from me. "Are you trying to tell me something in a roundabout way?"

She smirked but lifted a suggestive eyebrow. *That* look I knew well.

"You want him too, don't you?"

"Yes," she whispered, her smirk fading, gaze going unsure as though afraid I might deny her what she desired.

As if.

A gentle tug removed the band from her hair, and I ran my fingers over her scalp, spilling dyed tresses across her pillow.

"We talked about you all the time. Imagined you between us." My length pulsed at the memory. "Fantasized about it together."

Her pupils swelled as pre-cum oozed from my slit. "Oh shit."

The sounds of our breaths filled the space between us, and I fought the desire to pull her against my groin and grind on her thigh like a damn dog.

"Are we okay, Hal?" I asked, needing the truth before we went any further.

"Yeah." she breathed out the answer I hoped to hear, her smirk softening. "If I can set things right with him too, want to give it a shot?"

"Fuck yes," I didn't hesitate to answer, tightening my hands in her hair, "but right now, I need to try something else out first."

"Oh?" Her eyebrow flicked up again as I mobilized her head with my grip on her hair.

"I've been holding back for fucking *months,* Hal. Why do you think I was crunching on those fucking Blow Pops every night?"

"Because you have an oral fixation?"

I grinned, my entire body floating higher than it had been since the night I'd finally gotten my hands on her. "Well, that too."

Our gazes stayed locked, our smiles slowly fading. I didn't feel the need to put distance between us or pull a pillow over my groin like I used to do if the air grew too heated. One hand on her lower back, I tugged her in closer—until she pressed against me from my chest to aching groin.

"Oh God." A shudder rippled over her, tensing every muscle in my body. My snuggle bug brushed her nose over mine, her warm breath tempting my lips. "I want to be more than friends, Garrett. So if we're on the same page—"

I took her mouth, letting her know exactly what I wanted.

Fu-cking-hell. I whimpered a needy sound as a shudder tore through me.

She tasted like tart wine and sweet strawberries, so goddamn luscious my balls throbbed and heart swelled to bursting.

Her hands swept down my back and yanked at my T-shirt's hem. I pulled away long enough to rip the damn thing off and dove back in, hands on her face, claiming her mouth with need I felt clear though my toes. Her mouth was life. All I'd dreamed about and more. Torture of the sweetest sort—a delicious promise of more than simply release.

Our tongues stroked, teeth nipped, and she let me suck on her lower then upper lip.

And her fingers—her fucking fingers mapped out my chest, my contracting abs, lingering on the V of muscle dipping into my jeans.

It was after midnight, and I'd been exhausted from a long day at work, but I'd never felt so alive—awake and hopeful for my next breath.

"Fuck, Hal." I gasped into her mouth and grabbed hold of her tight ass, yanking her on top of me as I rolled to my back.

Our lips stayed fused as she settled in to straddle me, but I pushed her upwards, frantic to get that damn sleep shirt off her body.

No bra bound her perfect tits. Dark pink nipples, tight and mouthwatering called out to me.

"Fuck," I groaned the word and lifted my upper body toward her, latching on.

Haley let out a gasp and grabbed hold of my head as I set to fulfilling my oral fixation with her—fucking *finally*. I nibbled and licked, suckled on her sweet, soft skin, moaning over how heavenly she tasted.

"Fuck, your tongue feels good," she groaned, a shudder trembling her atop me.

Worshiping my Hal became my newest, favorite addiction, and I fed off her until she pushed my head toward her other nipple.

I devoured that one as well until she writhed over my groin as though seeking release.

"God, Garrett. I'm so damn wet for you."

"Mmm." I sucked hard and popped off. "So damn delicious." Hands grasping her tits, I smooshed them together, getting both reddened tips between my lips.

"Oh fuck." She yanked on my hair and gyrating her hips. "Yes. Don't stop."

As if I would.

A goddamn earthquake could shake the building down around us, and I wouldn't tear my attention off the girl I'd been dreaming about for half of forever.

She panted, letting out soft moans that kept me hard as fuck beneath her gyrating heat.

"Can you come from this alone?" I asked, thumbing over the tight buds.

"Fuck yeah." She yanked my head forward, and chuckling, I gave my girl more of what she wanted.

She moaned and gasped, pulling at the longer strands atop my head while grinding her core over my aching dick. Haley hadn't lied about being wet. Her arousal soaked through her panties and my shorts.

My length throbbed beneath Haley, pre-cum leaking from my slit and mingling with her hot arousal seeping through the thin materials separating us.

"Haley," I groaned around my mouthful of tits, thrust up against her, and bit down on both her nipples.

She came with a shriek, her body shuddering—and gushing hot cum to soak my groin.

The sound of her release, knowing I had caused it, had been the sole source of her pleasure, sent longing rippling through me like I'd never experienced. My balls drew up tight, my dick aching to bury in her wet heat.

"Haley." I choked on her name, my pulse thrumming, my entire body tight. "Need you."

She let out a sigh as a shiver rippled over her, pebbling her skin, and she rolled, sprawling onto her back. "Then take me."

I damn near swallowed my tongue. All I'd lusted for over the previous eight months lay at my fingertips— and I couldn't wait to find heaven.

Chapter 36

Haley

I sprawled on my back, my limbs tingling from my climax, but I was far from sated. My core ached to be filled.

With nothing between us.

Biting on my lower lip, I soaked in the man I loved sitting up in a ripple of muscle over his torso. I'd come so damn hard that I'd creamed all over the front of his shorts. He rolled and shifted, shoving them off his body.

He'd gone commando.

And fucking hell, my mouth watered over the memory of his taste. "Want it," I strangled the whisper, my gaze locked on his stiff dick, my fingers fluttering with a gimme gesture.

Garrett chuckled and crawled toward me. He grabbed one of my ankles and pulled, moving me sideways across the bed. Settling between my spread legs kept his cock out of my hands.

Our gazes caught, and only our heavy breaths filled the air.

No words passed between us, but they weren't necessary. The barrier hiding the truth had crumbled to rubble, and I damn near drowned in the desire, the love, pouring from his beautiful eyes. Wetness once more welled in their depths.

The ache inside me could only be soothed in one way.

"Take me," I repeated my earlier whisper.

"Condom."

I clutched at his arm as he started to roll toward my bedside table. "I want to feel you, Garrett. Every inch of your skin against mine—inside and out."

There hadn't been much we didn't share, including the test results we'd gone together to get not long after he'd moved in. We'd both been celibate except for Wyatt since.

Wyatt.

I swallowed hard at the intense longing I felt for both men—

"I've never…" Garrett's voice trailed off as he searched my face.

"Yeah," I said, wrapping my legs around the backs of his thighs. "Me neither, but I don't want anything more between us—until its Wyatt."

"Fuck, Hal." Garrett groaned and shifted his body upward, bracketing my head with his forearms. The feel of his rippled torso sliding over mine sent a spasm through my core. The tip of his dick kissed my aching pussy.

He hesitated, our gazes locking. Garrett was aware, same as Wyatt, that I wouldn't ever go without protection until I knew without doubt what I wanted in my life—who I needed beside me.

"Garrett," I whispered, my hands clutching at the muscles along his spine, my thighs grasping tighter to hold him close. My pulse thrummed, fluttering through my chest and stealing my breath.

"You're sure?" he asked.

"More than anything, yes."

He pushed forward, sliding through my slick lower lips to breach my body with his thick cockhead.

"Oh Jesus," I whimpered when he paused, the delicious stretch of his invasion rushing more arousal to ease his way.

His eyes darkened, a deep groan rumbling in his chest. "Fuck you're so hot."

Breath held, I watched his gorgeous face as he sank deeper. The flicker of his eyelashes as he blinked as though trying to hold my gaze rather than rolling his eyes back into his head.

A slow hiss escaped his parted lips, and I squeezed my inner walls as he buried the last inch of his dick in my body.

We both let out a shuddered breath, his length throbbing inside me, right the fuck where it belonged— where it should have been for months on end.

But we had a future to make up for that lost time.

And Wyatt would be with us. I refused to believe anything else.

I clung to Garrett, my heart pounding, my chest threatening to explode with the overflow of emotions rolling over me. "Love you so damn much, Garrett."

"Love you more," he whispered, his hot breath sweet across my lips.

My heart *ached*. "Not possible."

Souls locked together through our eyes, he dragged out of my wetness, groaning a curse. "Better...so much better than I fantasized. Fuck, Hal."

I tightened my legs, pulling him back in, the neediness in my core filling to the brink. He fit me perfectly, the heat of his shaft, the lack of latex between us...

So good. So *fucking* good.

A breathless gasp pushed from my lips as he flexed his ass beneath my heels, bumping against my cervix.

"Christ, your body is heaven wrapped around me." He swallowed hard and backed out again, taking his good old fucking time dragging his dick over my slick walls.

"Can't wait to feel Wyatt's cock shoved in here with me."

My pussy spasmed. "Fucking *hell*, Garrett."

"Mmm."

I lifted my hips when he pushed back in, both of us panting moans at the delicious friction.

Nothing lay between us. No walls. No barriers. No secrets—not even in our eyes. Raw need darkened his, and I remained vulnerable, allowing all my emotions, my feelings for him to pour from mine.

Love wasn't an adequate description for what tied us together as he slowly rocked in and out of my body. I felt like pieces of our souls fused in a bond as tight as our friendship had been.

"Hal," he croaked my name and twined his fingers through my hair, tipping my head back.

At the brush of his lips over mine, my pussy pulsed around his length. He groaned, and our tongues met in a slow fuck, moving in time with our writhing bodies.

The outward expression of our love was a long time in coming, and we both relished in the gyrations of our entwined bodies. His low moans, more breath than tone every time he pushed into my body, ramped up the need coiling in my belly.

I could come just from the noises he made, the delicious rumble in his chest, the shuddered exhales, and the muttered curses.

My toes tingled, the promise of a sure climax.

And neither of us touched my clit.

Euphoria rippled from where he filled me, and I cried out, clinging to his body, wishing Wyatt's lay beneath me, his arms wrapped around us both.

Garrett pulled his head back and caught my gaze, watching—drinking me in—as I fell apart beneath him.

"My God, Hal...you're so goddamn beautiful." He continued to stroke in and out of me with slow, slick glides, unhurried in carrying me through my climax. "Love you so fucking much it hurts."

I shuddered, completely wrecked, and he took my mouth.

At the first harsh thrust of his hips, I cried out, tingles of sweet pain from where he rammed into my cervix, arching my spine.

"Mmm," he moaned into my mouth and thrust again, driving my back over the mattress.

Every snap of his hips caught my breath and released a gasped groan from his lips devouring mine.

So. Fucking. Hot.

I came again, my entire body clenching up tight.

"Hal." He choked my name, and a burst of heat exploded inside me. "Oh fuck." Garrett grunted.

Our gazes latched as we fell together.

Madly. Deliciously. Soul-shattering bliss.

Tears slid over my cheeks when reality returned through the ringing in my ears. Our foreheads rested together. We shared breath. Sweat and heat lay between us. Wetness leaked around his semi still buried inside me, dripping down my ass crack and onto the bed.

I couldn't move, didn't want to break the connection between us.

Our hearts beat in time, slowing together.

Garrett let out a groan and shifted downward, pulling his cock from my body. Cum slid out in his absence, and I whimpered at the loss of him inside me.

He kissed my lips. My chin. My collarbone.

Then he lay his head on my chest, his hot breath wafting over my left, oversensitive nipple.

I speared my fingers into his hair, scratching his scalp in the way he loved, and he let out a heavy sigh.

I'd never felt so satisfied, so filled.

But with our passion finally abated after months of buildup, something lacked in the quiet between us. My hands stilled in his hair, and we both inhaled fully as though on the verge of speaking...

"Wyatt," we whispered at the same time.

And burst into giggles.

"Were you imagining him while fucking me?" I asked while snickering, my fingers once more combing through his hair.

He wrapped his arms tight around me. "No—honest to God. I'd wished his hands were on me, but I wasn't thinking about anything but your tight pussy sucking on my dick," Garrett said, his deep voice rumbling the chest pressed to my belly.

"I didn't compare you to him," I replied. "Promise."

Garrett lifted his head, his eyes like melted chocolate, soft and warm. "But you *do* still want him."

I grabbed hold of his scruffy cheeks. "Yes, but not because you aren't enough."

His slow smirk curled my toes. "I know." He turned his face, kissing my palm. "I want to try to make things work with him too, Hal, because as much as you own my heart and soul, he's in there with you. Does that make sense?"

I saw Wyatt's gorgeous blue eyes in my mind, remembered his kiss, the feel of his fingers entwined through mine. The sense of comfort and rightness I experienced every time we shared space.

But it was his guidance, the safety my heart and mind felt in his presence that made me yearn for him the most.

Garrett was my koala.

Wyatt was my true north.

"Yeah. I do," I murmured.

"I want him in all the ways I do you, Hal."

Longing for the same flooded through me, and I ran my thumb over Garrett's lower lip.

He sucked my finger into his mouth, his tongue swirling around the tip.

Arousal hit me hard and heavy in my core, and just like that, my thoughts went to the physical and fantasies. "You know what I would really like? To watch you suck on his dick like a lollipop."

Garrett groaned and dropped his forehead to my sternum. "Fuck, woman."

"That can come after. Preferably both of you in me at the same time just like you were thinking while sinking deep into my pussy."

"Shit." He lifted his head, dark eyes heating. "Let's get our man."

"It's after one in the morning," I said, once more tracing a fingertip over his lush mouth. "I want to wake up with you in a few hours. Share sleepy kisses and maybe a couple more orgasms. Call me selfish—"

"You're not."

"—but I need this alone time with my koala."

Garrett snickered and finally rolled off me.

"Where are you going?" I pouted, knowing he wouldn't leave me for long.

"Bathroom."

Fuck, that ass. I stared at Garrett's flexing backside, wondering what Wyatt's face would look like as he buried deep inside my koala's body.

I slid my fingers down over my belly and into the mess Garrett had made in my pussy.

Imagining the two of them thrusting into me at the same time, listening to their groans while coming…

Fuck.

"Hurry up, Garrett!" I hollered. "I need your dick again!"

His laughter spread a grin over my face, and I held out my cum-soaked fingers to him when he filled my bedroom doorway, beckoning with that gimme motion.

He sucked my fingers clean, then gave me what I wanted until we both passed the fuck out from exhaustion.

Chapter 37

Wyatt

River stood close to six feet, a willowy woman with perfect curves and stunning, feminine beauty. Even without a stitch of makeup and dressed like a flower child in some billowy dress, she drew heads when she walked into the diner we'd agreed to meet at for breakfast.

Our gazes clashed, and we both grinned like a couple of dorks even though part of my heart lay dead in my chest.

I stood up from the table I'd been wallowing at with a cup of coffee, and she let out a silly squeal, arms opening wide.

She launched herself at me in a clatter of jangled bracelets and hippie-like gauze material, and I held my sister up against my chest, hugging her hard. But she didn't allow me to enjoy having what I didn't know I'd been missing wrapped in my arms.

River pulled back as quickly as she'd thrown herself at me, grabbing hold of my scruff-lined jaw. "Let me look at you," she demanded, her voice as loud as her presence.

Blue eyes, as clear as the summer sky, roamed my face as her grin stayed put. "You're hotter than me."

I barked a laugh. "Grow another three inches, put some meat on your bones, and no one would be able to tell us apart."

Tears welled in her eyes. "Goddamnit, Rowan, I've been waiting so long for this moment." She planted a hard kiss right on my fucking lips and laughed, untangling herself from my body.

I could imagine the stares we got but couldn't be bothered to glance around.

My little sister, the one person on the planet who shared my DNA, sat mere feet from me. Her presence eased some of my hurt over the lack of communication from either Garrett or Haley. I'd turned my cell off a few minutes earlier, determined to focus on the day ahead, the sister in front of me, and the woman we would face in the near future.

"You're one hell of a free spirit," I told River, settling my mind on the *now.*

"And I'm thinking you need to let loose a bit."

We both still smiled, our gazes locked even as the waitress came over asking River if she wanted a coffee.

"And waffles," she and I both tacked on at the same time.

"Bacon?" I asked, one of my eyebrows raising.

"Sausage patties—if you have them," she added, glancing up at our server.

The waitress murmured they did before ambling away, and once more River and I sat alone.

"So." She reached over the table, and I gave her my hand.

Our fingers entwined, and I wondered if we'd done the same in our mother's womb.

River felt like an extension of me, the warmth of her hand bringing tears to my eyes.

"Is it weird to say that I somehow...recognize you?" I asked quietly. "I mean, even if we didn't look alike, I would know you."

She squeezed my fingers. "It's not weird at all, Rowan—can I call you that?"

"You can call me whatever the hell you want, little sister."

A twinkle lit in her eye. "What if I'm the older one?"

"You'll always be my little sister, and now that we've found one another, you'll never go without my having your back."

Her smile softened as her head tilted to the side. Warmth radiated from her entire face. "And you'll never be alone again."

Like I'd been all night long, laying in my bed, the silence stifling as I imagined Garrett and Haley together, loving each other.

Without needing me.

I swallowed hard.

"I can see pain in your aura, Rowan. What's going on?"

My mouth opened, and words leaked from my tight throat like a broken spigot, spilling the story of my love life—or rather, the lack thereof.

"That's what prompted me to call you last night," I said, my voice hoarse. "I was so damn lonely, my insides shredded. I'm sorry it took me so long to agree to meet with you, but with everything that's happened..."

I shrugged, unable to say more.

River squeezed my fingers she still clasped even though the waitress had dropped off her coffee a few minutes earlier. "Have you heard from either of them?"

"No. And it fucking hurts so bad, but I need to focus on one thing at a time. I'm not turning on my cell and checking again until we get this confrontation with Dahlia behind us."

Our waitress arrived, food in hand, so River released her hold on me, and we both sat back.

"If you need anything else, just let me know," our server said while setting our plates in front of us.

I cut into my waffle with my fork, unable to help wondering if Garrett and Haley ate breakfast or if they still lay in bed.

If I'd been in their shoes, it would have been the latter. Snuggled in warmth, soft caresses, and hungry kisses.

"Hey."

I lifted my unseeing focus off my plate, realizing I chewed a bite I didn't remember putting between my lips.

"One thing at a time, okay?" River reminded me with a kind smile. "And if it's meant to be with your two lovers, it will be." Her simple statement didn't sound cliche. The words spoke to my heart, made me remember my powerlessness to do anything about the situation of my love life.

She hadn't traveled north to act as my therapist, so I detoured our conversation toward the reason behind our finally meeting face to face.

Our mom.

And River went along with my steering away from heartache—even though I thoroughly expected another kind in a few hours that would be no less hurtful.

Having looked up our birth mother's address, I knew River and I had a three-hour drive ahead of us, so we didn't linger over our breakfast. Our easy banter, the catching up of thirty-plus years poured from our lips from breakfast and all the way up Route 5.

The closer we got to Fresno, the less words passed between us.

I got lost in thoughts of what Dahlia would look like. Any and every possible reception. The abandoned child inside me hoped for a tearful reunion and learning we'd been taken from her loving arms rather than abandoned to the system.

But she hadn't looked for us, hadn't gotten in contact with us.

Maybe she couldn't find us.

Fuck, how I hoped for that outcome since the opposite hurt too much to dwell on: a denial of identity, a complete lack of opening or willingness to talk to us.

I wasn't sure I could handle that atop missing my two lovers.

River reached for my hand, and I clasped hers tight while taking the exit Siri dictated. Her gentle touch soothed me, but in that moment, I yearned for Haley's comforting presence.

I remembered her soft hands clutching mine, the way she played with my hair and held my head to her chest. The memory of her peaceful heartbeat in my ear, the satiny skin cradling my cheek.

Memories of Garrett's steadying touch tingled my lower back. His assuring gaze and firm lips had grounded me whenever they brushed mine.

Fuck, did I need them both.

My throat thickened, but as we drove deeper into our mother's part of town, the seedier it became, pulling my focus back on the present. I'd expected the squalor but couldn't help my grimace.

The woman who bore us sure as hell had made some godawful choices in her life—or had she been a victim of circumstance, suffering for others' decisions or actions?

Until we sat silent in front of the dilapidated apartment building my directions had led us to, I half didn't even want to find out the answers to my questions.

A group of twenty-somethings hung out by a pimped-out car close to the entrance, some vaping, some smoking, all appearing as rough as their surroundings.

"This place has negative and volatile energy." River rubbed her bare arms, leaning forward to peer up at the building. "I should have had my cards read before doing this. Shit. Okay." She nodded as though she'd made up her mind and grabbed her bohemian purse off the floor from between her feet. "Let's go."

I hopped out first, rounding the front of my car. No way in hell would I allow her to walk less than a foot away from me. I also beeped my car's alarm nice and loud before heading toward the complex.

"Any shit goes down, stay behind me," I muttered, my hand on her elbow, the cloudy sky as glum as my expectations.

"Gladly."

A few catcalls whistled our way along with a handful of Spanish words I didn't know—or care to understand. We ignored the punks and stepped inside.

"Oh shit." I damn near gagged at the stench of wet dog and piss. "Hopefully, the whole building isn't this nasty."

It was.

River and I exited the filthy, trash-littered stairwell into the second floor's long hallway. The scent of stale cigarettes and skunk-like weed overshadowed the foul smells from below. Not as nauseating but far from pleasant.

I rubbed my sweaty palms down my jeans when I came to a stop in front of the fourth door on the right—206.

River tossed some of her long hair over her shoulder and lifted her chin, her entire body going from hippie flower child to statuesque goddess in a blink.

Our palms came together and fingers clenched on their own, and I let out a slow exhale.

I knocked with my free hand, my pulse thrumming, stomach in knots.

"The fuck you want?" A female hollered from inside, her voice husky as though she'd smoked her life away.

Hopefully, a roommate or friend.

"We're looking for Dahlia," I called back, and River squeezed my fingers tighter.

The door creaked open, blue eyes and thinned lips appearing in the inch-gap. A huffed snort escaped the person, and the door swung inward.

An older, broken-down version of River stood before us.

Sallow complexion, lanky, gray-streaked dark hair, I noted first. Track marks covered her bruised, thin arms. A gray tank top hung over her bony shoulders and braless sagging breasts. She wore stained underwear and nothing else.

"Wondered if you little shits would show up some day."

Her rasped words hit me like a fist to the solar plexus.

"I ain't got nothing for you, not even the name of whoever the fuck it was knocked me up." She glanced over us, her lip curling, revealing rotted teeth. "Go back to the rich folks who took you off my hands."

The door slammed in our face.

I blinked in the sudden silence, my feet rooted, all brain functions paused.

River snorted a sudden laugh that reminded my lungs to inflate. "Guess we have our answer!"

My sister spun on her heel in a flutter of gauzy skirt, tugging on my hand. "The trash took itself out, Rowan. Time for us to move on."

I stumbled down the stairs on numb legs beside her. We exited the disgusting building, and my heart thumped heavy in my deadened chest.

More catcalls followed us, but I barely heard past the ringing in my ears.

I hit the fob's button on autopilot and found myself locked away in the safety of our car before a thought entered my head. I clutched the steering wheel and stared unseeing out the windshield as reality attempted to seep in.

What had happened? Our mother hadn't spoken all of a dozen words before slamming the door. I couldn't remember her voice, only the abrupt message that left me gaping and numb.

"Hey." River's soothing tone rippled through my fuzzed brain, and I glanced over to find her studying me, not a single bit of evidence on her face that she'd experienced the truth taking a while to settle in my mind.

Compassion filled her eyes, and she clutched my forearm. "You okay?"

Was I? The little boy inside me sure as fuck wasn't, but the adult, the man I'd grown into thanks to Lionel and Tina...

Thank *fuck* they had chosen me. Loved me. Accepted me.

"Yeah." My voice came out as a ragged whisper, so I cleared my throat and nodded, all systems in my body coming back online. "No point in crying over her, is there?"

"Absolutely none." River settled in, dropping her bag to the floor between her feet. "It's time to face forward toward the future."

A sense of readiness rolled over me, completely lifting the fog.

I was ready to do what she'd said.

"Hey, Siri, call Mom." I said while attaching my cell to the magnetic plate atop my dash.

River grasped my shoulder, reminding me so damn much of Garrett's sure touch that my throat tightened again.

"Wyatt?" Tina answered, her tone hesitant.

"Hey, Mom." I choked—and broke down sobbing.

River took my hand while I apologized to both my parents once Mom put me on speaker. I told them about River, our birth mother, and how the reality of where I'd come from had opened my eyes to all I'd been blessed with.

"I'm sorry for being such an ass," I muttered through my tears.

"It's okay, baby," Mom said, her tone soothing. I imagined her brushing back my hair and kissing my forehead like she used to do when I was sick in bed as a kid. "Your dad and I realized we never should have hidden the truth from you. We're so sorry."

"I understand why you did," I said, swiping the back of my hand over my face. "One of these days, Dad and I can sit down and talk about what he went through too. I'm sure it would be helpful for both of us."

I recalled how easily I'd connected with Garrett over the whole adoption thing and realized I'd missed out with an even deeper bond with my dad.

But that would change—I wanted that closeness back, that sense of belonging with my parents. I looked forward to it.

"Love you, Mom," I whispered, thankfulness flooding through my heart. "You too, Dad," I added since they shared the couch and had me on speakerphone.

"Dinner Tuesday night?" Mom asked.

"Wouldn't miss it," I promised, breathing easier since facing Dahlia Angel.

We hung up a few minutes later, and I reached over the console and hugged my sister tight. "Thank you for never giving up. For looking for me. For agreeing to put this shit to rest alongside me."

"I'll always be here for you, Rowan." She patted my back and pulled away to click her seatbelt. "Now let's get out of this hellhole and back to where we belong," she suggested with a sweet smile.

That's exactly what we did, laughing and sharing childhood stories the entire way.

I said goodbye to my sister at the diner where she'd left her car, holding her in my arms. We made promises to get together at least once a month.

"And next time, I want to meet Haley and Garrett."

I wasn't ready to face rejection since I rode a high like I hadn't experienced in a long fucking time. "Not sure they'll be in my life *for* you to meet."

"I have a good feeling about them, Rowan." River stated with her matter-of-fact voice and hugged me again. "Maybe you ought to finally check your phone's messages."

I shoved my hands in my jeans' pockets, watching my little sister pull out of the parking lot. It wasn't until I climbed from the shower twenty minutes later after washing the stench of the day from my body that I found the nerve to swipe my cell to life rather than have Siri do it for me.

A message from Haley waited for me.

My heart rate jacked, and holding my breath, I clicked to open her text.

She'd reached out to me minutes after River had arrived at the diner that morning.

Haley: **So, I've got this roommate in my bed who agrees with me that we need our dry line or we're going to be left laying crooked paver blocks in life. Will you come be with us—and stay this time?**

A mixture of relief and excitement caught my breath on a sob. I pressed a fist to my mouth and reread her words.

They were together—and they wanted me.

Rather than text or call, I yanked on shorts and an old work T-shirt, shoved my feet into the closest pair of slides, and sprinted toward my front door, tripping on the way. Water still dripped from my hair, but I pushed it back, uncaring of my appearance.

My heart raced, light as a goddamn feather inside my aching chest.

Dahlia Angel didn't give a shit I existed, but she didn't matter when the two I yearned for the most did.

Chapter 38

Haley

Garrett and I lay together on the couch watching a movie with him being the big spoon. Both of us were worn the fuck out from countless orgasms and the Chinese food we'd devoured.

He slipped his hand up my sleep shirt, his fingers splayed on my belly. His thumb ran in circles, keeping my tumbling emotions from spiraling into darkness. A Blow Pop clacked against his teeth, the scent of cherries on his every exhale above my head.

"Maybe you ought to try calling," he murmured.

Wyatt hadn't texted back, and as the hours had slipped past, anxiety built up inside me. He never went that long without getting in touch with me whenever I used to reach out first. Had something happened to him? Had he changed his mind about me? Us?

Even though my heart was full from finally having my koala back, sadness and regret hung over my mind. Wyatt hadn't done anything to warrant my silence. It had been the abandonment wounds of my childhood that slapped walls between us—all my doing.

Had I fucked things up beyond repair?

"I'm afraid to call," I finally admitted, my voice small and insecure as fuck.

"There's nothing to fear, Hal. He's been hurting just as much as both of us. Trust me. Trust *him*."

I huffed an exhale. "I hate being patient."

"I think he'll be worth it," Garrett murmured, snuggling in closer, his hard body cradling me from head to toes.

His warmth seeped through my sleep shirt to my skin, and I closed my eyes against the action flick I wasn't paying attention to. Wyatt between us would definitely be incomparable, but anxiety kept my insides restless.

I couldn't lay still and kept rearranging my body, trying to get comfortable.

Garrett shifted with me—and a wet, sticky pop pressed against my lips. "Here. It's the best kind of distraction."

I grabbed the Blow Pop from his hand. "There are things way better than candy to distract my mind," I muttered.

"Yeah, but my dick is toast, and the last time I tried to kiss your pretty little pussy, you slapped my head because of overstimulation."

I snickered at that memory. "Never in a million years did I think I would tell a man to stop eating me out."

"Mmm." Garrett snuggled in close again, burying his face in my neck. "You smell good."

We'd showered together, and Garrett had worshiped every inch of me before tenderly drying me off and slathering my lavender lotion over my skin. It's a wonder we didn't just fall back into bed and pass the fuck out considering how little sleep we'd gotten.

But our stomachs had needed substance from the day-long fuckfest we had partaken in.

I closed my eyes, crunched the lollipop to smithereens, then put the gum back in the wrapper on the coffee table in front of me.

"You didn't even enjoy it," Garrett said with a chuckle.

"Sure I did." I tried to get comfy again, pulling his arm over my torso, threading our fingers atop my heart. Heaving a heavy sigh, I closed my eyes and focused on the weariness that physical and emotional exhaustion held over my body. "Wanna sleep."

Garrett nosed at the back of my head. "I'll snuggle you while you do."

The warmth of him eventually dragged my beat ass into calming darkness.

Strong arms held me, and the world swayed beneath me while I floated on air.

I snuggled against my koala's hard chest, sighing in my contented, half-conscious state as he carried me into my bedroom. My smile expanded when I curled on my bed, ready to be the little spoon.

Garrett wrapped his body around my back.

The mattress dipped in front of me, and my eyelids jerked open.

Wyatt slid beneath my comforter, scooting toward me.

I launched forward out from beneath Garrett's arm and plastered myself to tattooed skin and thick muscle. Wyatt smelled of soap and male virility, and I breathed him deep into my lungs as tears stung my eyes.

"I'm sorry," I whispered, throwing my leg over his bare thigh and latching onto him like a damn leech, my face smooshed against his neck.

Wyatt ran his fingers through my hair with tender strokes. "*I'm* sorry for thinking I knew what was best for the three of us and leaving without a word. I should have figured out how that would make you feel."

"And I should have gotten my head out of my ass and realized how my silence would affect you. Damnit, Wyatt, I'm so fucking sorry for being such a selfish bitch."

"I don't think you have anything to apologize for, but I'll gladly give you my forgiveness if that's what you need, my sweet Haley."

His possessive words drew a sigh from my lungs. I pulled back enough to see his gorgeous blue eyes. "Will you stay this time?"

He cradled my face in his hands, his steady gaze open and so damn vulnerable my heart swelled with longing. "If you'll have me."

I snorted and reached behind me, grasping for the man who should have followed along after me to keep my back warm. "Of course we want you, Wyatt. You belong with us. I'm guessing you and Garrett already made up?"

"Yeah," they both murmured at the same time, a hint of a smile in their husky voices that quivered my insides.

"And I fucking missed it," I grumbled, my own lips curled upward. "You're gonna have to give me a show tomorrow when I'm fully awake and can enjoy the hell out of watching you two love on each other."

"Whatever you want. Anything," Wyatt promised, his breath hot against my forehead.

I tipped my head back. "Kiss me."

Wyatt chuckled and lazed his mouth over mine, and even though I wanted to climb aboard and ride him until I fell over, my body didn't have the energy to rouse from near slumber.

"I'm sorry," I said against his lips, my chest full and aching as every single piece of me—around me—clicked into peaceful place.

He kissed my nose and forehead again as I shimmied down a bit to nuzzle my face over his chest. "So am I."

"We're good?" I mumbled, my eyelids sliding shut.

"So good I don't even have the words," he murmured against my hair.

Garrett pressed in tight against me, reaching over me to clutch at Wyatt's back. Both men made contented sounds that rumbled through me, and a shiver slid over my skin, pebbling every inch of my body.

"Oh, my fucking *God*, this is divine." I soaked in the warmth, the feel of two hard and sexy as hell bodies wrapped tight around me.

I pressed my cheek against Wyatt's smooth skin, listening to his heart thrum in my ear. Garrett's beat heavily against my spine. Sexual exhaustion still clung to my body even as I tried to stay awake and enjoy being right where I hoped to spend eternity.

My lips tingled to taste Wyatt's again. I wanted to watch Wyatt and Garrett devour each other's mouths.

But the warm comfort, the sense of *rightness* from being nestled between them, weighed against my mind.

I passed the fuck out.

* * *

Darkness outlined my blinds when I opened my eyes.

I burned like a damn furnace and couldn't move to kick my blankets off.

Hot flesh on my front.

Even hotter skin against my back.

A calloused hand rubbed over my hip, and another softer one ran up my same thigh. Both dipped lower on opposite sides of my body, and I gasped as fingertips grazed over my bare mound and my ass crack.

Oh hell.

Arousal flooded my system, bringing me fully awake.

"Fuck," I whispered, drawing chuckles from both chests still pressed against me.

"Sorry if we woke you up," Garrett murmured against my hair, his fingertips feathering over my clit.

"No you're not." I lifted my leg, tossing it over Wyatt's waist, baring myself to both of their wandering hands.

"Haley." Wyatt nosed along my cheek bone, down toward my lips, and I tilted my head back to meet him.

Soft and gentle, he teased my mouth with his, same as his fingers ghosted over the hole I'd promised him.

My core spasmed at the thought of being stuffed full of dick, and I opened to Wyatt's flickering tongue. He sank into my mouth with a groan. Middle of the night breath, sweeter than should be legal, filled my nose as Wyatt blew my ever loving mind with his sensual kiss. He stroked between my lips as Garrett's fingers probed deep into my slick core.

I reached back and grabbed hold of Garrett's head, and he rutted against the back of Wyatt's hand still teasing my asshole.

Wyatt's hard length pressed against my leg, but he began moving in time with his tongue, smearing pre-cum close to the junction of my thighs.

Breathing heavily in my ear, Garrett slipped his fingers from my pussy.

I moaned a complaint against Wyatt's mouth, but the thick head of Wyatt's length rubbed over my lower lips with intentional strokes.

Garrett's doing, I realized as Wyatt stuttered for breath and Garrett's knuckles brushed over my inner leg.

My koala knew exactly what I wanted—and how.

So. Fucking. Hot.

A shudder ripped through me, and I grasped at Wyatt's shoulder. "Please," I whispered on his lips.

He pulled away from my mouth completely as Garrett continued to tease me with the thick head of Wyatt's dick. "Bare?"

"Remember what I told you the first time we discussed sex?" I murmured, trying to see his eyes in the darkness. No such fucking luck, goddamnit.

Wyatt let out a shaky exhale and clutched at my ass tighter. "Did you already give yourself to our man?"

"Yes," I didn't hesitate to reply, and Wyatt's low groan fluttered my pulse.

"And you want that with me too?"

"Desperately," I assured him of the longing in my heart where there was more than room enough for both of them.

Garrett cupped my pussy—and Wyatt slid between his fingers, breaching my body.

"Oh God," I croaked, fingernails digging into Wyatt's skin.

He let out a slow hiss while sinking into my core. So hot that sweat broke out on my upper lip. So thick I winced at the sting in my pussy from overuse.

"Okay?" Garrett whispered against my ear, gently rubbing my clit he'd taken to beyond sensitive the day before.

"Mmm." I pressed my lips tight, thankful as fuck Wyatt held still inside me, allowing me to adjust. "Want you too," I told Garrett, reaching back for his hair again.

"No fucking way you can take us both, Hal. I used you too damn hard yesterday."

"Not my pussy. In my ass."

"Oh fuck." Garrett groaned the word out, his forehead hitting my shoulder.

"Lube up," Wyatt told him, his cock still too thick and throbbing deep in my core. "Give our girl what she wants."

My throat went tight at his possessive, commanding words. Nothing had ever sounded so right or settled peace inside my heart so much.

Garrett rolled away, and cool air licked over my back, but he returned seconds later. At the snap of a cap, I shivered even though fire seared my insides. He kissed my shoulder, moving in closer. Wet fingers traced over my hole.

"You sure?" Garrett murmured against my skin.

"Give it to me."

"Goddamnit do I love when you two get bossy." He dipped his slick fingertip into my ass.

"More," I demanded, bearing down enough that he pushed all the way in to his knuckle.

Wyatt cursed, his dick jerking inside me where he hadn't made a single move to fuck me.

"Wait until it's his cock." I moaned at Wyatt as Garrett felt around inside me.

"Garrett," Wyatt warned, his voice nothing more than a low rasp.

"Gotta get her ready." Garrett stroked a few times while I shivered, and Wyatt cursed.

Another finger slid in, and the scissoring began.

"Move," Garrett said, and Wyatt shifted out a mere inch and gently thrust back in.

Fucking stars exploded behind my eyelids. "Shit." I swallowed hard and groaned, my nerve endings lighting up. "If you don't put your dick inside me right now, Garrett Moore—"

Three fingers.

"Oh fuck." I tipped my forehead to Wyatt's chest and panted, every slow glide of his thick cock in and out of my slick pussy heightening my pulse and the readiness for release. "Garrett—please. Fucking hell, I need you."

My asshole gaped at the sudden loss of his fingers, and I gasped.

"Easy," he said, his mouth once more on my shoulder. "Let me in, baby."

Too fucking broad of a cockhead rubbed over my hole, and I forced myself to relax.

Wyatt backed out all the way, leaving me completely empty, but Garrett pushed.

My back arched on instinct, and I bore down, determined to take him. It had been years since I'd given my ass to someone, and Christ in heaven, the burn…

"Fuck. Holy shit." I gasped—and he breached the first ring of muscle.

"Jesus fuck." Garrett shuddered against my back. "You're so fucking tight."

I swallowed repeatedly, desperate for the ache to ease.

Wyatt moved his mouth over mine, and I sank into his kiss, quickly losing myself to his breath, his tongue stroking with languid licks.

I settled, relaxing into their gentle hands.

Garrett pushed, gaining a few inches. Slowly, he worked his way into my ass, his hands roaming my belly, my breasts. He tweaked my nipples, pinching lightly.

I went lightheaded with arousal, breathless from Wyatt's kiss.

Ready to tumble into oblivion with my men.

Chapter 39

Garrett

Hal's hot ass clutched at my dick, and I had to keep my teeth clenched so I wouldn't fill up her hole with cum before Wyatt even put his dick back into her.

"You're doing so well, Hal," I half-hissed the words, my lips pressed against her shoulder. "So hot and tight. Fucking perfect."

She'd taken all but two inches of me.

I pulled out to the head, the copious amount of lube I'd used to ensure easy entry making wet noises.

"Fuck." I grabbed hold of her hips, looking down and not able to make out a goddamn thing. "Turn the lamp on, Wyatt. I need to see her—both of you."

The bed shifted as he moved, and sudden light spilled over our sweaty bodies.

Haley's ass stretched around my girth, so fucking pink and pretty that my balls pulled up tight.

Slowly, I pushed back into her body, sliding deep...so fucking deep...

She released a low, guttural groan as I bottomed out, my balls resting against her body.

"Fuck, Hal." I choked on an inhale, panting through my nose. "Wyatt."

He snaked an arm beneath her—and me—to clutch at my shoulder.

His other hand moved between them, and he smeared his pre-cum slickened head over my balls.

I let out a hiss, and met his eyes.

Same as when I'd met him at the front door before devouring his mouth, black pupils overtook the sky-blue, shot through with lust and a ton of emotion I didn't have words for. I ate that shit up like a goddamn cherry lollipop.

He held my gaze and shifted.

"Oh God." Haley's head tipped back against me, and I gritted my teeth as Wyatt eased into her pussy, a mere fucking membrane of skin between our dicks, making her ass even tighter around my girth. "Shit. Fucking hell...oh my *fucking* God."

Haley groaned. Shuddered. Shifted between us.

"Shh." Wyatt finally tore his focus off my face and leaned down to brush his lips over her mouth. "Need me to stop?"

"Fuck no," she shot out, grabbing hold of his head. "Kiss me."

He sank his tongue between her parted lips, pushing into her pussy with his thick dick at the same time.

Their groans mingled, and I tugged down on my balls to keep from erupting.

So. Fucking. Tight.

I fought like hell to keep still until he buried deep with me. My entire groin throbbed, muscles tensing with the instinctive need to thrust.

Haley finally went lax between us, her shuddered breaths swallowed by Wyatt's hungry mouth.

Fuck, were they beautiful together. So goddamn hot.

I didn't realize I began moving my hips until they both cursed.

But there was no stopping what I'd started.

As I shoved in, Wyatt backed out, and Haley's groaned curses didn't contain a hint of discomfort. She began rocking along with us, fucking herself on whichever dick thrust into her.

She scratched down Wyatt's chest.

Pulled my hair.

Clenched her perfect hold around my length.

"Fucking hell, Hal. Your ass is divine. Want to fuck you until you come all over Wyatt's cock. Soak him like you did me, baby."

"Shit." Wyatt clenched his jaw, once more catching my focus. He grabbed my other shoulder. "Roll."

As though of the same mind, we moved as a whole unit, Wyatt flat on his back, Haley settling atop him, straddling his waist.

Somehow, we stayed connected, my dick on the brink of popping out of Haley's ass.

I slid my knees firmly beneath me, grasped her narrow hips, and sank fully into her silken heat that rivaled Wyatt's for perfection.

Her hair spread out in a wave of maroon, over Wyatt's chest and the white sheet beneath his body. Cheek resting on his pec, she panted, clinging to his torso as though drowning in a sea of emotion.

The feelings inside my chest echoed what I saw through her actions, and the second my eyes latched onto Wyatt's, I fucking fell, my heart bottoming out beneath me. He owned my heart in equal measure as Haley—completely, without question.

"Come here." He grasped the side of my neck, and I went willingly, giving him my mouth. My goddamn soul.

His tongue tasted as sweet as cherries with a hint of Haley on his exhale.

We stroked in and out of her in opposing movements, our tongues fucking each other's mouths.

Overstimulated by the feel of him dragging through Haley's pussy, I quickly lost myself to the instinct to move.

Faster. Harder.

Grunts pushed from Haley's lungs accompanied by moans for more. "Please," she whispered, her voice breaking.

I tore my mouth from Wyatt's and rocked back onto my heels, spreading her cheeks.

Wyatt thrust into her pussy, backing out to make way for me up her ass, and I groaned as her pink hole clutched at my girth.

The scent of sex and sweat mingled in the air with the sounds of wet fucking, lewd schlicking noises of lube, pre-cum, and the cream of her arousal.

Too much.

Not nearly enough.

Planking on one arm over my lovers, I reached between their slick bodies—contracting abs and soft flesh.

I found her clit, swollen and hard.

She mewled, and I rubbed.

Wyatt cursed, his head tipping back and neck cording. "Need you to come for us," he said through gritted teeth.

"Hal," I whispered and pinched, thrusting in deep.

Wetness erupted over my fingers, her shriek filling my ears.

"Fuuuuck, yeah. Such a good girl." Wyatt groaned, his dick throbbing against the back of mine.

I stroked once more. Twice.

A shudder ripped through my spine, bowing me forward. Cum shot through my dick, pulsing, flooding Haley's ass with spunk.

"Jesus." I gulped and thrust again, her tightness like fucking heaven clutching at my pulsing dick.

Planked over them, my head hung low as one last spasm twitched my length inside her body.

"Holy shit." I panted and sank back onto my heels, slowly dragging my cock from Haley's ass. Globs of white slid from her gaping hole before it closed.

I shoved my cum back into her body.

She hissed like a feisty cat, and I kissed the base of her spine with a chuckle.

"Love you, Hal," I said, stroking my cum-soaked thumb into her one more time.

"Go suck a dick," she muttered, then melted over Wyatt's chest like butter when I slipped my finger free from her body.

"I would, but you're still sitting on the only one I want."

Wyatt's eyelids cracked open, sated eyes peering up at me. He raised an eyebrow.

I raised one in return.

Lifting Haley off him earned the next hiss from her lips, but he tucked her in tight against his side, neither caring over the mess dripping from her core.

"Suck his dick," Haley murmured again but with lust in her tone rather than annoyance.

He was still hard even though I'd felt his release pulse through his cock. Spunk-covered, he was thick and fucking perfect.

I sprawled out on my belly between his thighs, nosing along his wet, soft sack. He smelled like Haley's pussy, musky and mouthwatering. A flick of my tongue coated my taste buds in her familiar flavor and the bitter saltiness of his release.

Lapping again earned me a low moan from Wyatt, and Haley pushed up onto her elbow.

Her gaze caught mine, and I grinned while licking up the backside of Wyatt's dick. She bit her lower lip as I closed my mouth over him, sucking him in deep.

"Oh my god, you two." Haley wiggled her ass like watching me blow Wyatt made her needy again. "You're so fucking hot."

"Mmm." I hollowed my cheeks and gave Wyatt my eyes.

The blue of his had hazed over, his free hand clutching at the sheets as he fought to lay still and just enjoy my attention.

I popped off, teasing his slit with the tip of my tongue, probing and searching for a hint of pre-cum. Licks and nibbles—but never taking him into my mouth. His gaze went hot, and I didn't relent in my intention to drive him to the brink.

"Christ." Wyatt shifted his arm from beneath Haley, and he grabbed hold of my head.

Yes.

"Open up."

Like Haley, his bossiness made my dick want to harden again.

I stuck out my tongue and relaxed my throat, knowing exactly what he wanted.

He yanked me down, and I closed my lips around him once more, allowing him to fuck into my throat.

Wyatt didn't hold back, and I never would have guessed he'd emptied a load in Haley's pussy minutes earlier if I hadn't seen it happen. Pre-cum coated my tongue, a salty tang I couldn't get enough of. I wanted to shove the tip of my tongue into his slit again, but he didn't offer me a chance.

My throat went raw, my jaw ached from his thrusts, but still I held his stare, gladly submitting to whatever the fuck he needed to release inside my body.

Haley found my hand grasping at Wyatt's thighs, and she laced her fingers through mine. I hung onto her and pleased our man. We had gotten Wyatt back into her bed—*our* bed—and I wanted him to know the same sense of belonging I'd felt the second he and I had both pressed in tight against Haley.

Giving myself to Wyatt was no mistake, same as loving Haley had never been. In my heart, I recognized we were meant to be together.

"Shit…" He cursed again, his voice nothing but husky rasp on the verge of release. "I'm gonna come."

"Mmm," I hummed my approval and swallowed around the length shoved so fucking deep I couldn't breathe.

"Take it all, Garrett—"

Wet heat erupted down my esophagus, and my ears drowned in Wyatt's groans.

Haley squeezed my fingers and sighed. Life couldn't be any more perfect.

Chapter 40
Wyatt

I collapsed onto the mattress beneath my back that was wet from sweat and cum. Blessed oxygen flooded my lungs, and I gasped for more, my mind buzzing, my limbs tingling.

One last twitch shuddered through me, and I moaned, going lax.

"I want to taste him on your tongue," Haley murmured, climbing over me to reach Garrett's mouth.

He popped off my softening dick, swiping a drop of cum he'd missed from the corner of his mouth with his thumb while propping himself up with his other hand. "Here." He held his thumb out, and Haley wrapped her lips around his finger, sucking.

"Holy shit." I choked on an inhale, gaze plastered on the two of them as she went to move away.

He twined his fingers in her hair and pulled her back in, taking her lips in a slow, sensual kiss that had to curl her toes. I knew how Garrett used his mouth, and goddamn, I wanted to be his Blow Pop over and over again.

Every fucking morning.

Every goddamn night.

My dick attempted to twitch back to life at Haley's soft sighs.

I twisted my upper body so I could see them better, staring as he suckled on her lower lip, nipping, and licking.

"Love you, Hal," he whispered, and a pang radiated through my chest.

"Love you too." Her declaration, her wide smile as they pulled back and stared at each other knocking the air from my lungs.

I'd seen it—

Now, I've heard it.

Unease began to twine around my guts regardless of Haley allowing me inside her body without a condom, and I shifted out of an instinctive need to protect myself.

Garrett's vise-like hands grasped my hips, holding me still.

Haley laid her palm against my chest, right above my heart.

Both sets of eyes roamed my face as though seeking out my thoughts.

"You belong with us," Haley stated firmly, the heat of her hand, the press of her fingertips on my skin seeming to mark me clear through to my soul.

"Maybe we weren't persuasive enough?" Garrett suggested, a smirk curling up one corner of his mouth before he sucked his lower lip between his teeth. "What do we need to do to make you realize that you're under our skin? In our heads—our hearts?"

"It's too soon," I tossed out what my mind grasped at— what my conscience assured me of. There was no fucking way they felt for me what they did for each other after a few short weeks.

"Is it?" Haley asked, her voice soft and soothing. She moved her hot touch off my chest, her fingers peeling mine from the sheet. Grasping the back of my hand, she lifted my palm, placing it over her heart. "Feel that?"

Holding her stare, the dark eyes I wanted to fall into, I nodded.

"It's split in two."

I blinked, thinking she'd been hurt—

"One half belongs to Garrett. The other to you," she whispered, stopping the way my mind had gone. "I don't know how, can't explain it, but you're...a part of me. A piece of home I hadn't realized I'd been missing. You're security—the perfect line the two of us needed to create beauty where a whole lot of rot existed before this began."

We were covered in sweat and cum, but I didn't give a shit. Tears welled my eyes, and I pulled them both up beside me in a tangle of limbs.

"I—I have to tell you what happened yesterday." I swallowed hard, and holding their hands, I shared with them the story of a little boy who'd had his heart broken—but how the man had come to realize that he'd already found his place and no longer needed to go searching for more.

We showered together, cramped in Haley's bathroom, but none of us were willing to let the other go. Giggles and full-on laughter accompanied my sudsy, slick attempts at cleaning them both from heads to toes.

At least things didn't progress into a sexy feast of body parts.

There was no goddamn space to maneuver.

I had plenty of room in my house though, a big enough shower for the three of us to get feisty and fuck whenever the hell we wanted.

We stripped Haley's queen-sized bed, put on a fresh set of sheets, and they ended up cuddling the hell out of me. I had so much love and affection to lavish them with, and they gave themselves to me, showing me all I'd been missing. With her AC window unit cranked to high and no blankets atop us, we managed to enjoy the warmth of one another without overheating.

Lingering kisses, a few wandering hands with loving caresses, and I ordered them both to sleep.

On my back, staring at the dark ceiling I couldn't quite make out, I hugged Garrett against my left, his hot breath ghosting over my chest. Haley snuggled into my right, her small hand tangled with Garrett's atop my heart, her hair a wild, damp mess cascading over my shoulder.

We all smelled like her bodywash—herbs and flowers, a soothing scent that filled my lungs and pulled me into oblivion with a smile on my face.

Wet suction on my dick roused me back to reality.

Early morning sunlight streamed around the edges of Haley's blinds. She still clung to me, her breaths steady and even.

Garrett had made himself at home a bit lower, using my body to satisfy his oral fixation.

"Run out of lollipops?" I asked, my voice hoarse from sleep.

"Mmm." He swirled his tongue around my swelling head, his tongue dipping into my slit. "I like the taste of you better."

I groaned, and Haley stirred against me. She stretched.

He sucked.

"Oh fuck," she whispered, her breath hot on my pec where her face rested.

Garrett popped off me in a mess of saliva dripping over my balls and grinned. "If that's what you want..." He straddled me, grabbed my hardened dick—and sank over my stiff cock with one downward thrust.

"Holy shit!" I bowed upward at the sudden slick heat clamping around me, jostling Haley off me. "Oh my god...fucking hell, Garrett." I choked on a breath and laid back again, my hands finding his thighs.

He'd lubed up his ass for me...

"Dickmonger," Haley said with a chuckle and settled back against me, her fingers finding my nipples to tweak at the suddenly stiffened peaks. Zings of lust shot straight to my groin.

Garrett gyrated his hips, his hot ass clamped around my throbbing length, and I bit my lip to keep from begging him to fuck himself harder. Faster.

"How long were you laying here fingering yourself open for him, hmm?" Haley asked, her other hand wrapping around Garrett's leaking dick.

"Ten minutes." Garrett swiveled his hips and rose up, only to sink back down again, his abdominal muscles rippling, that goddamn V beneath my thumbs flexing.

My eyes rolled back into my head, and I dug my fingers into his skin, trying to stay still and let him have what he wanted.

"I've been dreaming about this moment," Haley murmured, jerking him and pinching me. "Show me how well you take dick, Garrett."

Fuck, I loved how she bossed him around. Even more, I loved how Garrett attempted to give her everything she asked for, riding me hard, moving his body and angling to rub my dick over his prostate.

"Oh yeah." He bit his lip and sank down onto me again. "Right there."

"Fuck, I wish I had a dick," Haley murmured, her gaze plastered to where I filled Garrett. "I would love to own that piece of you."

"The strap-on offer still stands," Garrett gasped out, and I clenched my jaw to keep from filling his ass prematurely.

My hips moved on their own, thrusting up into Garrett's hot ass, and he let out a low, guttural moan.

"Just like that," he said, arching his back. "Fuck, Hal... your hand feels so fucking good wrapped around me.

"Suck him, Haley," I told her, knowing her lips and tongue would be ten times better.

"Want my mouth?" she whispered at Garrett.

"Yes." he gasped as I thrust upward, buried to the hilt. "Fuck yes."

She scooted, and I released one of Garrett's hips to make room for her, my entire body tight and ready to explode.

My fingers dug into Garrett's thigh, my other hand grabbing Haley's pert ass cheek.

"Ah, fuck." I gritted my teeth and tried to hold still and not blow early while Garrett rode me and our sweet Haley sucked him down. The wet sounds, their moans and groans...fuck, I wasn't going to last much longer. "Goddamn."

Haley stilled, allowing Garrett to find his own rhythm, fucking onto me, then lifting into her mouth.

I wished for a closeup video of what went down atop my groin and told myself someday...

"Hal." Garrett croaked out her name, grabbing hold of her hair. "Gonna come."

"Yes—fuck yes," I moaned.

Haley hummed her agreement.

"Fuck." Garrett's throat went corded—and his ass clamped down on my cockhead.

"Christ!" I thrust up, burying myself in his heat. Cum shot up through my dick, filling his ass as he flooded Haley's mouth, gagging her. My fingertips bruised against their skin, but I held on for dear *fucking* life while emptying my spunk. Marking my territory like a damn dog who panted for breath.

Mine.

Both of them.

A shudder ripped through me, and as Haley went to slide off my torso, I pulled her up to my mouth. Her tongue tasted like salt and bitterness with a hint of her sweetness beneath, and I stroked deeper, seeking out more.

Still impaled, Garrett sank over us, his lips finding my neck.

We were a cocoon of warmth, sweat, and rightness.

I'd found my place, and nothing and no one would make me leave them again.

I considered the smallness of her shower, her bed. While I felt it was too soon to invite the two of them to move in with me, I decided to be selfish for once. I was going to make what I yearned for happen for a change. I wanted them with me all the time, and since they stated they needed me to help guide their messy lives, I was going to take the reins.

Chapter 41

Haley

The scent of coffee filled my lungs, and I breathed deeply, starting to stretch.

"Ow." I grimaced at the sting between my thighs, the day and night before flooding my head with delicious memories.

So. Fucking. Worth it.

A wide grin replaced the pinched expression on my lips, and I relished in the sweet ache.

A low murmur of voices made me crack my eyelids open, and I realized I was the only one in my bed. One more languid stretch and I rolled off the mattress.

Wyatt's T-shirt lay on the floor, and I snatched it up, filling my lungs with his scent as it settled over my head and fell to mid-thigh. Tingles spread through my core, and I bit back a smirk.

There was no way I was taking a dick again anytime soon—in either hole.

I padded on silent feet down the hallway, pulling up short in the kitchen doorway.

Garrett leaned against the counter beside the coffeepot, Wyatt plastered to his front. Their mouths fused, and Garrett had a firm hold on Wyatt's backside. Both wore lounge pants low on their gyrating hips.

Heavy breaths.

Panted moans.

And coffee finishing its perking...

Warmth and arousal rushed through me, and I grinned like an idiot. A kid in a damn candy store.

I moved closer because *coffee*.

Wyatt stood with his back to me, and I grabbed hold of his ass alongside Garrett's hand, squeezing while reaching for the cabinet beside them for a mug.

Their mouths tore apart.

"Don't stop on account of me," I murmured. Hot dark and blue eyes both flashed over my face, and my grin widened. "Please continue."

Wyatt sank to his knees, taking Garrett's sweats to the floor with him, and my hand trembled while pouring myself a cup of coffee.

Garrett gripped the counter at his sides, and I held his gaze until he groaned and swallowed hard. Both of us looked down, and lust shot through my pussy at the sight of Wyatt's nose pressed against Garrett's groin, his mouth full of cock.

"My god." I croaked the words and shuffled backward for the table, my mug clutched in my hands.

My men were so damn beautiful, and I sank into a chair to enjoy the show.

I sipped on autopilot, not even tasting my coffee, my gaze riveted on Wyatt loving on my koala. Grunts and groans, the wet sounds of a sloppy blowjob, and curses filled my ears and dampened between my tightly clenched thighs.

Our honeymoon phase was going to be a fuckfest for the ages.

Nipples hard and core aching, I memorized the sight of Wyatt's dark head moving over Garrett's groin. Fingers pulling on mussed hair. Veined forearms. Rippling muscle over bare shoulders. Flexing pecs and a throbbing pulse along a neck.

Dark eyes hazed by passion firmly fixed on my face.

"Hal," Garrett rasped my name, sending butterflies to flight in my belly and goosebumps over my skin.

"Give it to him," I whispered.

"Fuck." Garrett's head tipped back, eyelids falling shut in a look I'd lusted over the day before. He came. Hard and in body-wrenching spurts, and I found myself swallowing as though he filled my watering mouth.

He gasped. Shuddered. Went lax against the counter.

Wyatt made an appreciative noise before standing, pulling up Garrett's sweats along with him. Their lips met in a languid kiss as Wyatt tucked Garrett's package away.

Smirking, turned on, but only wanting to enjoy my arousal, I sipped my coffee as my lovers shared the taste of Garrett's spunk on Wyatt's tongue.

Eventually, Wyatt backed off. He glanced over his shoulder, pink high on his cheeks, his eyes crystalline and more content than I'd seen before.

"Hi," I said, knowing my own orbs revealed the same thoughts and feelings inside me. "Thanks for the coffee." I grinned. "And the show."

"You're welcome." He winked and turned back toward Garrett, kissing him on the nose. "Sit. Let me get your coffee."

Garrett sank boneless into the only other chair we had at the table, and my gaze flitted between him and Wyatt moving around the kitchen to ready their mugs. Too much skin and delicious muscle.

"Sensory overload," I murmured, my brain absolute mush. Good thing I didn't have to work.

I pushed aside the flash of sudden negative feelings over my lack of a job as Wyatt turned toward us, a coffee in either hand. He glanced between us and the lack of a third chair.

"Living room?" he suggested.

Usually, Garrett and I would snuggle on the couch, but I realized things were going to change—definitely for the best.

I plopped down first since I refused to be the last one standing and needing to make a choice.

Wyatt sat on my left, and glancing between us, Garrett chuckled before settling on my right.

"How the fuck do poly relationships work?" he asked, angling toward me and lifting my leg over his.

"However we want," I said with a shrug. "Whatever feels right."

Wyatt sipped his coffee and stood back up. Garrett and I watched silently as he moved the coffee table and dragged the adjacent chair in front of us. He sat and pulled my foot not dangling between Garrett's spread thighs onto his lap.

His dark eyes flitted over us, that contentment still radiating.

What would be weird and uncomfortable to a lot of people swelled happiness up inside me as warm, calloused palms caressed my thigh and foot.

I grinned like an idiot, thinking I could definitely get used to their pampering. "So." I breathed the word. "Now what?"

"You come to work for me too, you both move into my house, and we live happily ever after."

Garrett coughed at Wyatt's firm statement, and I stared, searching Wyatt's face.

He was serious.

His gaze stayed on mine. "Garrett told me how you finally stood up for yourself, and I'm so damn proud of you."

My eyes stung.

"Lionel's Landscaping has expanded past the point of my ability to both manage and labor, and since I'm not willing to give up the latter... I need someone to organize my life, someone who's good with customers. How about becoming my secretary, sweet Haley?"

A ping shot through my chest. "You're offering me a job?" I asked, my lips quirking even though wetness hazed my eyes.

"It's yours if you're willing to accept it—same as my heart."

"Oh, fuck," I murmured as a rush of elation rose inside me to choking levels.

Garrett laced his fingers through mine and squeezed tight. I clung to him.

"We're really doing this, aren't we?" I asked in no more than a whisper.

The two men glanced at each other, that crackle of energy between them lifting the hairs on my arms, but when they turned toward me as though of the same mind, my breath left in a rush.

"I want you both," Wyatt said.

"I'm a greedy bastard," Garrett added.

"*Brat*," I corrected him, squeezing his fingers and snickering, my heart full to bursting.

"Well?" Wyatt pushed, pulling my focus back toward him.

"You're serious, aren't you?" I asked, the silliness fading along with my smirk.

"I already told Garrett he's going to move back in with me, but I need you there too, Haley. It'll be awkward as fuck sometimes, I'm sure. Uncomfortable. But I'm determined to try. I have so much love inside me, and my body aches to give you both the affection and attention you want."

"He's willing to be my living lollipop, Hal," Garrett added his two cents, and I burst back into laughter.

"You might change your mind," I warned Wyatt, my breasts and nipples aching at the memory of being on the receiving end of Garrett's oral fixation. "He's insatiable."

Wyatt grinned, so damn gorgeous that a pulse radiated between my thighs. "I wouldn't have him any other way."

I inhaled deeply and let the exhale leak slowly until my lungs emptied. "Yeah."

"Yeah?" Wyatt echoed, his eyes lighting.

"I'm willing to put in the work if you two are."

"Oh, thank fuck." Garrett set his mug on the table beside him and wrapped his arms around my waist. My fingers found his hair as always.

Wyatt's gaze caressed over us, a soft smile on his lips. "So." His focus lifted from Garrett's face to mine. "Can you start Monday morning?"

Sudden tears welled in my eyes at the raw honest vulnerability in his. "Yes."

"And is it too soon to tell you I'm desperately in love with both of you?" Wyatt asked, his gaze flicking between the two of us.

I choked on the tightness of my throat. "No—because I love you too."

"Fuck." Garrett swiped at his eyes. "You had to go and say the words I've been dying to hear...love you too, Wyatt. So damn much it hurts."

I wiggled my fingers toward Wyatt, and he sat on my other side. Threading my fingers through his hair, I glanced between my two men. Dark and blue eyes roamed over my face, landing on my lips.

"Kiss me."

They did.

And we ended up giggling in a tangled mess of limbs on the living room floor.

Chapter 42
Garrett

A staccato rap sounded on the door, and I shifted away from Haley's back where we sprawled on the hard floor. "I'll get it."

While still grinning like a damn idiot, I pulled open the door ready to share my joy with the world, holler it from the highest mountain—

I blinked at the man filling the apartment doorway, my lips falling flat. "Alec."

A rustle of movement sounded behind me, drawing my ex's focus off my face. A furrow flitted over his brow before he turned his attention back to me.

He smiled with a coy curl of his lips I used to find sexy as hell, the interest in his eyes that at one time had made me want to fall to my knees and worship his dick.

I stood unmoved, my heart a damn flatline when it came to Alec Henley. "What do you want?" I sounded more resigned than pissed off that he'd shown up and interrupted one of the happiest moments I'd ever experienced. I just needed him gone again so I could enjoy the beginning of the rest of my life.

"I missed you."

One of my eyebrows raised. It was more likely he hated the fact his dancing with that twink hadn't gotten under my skin and he'd lost that sense of power he'd always held over me.

"It took me awhile to find you, but I wanted to apologize." He licked over his lower lip but not in a sexual manner. More like he tried to bring moisture to his mouth. "And ask for a second chance. No one loves me like you do, Garrett."

I opened my mouth to tell him to fuck off, but he held up a trembling hand.

"I confronted Sindy. She admitted to lying about what went down that night. I'm so fucking sorry I didn't listen to you, baby, didn't let to explain. I can make this better—just give me a chance to remind you how good we were together—"

"Oh, please." Haley huffed a snort and manhandled her way into the entryway beside me, and the fire in her eyes, the imaginary claws extending from her fingertips turned me the fuck on.

"You manipulative little bitch," she spat at Alec, her hands finding her hips, and I bit back a grin. "This man's heart—his dick and mouth, are mine."

Alec scoffed, glancing down over her slight form covered in nothing more than the long T-shirt Wyatt had shown up in the night before. "You can't give Garrett what he needs."

She lifted her chin, seeming to look down at Alec even though he towered over her by close to a foot. "Maybe not exactly," she agreed, a smirk growing on her lush mouth, "but our *boyfriend* can."

Warmth caressed my back a heartbeat before Wyatt's arms wrapped around my waist, and he tugged me against his chest. His chin rested on my shoulder.

Haley slid in close, clutching to my side with her grabby hands.

Alec blinked as though processing what he saw—taking his good old time too. His brow furrowed, settling into a scowl as her words and both my lovers' actions registered. "You always were a greedy—"

"Careful," Wyatt warned, his low tone far from pleasant and neighborly.

Alec's lips clamped shut, and I lifted an eyebrow while threading my fingers through Wyatt's atop my stomach, my free arm wrapping around our girl.

"Obviously, my answer is no," I told him.

"You'll never make it in Hollywood," he hissed at me, his face mottling as it always did whenever he didn't get his way.

"I don't need my name in lights—that isn't my dream anymore. Turns out my reality is fifty times better than those old fantasies. Working beside the man who puts me first *every time*, coming home together to the prickliest, most empathetic woman who loves us more than anyone ever has...*that* is living. The *only* life I want."

I slammed the door in Alec's face and clicked the lock, shutting my ex and all things Hollywood out of my mind forever.

Haley snorted with laughter.

Wyatt hugged me tighter, his lips finding my neck.

"Boyfriend, huh?" I asked Haley, and she smiled up at me, her eyes luminous, the happiness on her face so fucking dazzling my chest ached.

"You've only got one." She stuck out her tongue. "I've got *two*."

"Yeah, well I have a better label for the two of you than that," I tossed out, grasping her ass and swinging her around in front of me so I was the one in the middle. "You're both *mine*."

"Damn right," Wyatt murmured, reaching around me to palm her other ass cheek.

Haley melted into me, her heart in her eyes. "It's about damn time."

Chapter 43

One Year Later

Haley

My father walked me up the aisle—or rather, held my elbow as we ambled barefoot through warm sand.

It had taken countless hours of therapy and tears for him and I to find understanding and forgiveness. Like I'd considered at my rock bottom all those months ago, I learned his own mother had been a narcissist who wrestled with psychosis.

Enough said.

We worked daily to create a relationship between us that we had missed out on, and just having him by my side on my wedding day made me realize we had done a good job of growing beyond our past trauma.

Flowers wove through my unbound hair rather than sitting in my hands, and I wore a simple gauzy white dress that fluttered around my knees in the ocean breeze.

River had picked it out for me. Perhaps a bit more bohemian than I'd have chosen, but it fit the venue. The men didn't care one way or the other where our wedding took place—they just wanted shit set in ink and vowed out loud.

The mortar between the pavers of our lives we'd set to lead us forward in life.

A handful of people stood as witnesses on either side of the path I traversed through the sand, but my focus stayed on the two waiting for me.

Wyatt to my right.

Garrett on the left.

Both watched me with smiles on their faces and tears in their eyes, and my own hazed over from the well of happiness filled to its brim.

It had been a long year full of ups and downs, misunderstandings, and attempts to not choose sides, but we made our polyamorous relationship work. We put in the hours, honored our dedication to always be truthful with each other, and I finally got the wedding I'd dreamed about but never hoped to have.

The Justice of the Peace we'd hired for our late afternoon ceremony behind Greyson, Blaine, and Lily's house had agreed to our strange request for three sets of vows even though only two could legally be on the marriage certificate.

My father kissed my cheek before handing me over to Wyatt and Garrett. He left us to settle beside my soon-to-be in-laws. Lionel and Tina had also claimed Garrett as a son. Me? I was their only daughter, thoroughly adored and spoiled rotten with motherly and fatherly love I soaked up like a sponge whenever given the opportunity.

Wyatt and Garrett threaded their fingers through mine, stepping in close so they could hold each other's against the small of my back.

Our friends and meager families hovered behind us, listening as the three of us exchanged promises to honor, love, and protect the ones we stood beside.

I refused to cry even as Tina sniffled behind me.

We had to separate to exchange rings, double bands that would be fused together the following day before we left for our honeymoon. Grey, Blaine, and Lily had gifted us a two-week vacation in Aruba, and I couldn't wait to escape for some much-needed rest after our busy summer.

Lionel's Landscaping had hired another crew and outfitted them to the nines in order to fulfill all our contracts.

Business was good, Wyatt claimed, because he had me at the helm and Garrett by his side. A dream team, he often called the three of us, and we were in every way.

We shared an awkward kiss as we often attempted in the privacy of our home and ended up in laughter along with our friends and family.

Our fingers entwined, we turned to accept congratulations and hugs.

Lily was the first to throw her arms around me, squealing and laughing. Her two men shook hands with mine, offering back slaps. The four had been forced to bond, and more often than not when we got together, they disappeared into a man cave to watch whatever sports was in season—if that was what it was called.

Lily and I shared a bottle of wine, not even bothering to try to understand talk about pucks, balls, or bats.

It was enough to just snuggle with her and watch our lovers laugh, bullshit, and rib each other.

That first night I'd been bracketed by Wyatt and Garrett's warm, hard bodies, I hadn't thought my life could get any better.

But I'd been wrong.

I enjoyed their affection on a daily basis. Heard words of edification and praise from both sets of lips.

Best of all?

Their unconditional love wrapped me up in the safest cocoon possible, giving my heart everything it needed to feel fulfilled.

✱ ✱ ✱

Wyatt

Rhett and Ash hung near the back of the group we'd invited to our small wedding, their hands clasped, shoulders touching. Rhett lifted the glass of champagne he held in his free hand, toasting me from afar.

I grinned and tipped my head his way.

It was because of the two of them that I'd found my place with Garrett and Haley—

River threw herself into my arms, ripping an *oomph* from my lungs and my thoughts off the couple I used to envy. My sister smelled like herbs—weed—and her laughter had me chuckling along with her.

"So. Damn. Happy." She hugged me hard and backed off, grabbing hold of my face and squeezing. "I knew things would work out. I could just tell. The aura around those two the first time I saw them—I could sense their love for you. Could taste it on the air. And now look." Her blue eyes sparkled like sapphires in the late afternoon sun as she waved her hand around what most wouldn't even consider a ceremony.

No archway to stand beneath.

No roses outside those in Haley's hair.

No string quartet.

But enough love to fill up my entire soul.

River's plus one stood off to the side, a wallflower compared to my sister—but no less beautiful. Sharon wasn't any taller than my sweet Haley, and the complete opposite looks-wise from my sister. Large dark eyes ate up the bulk of her pixie-like face, her white-blonde hair straight as a stick and barely brushing her shoulders.

She and my twin fit together like two pieces of a puzzle, madly in love and married within three months of meeting at their favorite medium's shop. River had said Sharon's aura had captured her heart, and the card reading had instilled what she'd expected.

She'd found her soulmate.

Lionel and Tina took up the space River vacated, Mom pulling me in for a hug, her mascara already ruined. Dad laid his hand on my shoulder, his throat working and eyes hazed with tears too.

"Thank you," I murmured against Mom's hair while pulling Dad in for a close hug. "For loving me. Accepting me—and the two I'm going to spend the rest of my life with."

Mom cupped my cheek, her smile wobbling. "You have been a blessing since day one, Wyatt. Love you so much. We couldn't be prouder of the man you've become. The choices you've made." Her voice broke, and I leaned down to kiss her cheek. One last squeeze, and she loosened her grip.

"Dad." I stuck out my hand, and we shook hard, both of us dipping our head as if to say ditto to all Mom had claimed.

A handful of other friends offered best wishes, and finally Rhett and Ash approached.

Ash tucked against Rhett's side, smiling with his lips but not his eyes.

"Congrats." He offered his hand while glancing at Haley talking to someone beside us.

They hadn't obtained the angel he dreamed about, the woman that would give him the children he longed for —and I felt a little guilty. Missing Link had been created for them—by them—and they still searched for their third.

I wasn't sure Rhett cared outside of wanting to please Ash, but it wasn't my business to get involved.

I shook Ash's hand and clasped his shoulder. "You'll find her," I murmured as River stepped in close again.

"I have a good feeling too," she said with a singsong voice, and I barely refrained from rolling my eyes. I expected the second we got inside that she'd be munching on the hors d'oeuvres the catering company had waiting for our small party.

She moved off as quickly as she'd intruded, Sharon's hand in hers as they started toward the stairs leading to Grey's balcony where cloth-covered tables and chairs offered a place to sit and enjoy the evening.

Rhett stared after the two of them, a...strange look on his face. Not disgust, but I could tell my sister wasn't his cup of tea.

"Yeah, she's a bit of a wild child," I agreed with what his expression said.

He quickly schooled his features when turning his focus back on me. "Whatever makes her wife happy," he stated with a shrug.

I expected if he had his way, Rhett's angel would be a straitlaced, stoic woman, content to be seen and not heard. Fuck knew the guy had a stick up his ass only Ash seemed to be able to extract on occasion.

As our last guests still on the beach, they ambled toward the stairs as well, Rhett lowering his head a bit to hear whatever Ash wished to tell him.

I turned to find my wife and husband beaming at me. "Shall we?" I asked, holding out both my hands.

They snuggled in on either side of me, same place as I often found myself.

Right where I belonged.

Garrett

My cuddle bug had promised her life to mine and Wyatt's, fulfilling me in a way I hadn't known still lacked, and I had offered her the same in return. Wyatt's wet eyes had flitted over my face as we took our turns, giving our oaths to protect, love, and cherish each other.

Husband and wife and husband.

Not recognized by the state of California, but Haley would be protected and provided for in the event of

Wyatt's death. Not wanting to share only one of our names over the other, she'd chosen to keep her own.

I had no immediate family in attendance, but I didn't need anyone outside the two I loved and the friends I'd made since fate had landed me on Haley's doorstep. People who accepted our relationship for what it was—love.

I'd travelled across the country with my grandparents' blessing to chase a dream almost three years earlier but had found a reality ten times more enchanting.

Peacefulness tucked into every cell of my body even though I never got to see *Garrett Moore* on billboards or walk a red carpet. Hearing my lovers cry out and groan my name fulfilled me in ways screaming fans never would. I'd found my place first with Haley, then with the gorgeous, generous man clasping my hand as we watched her dance on the sand, sans music except for the laughter and giggles of her, Lily, River, and Sharon.

Waves crashed on the shore behind our wife, the setting sun casting golden beams around her slender form. Just like in my dreams, flowers adorned her maroon-red hair cascading down her back.

She was absolutely stunning—and finally mine for life.

"I dreamed of this moment," I told Wyatt, leaning into his warmth, "but I never thought I would have it come true let alone be holding a man's hand when it did."

He kissed my temple, his lips lingering before he returned to watching our wife enjoy the hell out of our reception.

Haley caught sight of us staring and added an extra sway to her hips while dancing barefoot through the sand along with her friends.

"Look at our sweet girl," Wyatt murmured, the love in his voice matching the feelings aching through my chest.

"Prickly," I tacked on my favorite part of her, once more grinning from an overflow of joy.

"Yeah," Wyatt agreed, "but we wouldn't have her any other way."

I couldn't argue that fact. Haley fit us perfectly, no matter the situation we faced as a triad, no matter the angle or position we chose to love on each other.

"I love you, Garrett" Wyatt murmured what I never grew tired of hearing, squeezing my fingers.

"Love you too, Prince Charming."

He barked out a laugh. "If I'm that fictional character, then who is she?"

"Our Cinderella," I said, my face aching from smiling. "Our happily ever after."

THE END

About the Author

Lynn Burke is an international bestselling and award-winning author. A stay-at-home mom, she's a lover of coffee and vino, and with three spawn and two fur babies underfoot, noise levels dictate the daily switch-over time. In her few quiet 'me' moments, she can be found hunched over her Mac, trying to type as fast as her muse spews hot stories.

You can find more about Lynn at her website: www.authorlynnburke.com

Also By Lynn Burke

Abel's Obsession

Divulging Secrets

Healing Storms

In Between

Reluctant Lumberjack

Resisting his Mate

Blood Born Series

Bonds of Worship Series

Dark Leopards MC

Darkest Desires Series

Devil's Outlaws MC

Elite Escort Series

Fallen Gliders MC

Forbidden Obsession Duet

Found by Fate Series

Midnight Sun Series

Missing Link Series

Risso Family Series

Sandy Ridge Series

Sinful Nature Series

Vicious Vipers MC

www.ingramcontent.com/pod-product-compliance
Lightning Source LLC
Chambersburg PA
CBHW070228200726
48293CB00005B/1517